S0-CPF-895

Finally Yours

CLAIRE RAYE

Editing by Kelly Brennan
Cover design by Okay Creations

Other books by Claire Raye

Coming Home to You
A Rockport Beach Novel: Book One

Finding Home with You
A Rockport Beach Novel: Book Two

Making Home with You
A Rockport Beach Novel: Book Three

Always Yours
A Love & Wine Series: companion novella

Prologue

Fourteen Years Ago

Lauren

"I hate you!" I scream, shrill and ear piercing as hot tears sting my eyes. I'm certain every person within a mile radius has heard my cry. That is except for my mother and father, who don't bother coming to see if I'm okay.

"Aww, come on, Lulu. It was joke. It was supposed to be funny."

Nothing he ever does is funny.

He's not funny in the least.

Never has been and never will be.

As I stand attempting to shuck mud from my hair, I've never been more grateful that today is his last day here.

I can't wait for him to go back to that damn island nation he came from. The one filled with the world's deadliest animals, where I can only hope he's taken hostage by an angry mob of koalas or he gets bitten by one of those ridiculously over-sized spiders I've seen pictures of.

He begins to walk toward me and I take a step back, putting my hands up to tell him to back the hell off.

"Don't you even dare!" I yell, my voice now growing an octave higher than before. To say I'm angry would be an understatement. It's not just my hair that's covered in mud but basically my entire body. The only things possibly salvageable are the red rubber boots on my feet.

He doesn't listen and continues in my direction, although in his defense, his glasses are speckled with mud, and I wonder if he can even see me.

Just moments ago, I was mindlessly walking through the vineyard, enjoying the quiet when I was taken down from behind.

Normally I'd have been able to take him down, but he caught me off guard.

Jack can't weigh more than a buck with bricks in his pockets; tall and skinny, an awkward gangly boy with glasses and dirty blonde hair.

He's been my worst nightmare since his arrival over a month ago. My only saving grace has been school, something the average fifteen-year-old would never say. It is six and a half hours of non-Jack contact time, but I'm now on winter break and he has tried his best to ruin every second of it.

For some reason our parents thought we'd get along famously given we are the same age, but he's pretty much the most annoying person on the planet.

My parents own a vineyard and winery in Napa, California. Sounds great, right?

Not exactly. It's in the middle of nowhere and I've been trapped here with this jerk for my entire winter break.

My parents hired Jack's dad, some world-renowned winemaker, to come in and help get their new machinery up and running. He's been here for several months building wine barrels and teaching them the ins and outs of wine making.

Not that my parents are novices or anything. The business has been in our family for generations.

Eventually my sister and I will take over the business, but for now, she's away at college in Michigan and missing out on the wonderful experience of getting to know Jack Wilson.

Just his name makes me cringe inwardly. He's spending his summer break from school here, visiting with his dad, helping with tours and just being an all around pain in my ass.

The tourists love him though.

I'm spending my school holidays visiting my dad.

They find his accent endearing, and his stupid Australian lingo entertaining.

First of all, it's summer break, and why the hell does he add an "s" to the end of words unnecessarily? Every time he speaks I want to punch him in the mouth and knock his stupid accent out of him.

Today is no different, but my rage is definitely at peak capacity.

Jack is now within inches of me, his hand reaching out to wipe the mud from my face, but I swat at his hand, slapping it away.

"Don't touch me," I huff out, stepping back and turning in the other direction. I'm not sure where I think I'm going because behind me is nothing but rows and rows grape vines.

"Lu, where you going?" he calls after me, and I can hear the mud sucking at his bare feet as he jogs to catch up with me. "Let me help you get cleaned up."

I let out a riotous laugh, which slows to an offended chuckle.

He's got to be kidding me!

"What?!" I ask, my body whipping around to face him, the shocking disgust in my tone unmistakable. "Why, so you can cop a feel? Try to grab my boobs and claim it was an accident?"

He shakes his head, but says nothing, and the look of fake surprise on his face is almost comical. He's a great actor.

"While I was on holidays in the States, I felt up some stupid American girl I met," I mock, trying on my best Australian accent. "Great story, mate."

Without letting him speak, I flip him off and shove past him, heading back toward the house so I can get cleaned up.

Two hours and three showers later, I'm forced to say goodbye to Jack. When I say forced, I mean my mother literally had to pay me to come out of my bedroom, bribing me with twenty dollars and a bag of Twizzlers.

"He does these things because he has a crush on you," she whispered through the closed door and I rolled my eyes. If she thought that would make me leave the safety of my room she was sadly mistaken.

Eventually she changed her tactic and I emerged twenty dollars richer and a little less angry. I'm sure drowning my anger in Twizzlers will catch up to me someday, but for now my skinny ass is shoveling them down.

I'm standing with my arms crossed over my chest, now in the driveway of my parents' house as I watch Jack and his father put their suitcases into the trunk of the car.

Good riddance!

My mom, in her over the top ways, is crying and hugging both Jack and his dad, and my dad is shaking hands and wishing them safe travels, but I have yet to move.

It's Jack who leans in to hug me, and I make it as awkward as possible by not uncrossing my arms. But when his arms wrap around my rigid frame I feel my body relax with his touch. My heart suddenly begins racing, pounding hard and loud in my chest as my stomach fills with butterflies.

His touch ignites something inside me, something new and fiery and exciting; something that makes me think I just might miss him.

"Bye, Lulu," he says, a slight sadness to his voice, but it doesn't make me hate that nickname any less. With his mouth next to my ear he mutters, "I can still smell the mud in your hair, you dirty street rat." He pulls back with a smug grin on his face.

And just like that he makes it so easy to say good-bye.

Here's to never seeing Jack Wilson again.

Chapter One

Present Day

Jack

The captain comes over the loudspeaker to announce the plane will be landing in twenty minutes. I feel myself take a deep breath as I realize this will likely be the last time I hear my own accent for a while.

Unless of course I plan on talking to myself out loud, which I don't, because that would be fucking ridiculous. Obviously.

It takes forever to clear customs and immigration, and the whole process is made a million times worse by the fact that it was an overnight flight and everyone is exhausted, pissed off, and stinks.

I have to force myself to stay calm, even as the immigration officer grills me on my occupation, what my plans are for my stay, where I'll be staying, how long I'll be staying for, and generally a million other questions which have already been answered on the immigration form he's currently staring at.

Eventually I'm cleared through and I make my way to the hire car company. I'm not entirely sure how I'm going to go driving on the other side of the road. It was weird enough when I was a passenger as a kid, but actually having to drive? That could be a whole other story.

I manage to get myself what can only be described as a fucking pimp mobile. A giant black Cadillac complete with silver grill and a badge that can likely double as a gangster pendant if needed.

Rolling my eyes at the monstrosity, I throw my bags in the back, walk around and jump in the car only to discover I'm sitting in the front passenger seat, the steering wheel not in front of me but on the other side of the dash.

"For fuck's sake," I mutter as I get out of the car, walk back around and get in on the correct side.

After programming my location into the GPS, I navigate my way out of the airport and onto the freeway, grateful for all the cars on the road that serve as a constant reminder for what side I need to be on.

It's going to take me nearly two hours to get to Napa and as much as I wish I could stop somewhere, take a shower and mainline some coffee, I can't. I'm due to start work tomorrow and thanks to the three hours I spent in the airport, I don't have time for breaks.

This whole job and how I came to get it is actually kinda weird. An opportunity that only came up because someone was trying to get in contact with my dad, not knowing he'd retired and was currently traveling the world with Mum. Apparently, some equipment he'd set up at one of the wineries over here was now not working. Even though it was probably because it was fifteen years old, rather than replace it, they wanted someone to fix it, and when I'd answered the email and explained that I was more than capable, they'd given me the job.

That's the beauty about having my dad's last name though. He knew how to get shit done and he did it well. People always figured as his son, I'd be the same and fuck me if I didn't try my hardest to be exactly that. My dad was a legend in Australian wine making, a man who spent his entire career being lured from one winery to another. We'd lived in all the regions, from Margaret River in the West, the Barossa in the South and even the Hunter and Coonawarra regions over east.

As a kid I'd loved it and as an adult, I knew that I was always going to be living up to his name. And there was no way I was gonna fuck up that rep of his.

Plus, the timing was awesome given the fucking mess my life had become in the past few months. Technically speaking, I wasn't running away; I was between jobs and this gave me a month or so of work. In reality though, I was kidding myself if I thought escaping like this wasn't a huge drawcard.

So here I am, heading up to Napa, America's most famous wine region and a place my dad frequented a lot over the course of his career. Sometimes I was lucky enough to come and visit and while I don't remember all of the places he worked at, there is one particular winery and one particular girl who still sticks in my mind to this day.

Lulu.

Annoying, feisty, but unbelievably cute, Lulu.

Just thinking about her brings a smile to my face. God, how I loved to tease that girl and even though I have no idea if she still lives up this way, a part of me is tempted to look her up while I'm here, see if I can't have another go at riling that girl up like I used to.

Eventually the view outside the car gives way to hills of grape vines and as they do, I can't help but chuckle as I remember back to the last day I ever spent in the US.

Fuck me if I couldn't stop laughing my arse off at the sight of Lulu, covered in mud and screaming at me for what I'd done. And yeah it had totally been deliberate, but how could I resist, especially given it was my last day and I had no idea if I'd ever see her again.

She looked so fucking cute, covered in mud and trying so hard to stomp her feet at me, her little red boots stuck and only making her more frustrated.

The GPS interrupts my thoughts, telling me to take the next right. I move to indicate, instead clicking on the windscreen wipers, before saying fuck it and making the turn anyway. Christ this is going to take some getting used to.

As I do though, I'm hit with a memory of driving down this very road. Glancing around, a wave of familiarity washes over me and I can't help but smile.

I used to love her family's vineyard, although I know it can't possibly be theirs anymore, not when person who gave me this gig was called Ellen McIntyre. A part of me wonders why they sold it; a bigger part wonders where Lulu might be as a result.

As the landscape becomes more and more familiar with every kilometer I travel, the nostalgia becomes almost too much, the memories flashing through my brain. By the time I'm turning into the actual vineyard, the sense of déjà vu is overwhelming.

"I'm back," I say to myself as I drive past the sign announcing *Somerville's Winery & Vineyard* and head down the long drive, past the cellar door and out toward the sheds at the back, all of it so familiar; a trip I made countless times as a kid.

Whoever this new owner is, they've obviously kept the name and it's not hard to understand why. *Somerville's* was a brand and it had a reputation. A good one too.

I park the car by a dirt-covered four-wheel drive, killing the engine and hopping out. Almost immediately, this cocky-looking kid, who can't be more than seven years old, comes strutting out of one of the sheds like he owns the place.

"Hey," he says, stopping in front of me. "What can I do for you?"

I can't help but laugh. "You the boss around here then?" I ask.

He shoots me a weird look. "Why do you sound so funny?"

I roll my eyes. Here we fucking go. God, I remember being over here as a kid and the never ending *oh my god, I love your accent,* which was usually followed by, *I'm sorry, but what did you say?*

I got it nearly every time I opened my mouth. Fuck knows why they could never understand me though, it's not like I was speaking Swahili or whatever.

"Why do *you* sound so funny?" I throw back at him, the same exact words I said to Lulu when she asked me that question on my first day here.

"I don't," he fires back, a look on his face that screams *why are you such an idiot?*

I shake my head, wondering why the hell I am getting into an argument with a seven-year-old. "I'm looking for Ellen McIntyre?" I ask.

"She expecting you?" he asks, arms crossed over his chest now.

I laugh. "Look kid, I appreciate the welcome and I'm sure you run a tight ship and all, but yeah, she's expecting me. Can you tell me where I can find her?"

The kid gives me a hard look as though he's trying to work out whether to believe me or maybe he's just trying to work out what I actually said. Eventually, he seems to come to a decision and with a nod of the head, he says, "Follow me."

He leads me into the last shed on the left, which I remember contained all the tanks the wine was left to ferment in before barreling and bottling. My memory is right, and as soon as I walk inside, the familiar sweet scent of wine and sugar-filled grapes fills the air. I can't stop myself from taking a deep breath as I push my sunglasses onto my head so my eyes can adjust to the darkness.

"Good?" a voice asks.

When I look over, a woman, maybe a couple of years older than me and casually dressed in jeans and a white t-shirt is smiling at me, an amused look on her face.

"You must be Jack?" she says.

I nod. "Ellen?"

"Yes," she says, walking toward me. "Welcome to *Somerville's.* How was your flight?"

I shake the hand she offers me. "Long, drove straight up here too."

"Wow, okay, let's get you settled first," she says. "And then I can show you around, introduce you to everyone."

She leads me back out of the shed and indicates my car as if to suggest wherever we're going, I'm driving. I nod, opening the driver's side door this time, thank fuck, and get in.

Ellen slides into the passenger seat while the smart-mouthed kid jumps in the back, smirking at me in the rearview mirror.

"You're going to want to head down the back, take a left at the fork," she says, gesturing to the dirt road behind the shed.

"Yeah I've actually been here before," I say. "As a kid. I remember we stayed in one of the cottages down the back of the property."

"Is that so," Ellen says and when I glance over at her, she's got a strange smile on her face as she stares out the front window.

"So, this is your place now then?" I ask, wondering how it is Lulu's parents ever decided to sell the place. From what I remember, it had been in their family for years and considering how famous it was in this region, I have no idea why anyone would choose to let it go.

"Here, last one on the left," she says, gesturing to the smaller of the two cottages.

It's exactly as I remember it and I'm glad this is where I'll be staying for the month or so I'm likely to be here. Even though the winery might have changed hands, nothing about the place is different.

"Key's in the door," she says, opening the passenger door. "Get yourself settled and then come next door and we'll go over everything," she says, smiling at me. "Oscar, let's go," she adds, glancing at the kid in the back seat.

The kid gives me a dramatic eyeroll as he gets out of the car before offering me a wave and a "Later," over his shoulder as he walks into the cottage next door as though he lives there.

Ellen follows him inside, calling out "Only us," at the door as though it isn't where she lives. I don't hear a reply, but figure I'll meet whoever my new neighbor is soon enough.

Grabbing my bags, I head inside the limestone cottage that I'm now calling home. Inside is exactly as I remember it, the door opening to a front living room that's dominated by a large stone fireplace. The décor has been updated though and I'm grateful for the corner couch and large flat screen TV.

Heading toward the back, I pass the small, but newly renovated kitchen, the bathroom, my old bedroom and eventually the big bedroom my dad used when he worked here.

Throwing my bags on the large bed, I walk back to the bathroom, stripping off the clothes I've spent the last thirty-six hours in before jumping in the shower.

Afterward, I pull on a clean pair of jeans and a t-shirt, leaving my feet bare before heading into the kitchen. The fridge has been filled with food and drinks and I grab a coke, knowing I can't afford to sleep my jetlag away. Cracking the tab, I take a long sip before heading next door.

I knock on the front door, unsure exactly who lives here and not sure I can just walk in. The kid, who I now know is called Oscar, appears behind the screen door, staring up at me as though he's never seen me before.

"Come in," he eventually says, as though I've passed some sort of test. "They're in the kitchen," he adds before walking back into the living room and resuming his seat on the couch in front of the TV. Beside him is a girl who's about the same age as him and I watch as he leans over and pulls the remote from her hands and changes channels without asking. She turns and punches him in response and I have to bite my lip to stop the laugh.

Fuck me if this whole scene isn't straight out of mine and Lulu's playbook.

Shaking my head, I walk down the hall to what I assume is the kitchen at the back. The house has the same layout as mine, only bigger and decorated with a distinctly feminine touch. Not over the top girlie or whatever, just softer, vases of flowers and shit that suggests a female presence.

When I walk into the kitchen, Ellen is sitting at the large island, a glass of wine in front of her.

"Hi," she says. "Feeling better?"

I nod. "Definitely, thanks."

"Can I get you a glass?" she asks, gesturing to the bottle.

I look over, notice the *Somerville* label and wonder if it still tastes as good as I remember. It's not that it's been long since I had a glass of their stuff; it's sold in Australia. I just don't know when the place changed hands or whether that's impacted the quality.

I'm also not sure how alcohol is going to react with my jetlag, but fuck it; it's five o'clock somewhere.

"Sure," I say, finishing off my coke and taking a seat. "So, when did you take over this place?" I ask, remembering she never answered my question when I asked her earlier.

Ellen smiles as she grabs another glass and pours me some wine. "About two years ago," she says, topping up a third glass that's sitting on the bench. "But I'm only in charge of the admin side of things," she says. "My sister runs the actual vineyard. That's who you'll be working for."

"Okay," I say, reaching for the glass she offers me. She's got a weird look on her face, almost as if she's laughing at me. "And am I going to meet this sister of yours anytime soon?" I ask.

She nods and almost immediately, the sound of footsteps on the wooden floorboards signals her arrival.

"Speak of the devil," Ellen says as a set of long tanned legs walks into the kitchen. I feel my eyes tracing a slow path up bare, sun-kissed skin, a pair of cut-off denim shorts hugging curvy hips and a tight black tank covering an impressive chest, long blonde hair hanging over one shoulder

When I reach the face however, and the deep blue eyes that are currently squinting back at me, I can't stop the grin that breaks out, especially when I catch the *what the fuck* expression plastered all over my new boss' face.

"Hey Lulu," I say as I raise my glass in her direction.

Oh fuck me; this is going to be fun.

Chapter Two

Lauren

The look on his smug tanned face is exactly as I remember it fourteen years ago as he sits there staring at me from the stool at my kitchen island.

What in the literal fuck is he doing here!?

"Ellen, can I speak to you please?" I ask through teeth clenched so tightly that I swear I'm going to chip a tooth. "Alone," I add, now looking directly at that kangaroo-loving shithead. I always liked to believe he got lost in the bush somewhere trying to find that giant rock they all rave about over there. But I wasn't that lucky because he's now sitting in my kitchen.

Ellen follows me to my bedroom and I slam the door behind her, not making it any secret that I'm severely pissed off.

When she told me she had found someone to fix our crusher and destemmer machine, I didn't question it any further. The damn thing has been on the fritz for the last year and no matter how hard we've tried, we have yet to find some who can figure out what the hell is wrong with it.

I'm pretty sure if I had to listen to one more joke from a mechanic about stomping the grapes with my feet, I was going to lose it.

So original. Thanks *I Love Lucy.*

But those lame ass jokes are looking like a much better solution than having Jack Wilson involved. Honestly, I would even consider stomping grapes with my own feet right about now over my current option.

Who would've thought you could carry a deep hatred for someone after all these years?

"This is who you hired?" I demand, my hand flying at the closed door. As I listen voice I feel myself tense at just the sound of his accent. He's ruined me on foreign guys forever. "He's calling the kids 'mates' right now, Ellen." I huff indignantly.

This is all her fault.

"Hold up." Ellen's hands are up defensively. "I had no idea this was who they were sending and..."

"Bullshit!" I shout, cutting her off and not caring in the least if Jack hears me. "There's no way you didn't know. Why would you do this to me?" I moan, my voice coming out whiny and high, and I realize how immature I sound.

"Seriously, Lauren, I didn't know. I contacted his father's old company and they set everything up from there. I literally haven't been in touch with him until this point."

I roll my eyes dramatically and begin pacing the room wondering how I can get Jack to take a hike without actually speaking with him, without ever seeing his face again.

And as I obsess over this, I realize I'm going to have to throw out my beautiful Pottery Barn stools that I just bought because he touched them. His stupid ass was sitting on them! Fuck, what else could he be touching right now? I gotta get out of this room before I have to burn my entire house to the ground.

"Geez, Lauren, you're being incredibly irrational," Ellen says, as I try to storm past her. She catches my arm and glares at me, her eyebrows knitting together and her lips pursed.

"Grow up, and for the love of fuck, remember you're a professional."

"I am a professional!" I shout inches from her face and Ellen hauls back like she's going to smack me and I finch, making her laugh. "But I'm certain he's not. Did you see the way he's dressed? Ugh..."

Ellen cocks an eyebrow at me, her hands on her hips, "Listen, Pot, you and the Kettle out there aren't dressed all that differently."

"Oh my god, why are you taking his side?" I lament before defending myself. "For your information I was out trying to unclog that damn crusher..."

My words stop me in my tracks and so do my purple stained hands that I quickly shove into the back pockets of my shorts.

"Point. Made," Ellen quips as she turns to leave the room, but just before she opens the door she turns back to me. "You never told me he was so hot." She opens her mouth into a perfect O-shape and fans her face.

I slap at her and practically shove her into the door. "He wasn't," I hiss as I reach around her for the doorknob, opening the door and forcing her out before me.

"You never told me he was so hot," I mockingly mutter as we both leave my bedroom. Hot, if you like that tanned, blue-eyed, Australian accent, total dickhead, conceited prick look. Pffft...

"Come on kids," Ellen says, flagging them off the couch where they were already nestled up against Jack looking at pictures on his phone. He's so charming even they've turned on me.

Jack stands up and advances toward me with a look on his face that says he's thrilled to be here, and it takes everything in me not to charge at him and slug him in the face.

We didn't exactly part on the best terms. Hell, we didn't even start on the best terms. "You look good, Lulu," he says, smiling as his eyes trail over my body.

My hand whips up, "Don't even start, and let's get a few things straight: my name is Lauren. Not Lulu, Lu or anything else, just Lauren. And I am your boss. It might be Ellen who hands you a check, but make no mistake, I am in charge."

"You got it," Jack says shrugging his shoulders as he slips past me and back into the kitchen. He takes a seat on the stool that Ellen vacated earlier, picking up his wine, he indicates for me to sit down.

"How've you been going, Lu...Lauren?" he corrects, his tone casual like we're old friends.

"I'm fine," I reply, my response clipped, but that doesn't stop him from continuing.

"Your kids are quite cheeky, especially the boy," Jack says, his eye glancing at door they left through.

"We're not doing this," I tell him and he raises his eyebrows, a confused look on his face.

"Not doing what?"

"This," I motion a hand between us. "The pleasantries, the acting like we're friends."

"We are friends," he deadpans, and it takes everything in me not to burst out laughing.

He clearly forgot all the times I told him I hated him. All the times he made me completely miserable, but the biggest of them all, the day he left when he tackled me and I fell face first into a muddy gully out in the vineyard. That's the one that stands out in my mind.

"You going to ask me how I've been going?"

"No, because you're here to fix my crusher and that's where we're going."

I leave the kitchen, hearing Jack slide off the stool and push it in, following me into the mudroom where I left my boots. I bend down to pull on my boots and a nearly inaudible gasp leaves Jack's mouth, but it's enough to make me sit down and tug on my boots.

He does not need to be looking at my ass as I bend over. This is a professional relationship and the fact that Ellen let him into my house has already crossed that line.

He must take the hint that I have no interest in speaking to him, because he stays silent until we reach the building. But I notice him taking in the grounds, looking around at everything.

"So, here it is," I say, gesturing with great flourish at the oversized machine in the center of the room. My stained purple hands indicating that this machine and I are in a never-ending battle. "Things start to go wrong when it reaches the point where the crushed grapes need to move through…" My thoughts are halted as Jack walks around me and climbs the small stairs to look into the large metal drum.

He slides his hands into a pair of black rubber gloves that are clipped to railing and begins digging around without waiting for me to finish.

"No, not there," I mutter, climbing up behind him and squeezing next to him. Jack shifts sideways, making room and I point out the place where things seem to be going wrong, grabbing a handful of barely mashed grapes. "See," I say, showing him, my hand now dyed an even more bright purple than before.

"Few things," Jack says, a perplexed look on his face as he takes the grapes from my hands and dumps them into a bucket, hanging up the gloves. "I'd say your first problem is that you're contaminating your wine by shoving your dirty ungloved hands in there. Second…"

"Oh my god, and to think I thought you were here to help," I say on an exasperated sigh as I climb down the steps.

Jack grabs my wrist as I make my best attempt to storm out on him, practically yanking me back against him. His hand is warm and calloused, and I have no idea what happens but my heart rate skyrockets, sending an electric shock through my entire body. Every nerve is on fire from just one touch.

His thumb strokes the inside of my wrist and as much I want to pull away, something about it feels strangely right. It's been way too long since I've had sex because right now a part of me is turned on by this asshole's touch.

I shake my head, clearing the haze that has clouded my better judgment and I pull my wrist away with a quick tug.

I glare at Jack, hoping my expression forces him back to the land of professionals that we are supposed to be in. He wouldn't do this to a client, why would he think it's appropriate with me.

"I'm just taking the piss, Lulu." He winks at me and I'm sure he'd be able to charm the panties off of most women, but I'm not most women or am I? Because for the first time since his arrival, I get a good look at him, and holy shit time has been good to him.

His t-shirt is fitted allowing the outline of his muscled arms and chest to show through, and someone has never made a pair of worn out jeans look so damn good.

I hear him clear his throat, "Um, Lu?"

"Yeah?" I answer not even noticing that he has completely disobeyed my request to call me Lauren. "What?" I drag my eyes away from his amazing body and silently remind myself to dig that vibrator out of my nightstand later.

Jack is smirking, his chest pushed out, his hands in his back pocket. When my eyes meet his, I'm mortified that the expression on my face has totally given away what I'm thinking. I feel my face flush, and I look away quickly.

I can't find him attractive. I chalk it up to the fact that I'm just lonely.

"You never had the best poker face," Jack teases, pinching my side as he walks by me. "Anything going on with the crushers over here?" he calls, walking over to the two other machines in the room.

"No, but those ones don't..."

"Work as quickly," he says finishing my sentence.

"Yeah." As much as I hate that he can finish my sentence, he's obviously the right person for the job.

"I'm gonna go back and change into some work clothes, and then come back to take a look. That okay, boss?" Again that cheeky smile is back, and he's giving me shit just like he used to.

"Yeah, Jack, it's fine," I say, my annoyed tone not masking the fact that I know he's purposely being a shithead.

I begin to head back to my house and Jack jogs a bit to catch up with me asking, "When did your parents retire?"

"Couple of years ago, but Ellen and I have been working here since we graduated from college.

"You were working here long before that, Lulu. You knew this place like the back of your hand at fifteen."

"Yeah, but..."

"But nothing. Learn to take a compliment."

His comment brings a smile to my face and again I feel my cheeks grow hot, but that feeling is short-lived when the front door to my house swings open and Olivia rushes out.

Her big brown eyes are wide as she looks up at me. "Why's your face so red?" Her hands are on her hips, demanding an answer. "We're you running? We're you racing? Who won?"

"Go back in the house, Nosy Rosy." I squint my eyes at her, my lips pulled into a pucker, and she giggles loudly and runs back into the house calling Oscar's name.

"Cute kids," Jack says, and I recall his comment from earlier, and realize I never acknowledged it.

“Yeah, twins, they’re cute, but they’re a bit too honest for their own good.”

“World might be a better place if we were all as honest as kids.” He shrugs his shoulders and begins to look around, taking in the vineyards that surround my house and his rental. The houses are set a ways back, far enough to not be intrusive, but the view is still phenomenal.

“Place looks amazing, Lulu. Your parents would be proud.”

I swallow hard and nod my head.

Why is it so hard to take him seriously?

“What about your parents? Your dad?” I ask, changing the subject before things get a little too comfortable between us.

“Dad’s retired, and he’s off traveling through Europe with my mum,” Jack responds but offers nothing more. And before I can ask what he’s been up to, he says, “I’ll check in with you in a bit after I have time to look into things.”

“If I’m not here, I’ll be up front in the office.”

Jack gives me a curt nod of his head and leaves, making his way back to his cottage.

I take in a deep breath and exhale slowly, watching him walk away.

“Get a good look at my arse?” Jack calls over his shoulder, his laugh booming across the empty rows of vines.

“Shut up!” I yell back, slapping my hand over my face before I disappear, mortified, into my house.

I slam the door and I hear that Ellen and the kids are back, and she giggles as I storm into the kitchen.

She’s standing poised at the island with a glass of wine in each hand and a smile on her face.

“How’d that go?” she questions, and I can’t tell if she’s teasing or prying.

“About as well as expected,” I mutter, grabbing the glass from her hand and taking a big gulp.

“Dad would kill you if he saw you chug your wine like that.”

"I don't need your shit, too." I roll my eyes at her and plop down on a stool, as Ellen grabs the one next to me.

"Is he married?" she asks seemingly out of nowhere, her eyebrows going up along with the corners of her lips. Nosiness must run in the family.

"You're as bad as the kids."

Chapter Three

Jack

I'm grinning as I walk back into my cottage. It's funny how things have turned out, me wanting to look Lulu up while I'm here and her turning out to be my boss and neighbor.

Even better is the fact that I still have an effect on her, too. Good to see nothing's changed there. It's certainly gonna make my time here a whole lot more fun.

After I pull on some boots, I walk back to the building containing her broken crushing machine and take another look. Almost immediately I think I know what the problem is, but I also know I can't do anything about it. Not right now anyway.

Before I leave, I take a look around the shed, the two other crushers she's got to the side, the logbooks and signs documenting everything that goes in and everything that comes out. She's organized and methodical about it all, which is good. It's exactly how you need to be.

Eventually I walk out of the shed and head back to her house, but she's not there, no one responding when I call out.

I head back up to the main building, the one I know from my time here as a kid that houses the cellar door and tasting rooms and the offices out the back.

"Hey, Lulu?" I call out as I walk inside. "You in here?"

I hear the loud exhale before she calls. "Back here."

I walk through to the main office and see her standing behind a desk, an annoyed look on her face.

"What, don't tell me you've given up already?" she asks, a look of aggravation on her face as though this would legit piss her off if I had.

I grin. "No, Lulu, I have not. But, I do know what the problem is, so I will be able to fix it. The biggest issue is the grapes, they gotta go."

"What?" she asks.

"The grapes," I say shrugging. "I can't fix it with them in there."

"Shit," she mutters. "Think we can save them?"

"How long they been in there?"

Her eyes flick to the ceiling as though she's mentally tallying the days. "About a week?" she says, like she's asking me.

I let out a long breath. "Yeah, no, we can't save them," I tell her. "Maybe the untouched bunches at the top, but the rest, are toast."

"Shit," she says again.

"Kinda stupid putting fruit in a crusher that was playing up, wasn't it?" I say, taking a step toward her.

Lulu puts her hands on the desk and leans forward. "Oh, you think that's what happened, do you?" she asks, annoyed.

I smirk at her before I'm distracted by the clear line of sight I now have down her top. I can't resist looking and clearly I'm obvious about it because she immediately stands and takes away my view.

"Whatever," I add, waving my hand as though to say it doesn't matter. "But I will need some help getting those grapes out."

She shakes her head, hands on her hips. "The guys will be in tomorrow morning," she says. "I'll get them to help you."

I nod, even though a part of me wishes it were her that was going to be the one helping me. The idea of Lulu, half buried in crushed grapes, her arse sticking out of the crusher, her skin and clothes stained with purple juice, it's almost too much to bear.

Before I have a chance to ask her though, the door opens and a girl, maybe in her early twenties walks in and hands some paperwork to Lulu before turning to look at me.

Lulu nods in thanks and then looks up, sees this new girl and me eyeing each other. "Penny, this is Jack, he's here to fix our crusher and be a monumental pain in my ass. Jack this is Penny, she runs the tasting room," she says, clearly annoyed at what she assumes is us checking each other out.

"Hi," Penny says, grinning at me.

"Hey, how's it going?"

Penny stares at me before glancing at Lulu, then turning back to me again, a confused look on her face now.

Lulu sighs. "He's asking 'how are you?'" she says. "He's an Aussie, they don't speak properly down there."

"Aussie," I say, turning to Lulu.

"Yeah, that's what I said," she replies.

"No, you said, Aussie. But it's pronounced Aussie."

"What?"

"Aussie, like oh-zed-zed-why, Ozzy."

Lulu rolls her eyes at me. "You mean oh-zee-zee-why?"

I grin, crossing my arms over my chest. "Pretty sure it's zed actually."

Lulu mirrors my pose. "Pretty sure it's not."

We're standing staring at each other, Penny looking from me to Lulu to me again. "Did you guys used to like date or something?" she asks.

"NO!" Lulu immediately shouts as I burst out laughing.

"She wishes," I add.

"I do not!"

"Ohhh, come on Lulu, just admit you fancy me," I say, chuckling at how pissed off she looks. "Even just a little?" I add holding up my hand, fingers pinched almost together as if to indicate just how much I mean.

"I literally have no idea what he's saying," Penny says, turning to Lulu again. "You need anything else from me boss?"

Lulu shakes her head, her eyes never leaving mine. If looks could kill, I'd be a dead man right now because she is staring daggers at me.

"No, thank you, Penny," she says. "See you tomorrow."

Penny nods to us both before she leaves and as soon as she's gone, the tension in the room immediately ratchets up a notch or two.

"You," Lulu starts, a finger pointed in my direction as though she's about to unleash on me.

"So tomorrow," I say cutting her off. "I'll be in the shed by eight, have the guys meet me in there, okay? Thanks boss," I add before turning and walking out, not giving her a chance to say another word.

Back at my house I can feel the exhaustion catching up with me. I know I need to force myself to stay awake for a few more hours though, fight the jet lag so I can get into this time zone as soon as possible. So changing into a pair of shorts and some runners, I do the only thing I know that will keep me awake.

I stick to the Somerville property, looping around the yard at the back of the houses Lulu and I are staying in before heading back out to the drive and entrance. It's probably only a couple of kilometers the whole way around, so I run four loops, my legs burning as I pass by the main building for the fourth time.

Slowing to a walk, I immediately hear the sound of feet behind me. Turning, I catch Oscar, running, struggling to keep up with me. Grinning, I slow even more and allow him to reach me.

"You in training or something?" I ask.

Oscar is breathing hard, clearly struggling to catch his breath. "Nah," he gets out between puffs. "I always," he pauses, before trying again. "Always, do, this."

"Right," I say. "Well, I'm done now, so time for a cool down."

Oscar nods as though this is exactly what he was planning and he slows to a walk, gradually catching his breath.

"So," I start, knowing this kid is gonna be a great source of information for me. "You like it out here?"

Oscar shrugs. "Yeah," he says, still trying to catch his breath.

"Your dad around?" I ask, wondering exactly who he might be. Hopefully not one of the guys helping me tomorrow, that's for sure.

It was a shock finding out Lulu even had kids, and I'll admit, a part of me doesn't like the idea of her having done that with some other guy, even though I know there's not a chance in hell she's remained a virgin these past fourteen years.

But there was something about the idea of some other guy claiming her as his, of starting a family and tying them together forever that just didn't sit well with me.

"Here?" Oscar asks. "No, he's not here."

"So he and your mum aren't together anymore?"

Oscar looks up at me as though I've just asked him a really dumb question. "Yeah, they're together," he says.

I nod, trying to look like I'm not prying, when in fact, I am. "Okay," I say. "So he just doesn't work here then?"

Oscar shakes his head. "Nope."

"What time does he get back from work?" I ask, wondering when I'm going to be forced to meet this guy that's married

Lulu and knocked her up. Although truth be told, I'm not sure she is married, I didn't see a ring.

Still that could be because it's currently sitting on the bottom of the crushing machine on account of the fact she insists on sticking her hands in there without putting gloves on.

Oscar shrugs. "I don't know," he says. "Mom's been letting us stay here this past week."

Now I'm really confused, my jetlagged brain trying to process what this kid's telling me. Just as I'm about to ask him, it dawns on me. Chuckling, I say, "Ohhhh, so Lulu's not your mum?"

"Who's Lulu?" Oscar asks, glancing sideways at me.

My grin widens. "Lauren," I say, gesturing toward her house as we walk down the dirt road to it.

Oscar shakes his head. "No, she's my aunt."

I burst out laughing at this, suddenly relieved at the idea that not only are these not Lulu's kids, but that maybe she might not be married either.

"So," I say, hand on Oscar's shoulder. "Is your aunt Lauren married?"

Oscar shakes his head. "Nope. Mom says she's married to this place," he adds, looking around the property.

I laugh. "I see. Boyfriend?"

He shakes his head again. "Nope," he repeats again. "But I overheard Mom telling her that a good pounding from a hot guy is exactly what she needs," he says. "What does that even mean?"

I burst out laughing, actually stopping as I bend at the waist, hands on my thighs. Oh god, thank fuck for the honesty of kids, cause this one's gonna be a goldmine of information.

"Oh Oscar," I eventually say. "I think you and I are going to be good friends." A hand on his shoulder again as I steer him toward what I now know is his aunt's house.

"Cool," Oscar says, nodding.

When we get back to the house, Lauren is sitting on her front porch, feet up on the rail and a beer in her hand.

"There you are," she says standing, eyes on Oscar. "Get inside and get cleaned up," she says to him.

Oscar holds out a hand to me, giving me some complicated handshake when I offer him mine, before he walks off. Lauren stares at him until the front door slams, before turning back to me.

"Good kid you got there," I say, even though I know he isn't hers now.

"Hmmm," is all she says, not bothering to correct me.

I grin, lifting my shirt to wipe the sweat from my face. When I lower it, I see Lulu staring at me, her mouth slightly open.

"Get a good look?" I ask, grinning.

She swallows hard, before taking a long pull from the beer that's currently pressed against her neck. "What happened to your glasses?" she asks, the added, "Four eyes," clearly said to piss me off.

I chuckle, remembering all the times she called me that as a kid, thinking it did piss me off when really, it did nothing but confirm she was paying attention to me.

"Laser," I say, lifting my shirt again, partly to wipe the sweat, partly because I wanna watch her reaction once more. "Don't wear them anymore."

Lulu nods but in that way that says she hasn't heard a single thing I've said.

"You okay there, Lulu? You look a little tense."

She nods again, but says nothing.

"Well, I gotta take a shower," I say, hand gripping my t-shirt. "Laters, Lulu," I add, pausing before adding, "Unless you wanna join me?"

I watch as she stares back at me, a look on her face that I can't decipher, before her jaw tightens and she seems to regain control of herself again.

"Grow up," she says, shooting me a filthy look.

I chuckle. "What?" I say, hands out as if to indicate, I have no idea what she's talking about. "We're both adults."

Lulu rolls her eyes. "One of us is," she mutters.

"Well," I say, as I make my way next door. "The offer's there, should you change your mind," I add, opening my front door. I can feel her eyes on me, watching me as I walk inside my house. Just before I let the front door close behind me, I pop my head back out and bust her still watching me.

Grinning, I say, "Also, I brought a shitload of Tim Tams over with me, so you know, if you want some..."

I trail off, not bothering to hide the double meaning of my words *if you want some*.

Lu says nothing, but I can't stop the grin as a red flush creeps over her cheeks. Chuckling, I wink at her again before disappearing inside to take a shower, my brain picturing what it would be like if she joined me.

Chapter Four

Lauren

How after all these years does he still know how to push my buttons?

He knows I love Tim Tams and for the past fourteen years, I've been getting by on the American knock-offs, but they just aren't the same.

I could always sneak over to his cottage while he's in the shower and snatch some. I'm sure he wouldn't miss them, and then I wouldn't have to deal with begging him for a package. There's no way he'd hand them over willingly, and I'd then be forced to deal with his incessant teasing.

I can be stealth-like when I want to. And it wouldn't be like I was breaking and entering since I actually own the cottage. But if he catches me...

No cookie is worth subjecting myself to Jack and his obnoxiousness, but I do contemplate sending Oscar over there to con Jack out of a few.

I finish the last swig of my beer as I walk in the house. Oscar and Olivia are working on building this epic Lego rendering of my house and the cottage next door; something they've been working on for a solid two weeks since they started their summer break. I remember how much it sucked being trapped here as a kid, but they actually seem to like it. Oscar even more so now that Jack is here.

The kids have spent the past few nights with me, but with their dad returning from his business trip, I imagine Ellen will want to take them home.

"Aunt Lauren, why's he call you Lulu?" Oscar asks when I step through the door, a confused look on his face.

"I don't know," I reply, annoyed that my nickname has now traveled beyond Jack's lips.

"Can I call you Lulu?"

"No and stay away from Jack. He's... yucky." I stand with my hands on my hips looking down at Oscar who's smiling up at me with a silly grin on his face. By telling him no, I've just solidified that he will call me Lulu for the rest of his life. And Jack will now be his new best friend.

"Whatever you say, Aunt Lulu," he chides back, shrugging his shoulders and going back to adding the multi-colored chimney to the house.

"I think we should all call you Lulu," Ellen shouts from the back of my house, letting out a belly laugh that makes me want to pull my hair out.

Why are they all turning on me? He's not *that* charming.

"Get Tommy to empty some of your compost out when he comes in tomorrow," Ellen says, walking in through my mudroom with a bowl. "You barely have any room in that thing."

She's just finishing up making dinner that looks to be spaghetti and salad, and as annoying and motherly as she can be sometimes, it's been nice having her here. Most of the time I eat alone, but it doesn't bother me too much.

"Got it, Mom," I reply back, giving her an exaggerated eye roll.

One of the perks of living on so much land is that I have plenty of room for a garden and I always have compost.

Between the vines, the grapes, the cut grass and my own food waste; it's kind of never-ending.

"So, does he think he can fix it?" Ellen asks as she signals for the kids to come and sit down for dinner. She's dishing out spaghetti while I pour us each a glass of wine.

"He does, but we have to clean the entire machine out."

"Well, that sucks. We're gonna lose all the grapes in there. That's at least a dozen bottles of wine."

She's preaching to the choir here. I know this already and I'm just as pissed off at myself for continuing to use the damn machine when I knew it wasn't working properly. Something Jack didn't have an issue pointing out to me.

"How long does he think it'll take to clean it out and get the repair done?"

"Not sure. He didn't say."

"And you didn't think to ask?" Ellen responds, her tone teasing, because she then says, "Too busy flirting to do your job?"

I don't even dignify that with a response. I just begin shoveling my salad into my mouth.

"What's flirting?" Olivia asks, and I shoot a dirty look at Ellen. She damn well knows these kids are listening to everything we say and now one of us has to explain it to Olivia because she won't be satisfied with a half-assed answer.

"It's when two people who like each other..."

"It is not!" I say too loudly given the fact that we're all sitting together, and quickly cut Ellen off by saying, "It's when someone is really annoying like Jack." I whip my head back to Ellen, wrinkling my nose at her to show her I won this battle.

But then, just to prove that Ellen is always right, Olivia huffs and says, "Oscar is always flirting with me too, Aunt Lauren." She rolls her eyes dramatically, as if to say solidarity sister, but all I've created now is a mess.

"This is why honesty is the best policy, kids," Ellen responds, chastising my ability to lie so easily to my niece and nephew.

The rest of the meal goes on without mentioning Jack or his annoying tendencies. We talk about their upcoming vacation to Disneyland and what rides they are most excited about. The conversation is light and fun, and as much as I like my privacy, I'll miss having them with me every day. Not like they're going far or anything.

Ellen, her husband Will, and the kids live about ten minutes away, and more than likely will probably spend their whole summer, with the exception of their vacation, here. It's just been nice coming home to dinner and conversation.

Ellen's washing dishes, her eyes looking out the window over the sink as I put the leftovers in the fridge.

"He's not that bad, you know?" she says, and I quickly shove the containers in and move so I'm now looking over her shoulder.

Jack is on the back deck, his feet resting on the table, a glass of wine in his hand, and fuck me if he doesn't look amazing.

How can someone be so hot and so obnoxious at the same time?

I'm silent, not responding, not wanting to add fuel to her fire.

"You should've been a little nicer to him when you were kids. Who would've thought he'd grow up to look like that?" Ellen waves a hand at the window and I grab it, pulling it down just in case he happens to look over here. He does not need to know we are talking about him. It will just add more to his already overinflated ego.

"Give me a break, Ellen. He's still single. Who is thirty and not married? There's obviously something wrong with him."

Ellen drops the sponge into the soapy water and spins around to look at me. Leaning up against the sink, she raises an eyebrow at me.

"You can't be serious, right? You're single, nearly thirty, and hell, there's definitely something wrong you."

"I'm single by choice," I defend, and I give a little nod of my head.

"I don't think being left..."

"Too soon, Ellen!" I shout over her and walk out of the room joining Oscar and Olivia on the floor, inserting myself into their game of Uno.

It's after nine by the time they leave, the kids and I watching the *Lego Movie* for the millionth time, and my house is now back to being quiet.

It's almost too quiet, and as much as I know Ellen didn't mean anything by our earlier conversation, I can't stop thinking about it.

I like to believe I'm single by choice, but anyone in our family, anyone who works at *Somerville's* knows I'm guarded now.

This is not where I expected to end up. I love running the vineyard and the winery, but I never thought I'd be doing it alone.

I step outside into the cool evening air and take a deep breath. One of the greatest things about living here are the warm days and the cool nights, and tonight I need the cool air to clear my head.

I begin to walk, first up one row and then down the next, with each step I feel lighter. The sweet smell of grapes reminding me why I love it here.

The next row I walk up is the one where Jack knocked me down, my entire body covered in mud. I laugh a little at the memory. As much as he pisses me off, as much as I hated having him here that winter, he is in every one of my memories.

I look up at the cloudless sky, each star a bright white, making it look like a scene from a movie. The landscape and the night's sky working together, and I feel myself settling.

My eyes are closed when I hear the sound of footsteps; each step rustling the grass and the leaves on the vines begin to move.

My eyes pop open and I suddenly wish I'd grabbed a flashlight. This place is deserted and there shouldn't be anyone on the property, but in the past we have had trouble with local kids coming out here after dark. Playing hide and seek and eating grapes off the vines.

The grapes aren't meant to be eaten; these aren't your store-bought variety. And all I can hope is that I don't have to call the police again.

I call out, hoping to scare off whatever or whoever is roaming about, but the footsteps progress in my direction and my heartbeat quickens.

"Hey!" I shout this time, but it comes out shaky and high, giving the impression that I'm not here to scare anyone off.

Damn my nervousness!

I can barely see my hand in front of my face, but I can feel the presence of someone coming closer and instead of running in the other direction, I again yell out, "Go away!"

A voice responds with, "Settle down, Lu." His accent catching in my ears on the first syllable and I slap at his chest and shove him when he stops in front of me.

"What the fuck are you doing out here so late?" I demand, angry with him for scaring the shit out of me.

"I could ask you the same question," he responds back casually.

"Um, I live here."

I walk around him, making my way back to my house, but as I slip past him, he shines a flashlight right in my face, my eyes blinking rapidly to try and recover from the shock. I push my palms into my eyes, rubbing gently.

"You okay?" Jack asks. "You look sad."

"I'm fine, but shouldn't you be in bed?"

He doesn't need to know why I'm out here or that I am feeling a little shitty. Nothing I do is his business, as I pry into his life.

"I fell asleep earlier, but the time change is fucking with me."

He's following me as I walk back to my house and I stop, letting him catch up so we're now walking next to each other.

"How about you have a drink with me," he says, shrugging one shoulder, and he's not asking me, but rather indicating that I should.

"I'm not having a drink with you, Jack." I shake my head, my lips set in a firm line. He's really pushing hard at this friends thing.

"Why not?"

"Because I'm your boss," I quip back, but realizing how stupid I sound. I'm just looking for an excuse not to get close to him.

"What, you worried you'll fall for me?"

"Definitely not," I say, a small condescending laugh falling from my lips. "I'm worried I'll have to fire you for sexual harassment."

"It's not harassment if both people are enjoying themselves, Lu" he adds, winking at me. "Don't pretend you don't enjoy this love/hate thing we've got going on."

I blow a hard breath out my mouth and hold back from starting an unnecessary argument with him. It leans way more toward the hate end than anything, but a part of me shivers in response to his words, my stomach suddenly fluttering.

"You sure you don't want to have a drink with me? I brought a bottle of Shiraz from home," he says trying to sweeten the deal.

We got drunk off a bottle of Shiraz when we were kids. Jack stole it from the wine rack in the cottage and we drank it together one night under the stars. It was a cool evening, much like tonight, and we sat taking swigs straight from the bottle until the whole thing was gone.

I smile a little at the memory, and Jack catches the look on my face immediately and says, "What do you say?" Trying his hand at using our walk down memory lane to convince me, and if I'm being honest, he's almost there.

"Go to bed, Jack."

"One drink, I swear that's all." He holds up one finger and gives me that cheeky smile. He's strangely hard to say no to. Either that or my sudden loneliness is pushing me in his direction.

"Fine," I say, finally conceding and I watch Jack's face light up in a way that I've never seen before. "But you owe me a package of Tim Tams."

"Deal."

Chapter Five

Jack

She follows me inside, a strange silence settling between us now, as though neither of us expected our night to end up like this. Truth be told, when I'd woken up twenty minutes ago, the remnants of a dream about her lingering, I'd been overcome with a sudden urge to just hang out with her, like we'd sometimes been able to do when I stopped teasing her for five minutes back when we were kids.

So, I'd pulled on some clothes and headed over to her place, not really sure what I was going to say or how she was going to react to me just randomly dropping by. Only just as I'd gotten there, I heard her front door slam. Following her, I couldn't stop the smile on my face as she wandered down to the fields, slowly walking a path through the vines. I'd been half-tempted to sneak up and tackle her for old times' sake, but figured it was a shitty thing to do in the dark.

"Help yourself," I say, gesturing to the packets of Tim Tams sitting on the kitchen bench.

Lu looks over at them, an audible "Holy shit," falling from her mouth when she sees how many packets I brought over.

I smile as I grab the bottle of wine and two glasses before walking out to the back deck. Lulu eventually follows me out there and I hand her a glass and take a seat, propping my bare feet up on the rail. She takes a seat beside me, slipping off her shoes and mirroring my pose.

"Why'd you bring so many?" she asks.

I look over and grin. "Figured I'd look you up while I was here," I say. "And they might be useful as a peace-offering," I add. "Or at the very least, could be used for bribery," I continue, winking.

She gives me a strange look. "You didn't know I'd be here when you took the job?"

I shrug. "Your sister has a different surname, figured your folks had sold the business."

"Never," she says. "It's been in our family for generations."

I nod, but say nothing more. "Anyway," I say, holding my glass out. "Cheers, Lu. Here's to you and me, together again."

Lulu doesn't move, staring at me for a few seconds before she lifts her glass and clinks it against mine.

I watch as she smells the contents of her glass before taking a sip, slowly swirling the liquid in her mouth before swallowing it. In the low light, surrounded by nothing but silence and stars, the whole thing is strangely erotic and I feel my own mouth go dry just watching her.

"Wow," she says, reaching for the bottle. "This is amazing. Is it one of your dad's?"

I say nothing as she reads the back label on the bottle, the lighting only just bright enough that she can make out the small print.

"Holy shit," she says, looking up at me. "You made this?"

I nod, giving her a smile as I take a sip of my wine.

"It's...it's really good, Jack," she says, obviously shocked. "Like really good."

My grin widens now. "Bet that was hard to get out," I say, nudging her bare foot with mine.

Lu swallows hard, her eyes never leaving mine even as I leave my foot resting against hers on the railing. We're barely touching, but the heat it's generating between us feels like a furnace, as though it could combust at any second.

I have to swallow hard as she continues to stare at me.

Eventually she pulls her foot away. "Only you would say something like that," she mutters, looking away.

I chuckle, taking another sip of wine as I slide lower in my chair and stare out at the night. "It is good to see you though," I say, my eyes wandering over the rows and rows of grape vines. "Seriously."

Lulu says nothing and when I turn to look at her, I see she's also staring out at the night, a strange look on her face.

"How's life been these past fourteen years?" I ask, genuinely interested.

She shrugs, still not looking at me as she replies, "Busy, hard work. But of course, I wouldn't trade it..."

"For anything," I finish off, smiling a little. "I know what you mean."

"You ever think about getting your own place?" she asks, sipping her wine. "Instead of making wine for everyone else."

"Yeah," I admit, reaching over to top up her glass. She shoots me a look that says, *what happened to only one drink?* And I smirk at her. "There's no way we are leaving this wine open and unfinished," I tell her. It's an eighty-dollar bottle, Lu."

She raises her eyebrows in surprise and I can't tell if she's impressed my wine is worth that much or shocked I'm choosing to share it with her.

"Anyway," I continue, topping up my own glass. "For sure I'd love to have my own place," I confess. "But it's hard breaking into the market in Australia. Plus, it would be a huge capital outlay and probably not something I want to do myself, especially from scratch."

"So, no significant other waiting for you back home to help out?" she asks.

I turn to look at her and she meets my stare for a few seconds before looking away, suddenly embarrassed at how personal this conversation has gotten.

I grin even though she isn't looking at me. "No, Lulu, no one waiting back at home for me," I say, knowing just how true that is. "What about you?" I add, nudging her foot again. "Seeing anyone?"

I watch as she takes a deep breath as though contemplating whether she can continue the unspoken charade of Oscar and Oliva being her kids. Clearly she realizes she can't and I watch as she turns to face me, a strange look on her face as she says, "Nope, no one special."

My heart lurches at the look in her eyes, the sadness that now fills them. "Lu," I say gently, half sitting up.

But she shakes her head and looks away. "So," she says, taking a large sip of wine. "How long do you think it's going to take to fix the crusher?"

I focus on her, watch as she fights to regain her composure, hide the hurt I know I just saw. Wanting to lighten the situation, I say, "Don't tell me you're trying to get rid of me already?"

A half smile tugs at her mouth. "Well," she says, shooting me a sideways glance.

I grin. "Come on," I tease. "Admit you like having me here again," I say, nudging her foot once more. "Admit you've missed me all these years."

She rolls her eyes now, muttering something under her breath as she takes another sip of wine. She doesn't move her foot this time though and I chalk it up to a small win that she lets me keep resting mine against hers.

The heat is back again too and it's making my fingers itch. It's surprising how much being this close to her is affecting me. Despite wanting to see her, eager to know how she is after all this time, I hadn't expected it to have such a big impact.

Especially considering everything I was running away from in Oz.

We sip our wine in silence now, me topping our glasses up once more until eventually the bottle is empty. It feels peaceful and relaxing sharing this moment and this wine with her. And a million miles away from all of the fucked up drama I was dealing with back home.

And even though this country is so different to Australia, a part of me can't help but feel at home here. I don't know if it's because of the nearly two months I spent here as a kid or because of Lulu and the way I feel drawn to her, even after all these years apart.

Either way I'm glad I'd taken the job. Even more glad that I get to work with and see Lulu every day as a result.

"Well," Lu finally says, draining her glass and standing. "I should let you get some sleep."

Immediately, I want to ask her to stay, my hand practically reaching for her as though I can somehow make it happen. Swallowing, I stand and face her, our eyes meeting in the darkness.

Lulu blinks at me and I don't know what it is, but I feel myself taking a step toward her, my hand reaching for her, my fingers circling her wrist as my thumb brushes against the soft skin on the inside.

Inside my chest, my heart is going double time, the noise so loud I swear she can hear it.

"Lulu," I whisper, her eyes widening as I take another step closer, our bodies only inches apart now.

The space between us feels charged with electricity, the attraction intense, as though everything I felt for her as a kid has only been magnified by all the time we've spent apart.

I'm suddenly overcome by want, by an urge to pull her against me, wrap my arms around her and kiss her hard, convince her not to go but to come inside with me instead.

But as though she can read my mind, she suddenly blinks, pulls her arm from my grip and says, "Goodnight, Jack," her voice strange in the silence of this moment.

I watch as she walks down the back steps and over to her house, going in through the unlocked back door, not once looking back.

Shoving a rough hand through my hair, I finish off my wine as I attempt to get myself back in control. Whatever that was just then, I have no idea how to explain it, I only know she felt it too.

When I head back inside, I notice the packet of Tim Tams she obviously chose are still sitting on the kitchen table. Knowing this is likely a really bad idea, one that could get me yelled at, or worse still, fired, I pick up the packet and walk back outside.

Over at her house, I watch as the kitchen light switches off and is replaced by a light in what I assume is her bedroom. Without stopping to think, I walk quickly down the back steps, cross over to her yard and go quietly inside the back door, holding my breath in case she hears me.

I wait a second for my eyes to adjust and then before I can question what the fuck I'm doing, I walk through the mudroom to her kitchen, where I leave the packet of biscuits on the island and quickly walk back out.

The next morning, I wake early, my jetlagged body still struggling to adjust to the million time zones I've crossed to be here. Despite the wine and my exhaustion, it had taken me a long time to fall asleep last night, my mind whirling with confused thoughts over that moment on the back deck just before Lu left.

I still wasn't entirely sure what had come over me, nor was I sure what I was supposed to do about it either.

Shaking my head, I drag myself from bed and into a cold shower, before quickly dressing and walking out on to the back deck with a cup of coffee.

I watch the sun as it rises over the fields of grape vines, casting a warm glow over rows and rows of green. Next door, Lu's house is silent and I can only assume she's still asleep. Hasn't discovered what I snuck inside and left for her.

Glancing down at her backyard, I notice a compost bin overflowing, the lid barely containing all of the waste jammed inside it. Finishing my coffee, I leave the mug on the back table before wandering over to take care of it.

After I'm done, I head down to the sheds containing the broken crusher, knowing I'm early and the others aren't likely to be there yet.

Grabbing one of the empty plastic bins by the back room, I head over to the stairs and climb up to the machine. Peering inside I almost cringe at all the grapes she's going to lose.

"What a fucking waste," I mutter as I reach in and grab the bunches that just might be able to be salvaged. As I gently place them in the plastic bin, an idea starts to form in my mind. Working quickly, I clear out all the intact bunches I can, managing to fill four containers, which I then take to the back room and shove beneath one of the counters for later.

Just as I walk back into the shed, in walks Lulu, Oscar in tow.

"Morning, Lulu," I say, grinning at her. "Oscar," I say, holding out my hand to him as he proceeds to go through the handshake he's apparently decided we need to use for each greeting and farewell.

She watches us, rolling her eyes in obvious annoyance.

"Get out on the wrong side of the bed this morning?" I ask, glancing at her.

She exhales loudly. "No," she shoots back.

I chuckle. "You sure? You seem a little, I don't know," I pause, hand under my chin as I run my eyes up and down her body. "On edge or something?" I add.

Lulu stands with her hands on her hips, her eyes on fire as she once again shoots daggers at me. "I'm perfectly fine," she says through gritted teeth.

Laughing, I walk toward her, stopping when we are side by side. Leaning over so my mouth is against her ear, I whisper. "You know, I have the perfect solution for taking that edge off."

I feel her stiffen beside me and I can't resist laughing a little. "Just sayin', Lu, that offer I made, it still stands."

She whips around so she's facing me now, her cheeks red and her mouth open as though she's about to rip me a new one. It takes every ounce of self-control I have not to burst out laughing at how fucking adorable she looks right now.

"Honestly, Jack," she says, jaw tight. "I have no..."

"Aunt Lulu," Oscar says, interrupting her. "Everyone's here."

I bite my bottom lip to stop the laugh from escaping, and when we both turn I see there are now half a dozen guys standing inside the shed, staring at us. One of them looks extremely pissed off, his eyes flicking between Lu and me as we stand face to face.

Almost immediately I want to tell him to back the fuck off, to rein it in and take his eyes off his boss. But I don't say anything. As much as I might like to tease Lu, give her shit because I love driving her crazy, there's no way I'm going to embarrass or belittle her in front of her employees.

The stuff I do and say to her is private.

"Well, we can talk about it later," I say, my words loud enough for everyone to hear. Giving her a small grin, I gesture to the waiting workers and say, "You want to introduce me?"

Chapter Six

Lauren

He's always right there on the edge of me forgiving him for being a shithead, but he always manages to bring me right back to hating him.

This morning I woke up to a pack of Tim Tams sitting on the island in my kitchen, while creepy as it was, something about it was also really sweet.

The creepy Tim Tams are now looking creepier than ever and if he was hoping to leave them as a peace offering, he's going to have to do better.

Like hell if I'm letting him undermine me in front of my staff; a staff that respects me and knows I run this place like a well-oiled machine.

They're all standing there waiting for me to say something, because it has been years since I've brought someone new in and it's very clear that Jack is here for a while.

He's elbow deep in grapes, and by the way he's standing he's about to start ordering people around.

"Good morning," I greet, turning around and smiling at my crew. "This is Jack Wilson. Some of you may even remember him or his dad from when they were here many years ago."

Jack approaches and reaches out, shaking hands with each one of the guys and greeting them with his usual flourish of,

"Nice meet you, mate" and all the other accented over the top lingo he likes to drop.

Kangaroos, wombats, square poop, didgeridoo bullshit.

Feeling far too full of himself as he unloads his credentials and name-drops his dad to the guys, so I knock him down a few notches.

"Jack is here to fix the crusher. He is by no means in charge, so if you need anything or have any questions, as always, everything is directed to me."

I give Jack a side eye and he's smirking like he always does, totally unfazed by my comments.

Even worse, Oscar is looking up at him like he's an absolute genius and I take Oscar by the hand, tugging him close to me. I shake my head and widen my eyes at him, but he just sticks out his tongue in response.

"Listen," I whisper, bending down so I'm on his level. "You're siding with the wrong person here. Remember who has a tub of Twizzlers in her pantry."

Oscar laughs, throwing his arms around my waist before he runs out of the shed, disappearing into the vineyard.

It's Tommy who pipes up first stating, "We've had tons of people here to fix that damn crusher. What makes you think this guy's suddenly going to be able to?" He tosses his thumb in Jack's direction and shoots him a look that lets me know he's on my side.

Finally!

I give the guys the lowdown on why I believe Jack can fix it and on what needs to be done, letting each of them know their place and what I expect from them. We've never had to take on something of this magnitude and the last thing we need are too many chefs in the kitchen.

I put Tommy in charge because I have a shipment coming in and I need to be up front to collect that. I called Penny in early so she could help me check it in and get the shelves of the gift shop restocked. With the nice weather comes tourists, and we need to be prepared.

I'm about to walk out when I remember my composter.

"Hey Tommy," I call and he trots over to where I'm standing.

"Yeah?"

"When you get a chance could you empty my composter? Dump it in the usual spots."

"Yeah, no problem," he says, his hand resting on my shoulder.

"Already done!" Jack shouts from the platform above the crusher. He lifts his chin toward us like the pompous ass that he is.

"What?" I practically shout back and suddenly Jack is standing next to me, his hand on my other shoulder mimicking Tommy's stance.

"Yep, emptied it this morning. I noticed it after I left your place," he replies winking at me, and I swear if I were a cartoon character steam would shooting from my ears.

"You're deluded, because being invited to my house and sneaking into it are two different things."

"Where'd you dump it?" Tommy asks, his tone clipped.

"Right where it's supposed to be," Jack bites back, his arms now folded across his chest. "Some things never change, right Lu?"

"You can say that again," I mutter as I walk away, letting Jack and Tommy duke it out.

Several hours later and the shelves are restocked, the summer wine list has been updated and the tasting room is packed with people.

It's nearing lunchtime and my stomach growls reminding me to eat. I've been up since six and totally forgot to eat breakfast. I had downed a couple of Tim Tams from the creeper pack Jack left, but it isn't doing me much good right now.

I hear Penny laugh and I smile. She's young, cute and chatty with an infectious laugh. It's why I hired her to run my tasting room. People love her. They get drunk and buy things from her. It's a win for everyone.

I look out the window of my office onto the patio and every table is full. People are drinking and eating, and it's these kinds of days that make me grateful that I had the opportunity to take over this place when my parents retired.

I hear Penny laugh again, knowing she's killing it out there, but it's when I hear her say Jack's name that I bolt out of my chair and hightail it down the hall and into the tasting room.

Stopping in the doorway, I find him behind the counter with Penny, encroaching on her personal space and yucking it up with the customers.

I'm not paying him to flirt with my employees and bother my customers.

I watch Jack open a bottle of wine, giving Penny explicit instructions on how to pour it and telling her she's keeping the temperature of the chiller slightly too high. His arrogance makes me irate, but I let it play out just a little bit longer.

Again I watch as Jack attempts to wow the customers with his knowledge and for some reason, they are swooning over his every word, as is Penny. Jack's hand slides down Penny's back and before he can reach her ass, I clear my throat alerting them that I'm standing in the doorway.

"Jack," I say, but it comes out harsh and like a warning. Penny instantly shies away from him and returns to being the professional I hired.

I don't blame her for being attracted to him. He can be incredibly charming and listening to him with the customers kind of makes me swoon a little too.

As a kid he was nerdy and skinny, but that charm factor was always there. He just grew into it, and now the inside fits the outside.

I walk back down the hall that leads to my office with Jack following closely behind.

"Jack, I hired you to fix my crusher not flirt with my employees," I say giving him a stern look, but when I catch his eyes, he's grinning at me.

"Come on, Lulu. Don't be jealous. You know you're the only one I want to flirt with."

I roll my eyes and walk toward the door giving him a shove and telling him to get back to work.

"That's why I'm here," he says, halting my shoving by planting his feet and slipping his hand to my hip.

When his fingers slide along my shirt, lifting it slightly, I feel the warmth of skin brush against mine. It's like someone has set my skin on fire and the room grows suddenly hot.

I try to control my strange urge to press my body against him, but the gasp that leaves my lips slips out, letting him know he's getting to me.

"Have dinner with me tonight," Jack murmurs, his hand now resting on my lower back. The pressure of his hand forcing me to step closer and now the space between us is barely existent.

Goosebumps rise up on my skin despite the scorching temperature in the room and I swallow hard, trying to force back my obvious attraction to him.

I chalk it all up to loneliness. I haven't been this close to a man in months, and at this point I'm certain anyone could elicit this response from my body.

When I finally regain my ability to speak all I can get out is a breathy, "What?"

"Have dinner with me," he repeats and I shake my head, but my damn body betrays me and I brush against him as I try to move away. I need to put some distance between us.

"I'll take that as a yes," he says, reaching for my hand as I make my way to the door. His fingers glide along the inside of my wrist and brush the center of my palm, lingering for a second on my fingertips.

I don't argue with him because the most important thing I need to do right now is get away from him before I do something stupid.

I leave out the side door and nearly run into Ellen as I do. Jack is hot on my heels and when she takes in the look on both our faces she laughs out loud.

"Jack was just filling me in on how things are going with the crusher," I tell her, but my voice is high and I sound like I've been running.

"Oh really?" Ellen questions, her eyebrows going up in surprise at what seems like an obvious lie.

"It looks like I have to order some parts. Could be a few weeks before they arrive. The machine's gonna be down for a bit though."

Without waiting for Ellen or me to respond Jack walks off and I curse under my breath because I didn't have a chance to clarify that I absolutely am not having dinner with him. Probably all part of his plan.

"So, did you finally get your rebound bang in with Jack?" Ellen asks, laughing, and I storm away from her. I can't even deal with her constant teasing and Jack's ability to make me weak in the knees.

Ellen's teasing doesn't end there, but I continue to avoid her until our day ends. It turns out it's hard work avoiding two people despite the size of the vineyard, and by the time I grab a beer from my fridge and park my ass on the couch, I'm exhausted.

A knock comes on my door only a few minutes after I begin to relax and I let out an annoyed huff as I peel myself off the couch.

I open the door to find Jack standing there with a bag and a bottle of wine. I look down at the bag and see takeaway containers from the small restaurant we have on the property.

"Tell me you didn't con my restaurant staff into making you dinner."

"Never," he says, feigning like he's appalled that I questioned his integrity. "I bought this." He raises the bag up as if me seeing it closer will make me believe he didn't just charm them into giving him free food. "Hopefully you still love sauerkraut like you did as a kid."

"From what I remember you loved it too."

"Oh I still do, but you can't get a Reuben in Oz like you can here in the States."

He knows my weakness and I don't know if that's a good thing or a bad thing. It's kinda sweet that after all these years he remembers these things about me. It's not like I blocked everything about him from my memory either.

"I'm pretty sure I never agreed to dinner with you and showing up here with a Reuben is a low blow." But even as I say it the smile on my face tells him he won. I can't send him away now.

"I hoped it would work," Jack says, shifting his weight back and forth and I realize I've rudely left him holding everything and waiting for me to invite him in.

I take the bottle of wine from him and step aside. Jack walks in and heads right for my kitchen, setting the bag down, he begins unpacking.

He's brought two sandwiches, chips, fruit, and to make things even better, a pack of Tim Tams for dessert. He sure knows how to win me over.

"What were you planning to do with all this food if I sent you away?" I ask, as we both sit down and start eating.

"I guess I would've just eaten both." He shrugs his shoulders, taking a big bite of his sandwich. His eyes roll back and he lets out an incredibly sexy low groan. "Might still," he adds and I laugh as he tries to covertly slide his hand over to my plate.

My memory catches and I think back to all the times we'd meet up in the kitchen after it closed, when both of us knew we shouldn't be there, and we'd make our own Reuben. Mine piled high with a ridiculous amount of sauerkraut and Jack's with like thirty pickles on the side.

My dad caught us once and Jack took the blame. Claiming he didn't know we weren't supposed to be in the kitchen and that he convinced me it was okay. It was complete bullshit but because my parents thought Jack walked on water, they let it slide. After that we were better at sneaking in there.

"You get extra pickles?" I ask, and Jack reaches into the bag, pulling out a to-go container filled with them.

I laugh out loud as we relive our childhood in my kitchen.

Chapter Seven

Jack

It's nice being here with Lu like this, laughing as we remember all the shit we used to get up to as kids. Not having her be pissed off at me like she was earlier today is a bonus too.

I knew she'd been shitty when she caught me mucking around with Penny earlier, which is kind of what I'd been aiming for. After watching that Tommy guy strut about marking his territory, I figured I'd see what happened when I turned the tables a little.

It had been good to know I could get her so worked up, even if it had all been harmless. As nice as Penny was, she wasn't my type. Or the subject of all my fantasies.

But sitting here with Lu now, it's nice not having to worry about anyone else getting in the way or interrupting us, as we laugh about our frequent break-ins to the kitchen and tasting room back when we were teenagers.

"So, you really want to stick with the story that I was a total pain in the arse to have around back then?" I ask, smiling at her.

Lu takes another bite of her sandwich, her tongue slipping out to lick the corner of her mouth in a way that is far too sexy to be associated with eating food. "Well," she starts, swallowing. "You weren't *all* bad," she says, rolling her eyes when I grin and nod in agreement with her. "But you were a huge pain in my ass most of the time."

"Pfft," I say. "As if. You loved having me here, just like you do now."

"Mmmm," is all she says, before licking her fingers.

I reach for the bottle of wine to top up our glasses, anything to avoid reaching for her and sucking those fingers of hers into my own mouth. It's amazing how crazy she can drive me without even trying.

"What?" I say, as I take a sip of wine and force my mind to stop thinking dirty thoughts. "Does it really bother you having me here?" I ask seriously, my smile gone now.

Lulu looks at me, her eyes meeting mine. She says nothing for what feels like forever and just when I'm starting to think I have seriously misread everything about us and this whole situation, she smiles, lifts her wine glass to her lips and says, "No, it doesn't."

I grin now, reaching over and clinking my glass against hers as I say, "Finally, she admits she likes me!"

Lulu laughs, even as she says, "Now, let's not get too carried away."

My smile widens. "Just stating the truth, Lu, that's all."

We continue eating in silence for a while, a relaxed calmness settling between us. Eventually though, I find myself asking her about one of the guys from earlier today, unable to control my curiosity over just what his deal is with her.

"So, this Tommy guy," I start and Lulu immediately starts laughing.

"Oh, please don't tell me you're jealous," she says, shaking her head at me.

I shrug, feigning nonchalance. "Just wondering what his story is, that's all. He seemed to get his panties in a wad about me being over at your house."

Lulu grins at me and I can tell she loves the idea of me being annoyed by all of this. Shrugging, she says, "He's just a little protective, that's all."

"Protective of what?" I ask. "Of you from me?"

Lu bursts out laughing as she reaches for the packet of Tim Tams. "You *are* jealous!"

I shake my head. "No I'm not," I say even though the tone of my voice clearly indicates I am. "Just wondered that's all. Did you guys used to date or something?"

Lu swipes under her eyes, as though this whole thing is hilarious to her. "No, Jack, we did not," she says. "I don't mix business with pleasure," she adds, giving me a pointed look.

I'm not sure what she's referring to, but I smile as I meet her stare and say, "First time for everything, Lulu."

"I mean it, Jack," she says. "Stay away from Penny."

Now it's me laughing as I shake my head at her. "Now who's jealous?!"

"No," she says, her voice stern. "It's called being professional," she adds.

I chuckle, reaching over and grabbing her hand and threading our fingers together. "Like I said, Lulu, you're the one I like to flirt with," I say, winking.

Lulu lets out a long breath, her hand curling into a fist in mine before she eventually pulls it away. "The same rule applies, Jack," she says.

"Um hm," I murmur, resting my chin on my hand, elbow propped on the bench. "Well, you should know, I do like a challenge."

After dinner, we spend a couple of hours watching mindless TV together as we finish off the wine and the entire packet of Tim Tams. Eventually though, I realize I'm going to have to make a move, so I push up off the couch, before reaching for her hand and pulling her up too.

Before she has a chance to protest, I pull her into a tight hug, wrapping my arms around her shoulders.

"Thanks for a great night, Lulu," I whisper, my mouth at her ear. I feel her body sag against mine, even as her hands remain in tight fists between us on my chest. Smiling, I can't resist adding, "See how much fun it can be, hanging out together?" Before kissing her on the cheek and releasing her.

She stares up at me, her cheeks flushed as I grin down at her, brushing my fingers against her bare shoulder. Before she has a chance to tell me off, I add, "Goodnight," before turning and walking out of her house.

My good mood evaporates quickly though, the second I get inside and glance at my laptop, sitting open on the dining table.

My email is open and there are several new ones sitting in my inbox. Most of them are from Melissa with subject headings like *Where are you?* and *Please call me!* One of them even says *I went past your house...what the hell's going on Jack?*

Sighing, I delete all of them without bothering to open or read them. I don't give a shit what she has to say to me, just like I'm not interested in telling her where I am either. She lost all right to that information a long time ago.

There's another email from Matt too, asking pretty much the same thing, which I also delete.

The pair of them can go to hell, I think, as I contemplate grabbing another bottle of wine and heading back over to Lu's house.

But I don't, knowing I have no desire to explain all of this to her right now, regardless of how much I might want to hang out with her. So instead, I head to my room, strip off my clothes and climb into bed.

As I lie there, staring up the ceiling though, I can't help but smile as I forget about all the shit going on back home and think back to Lu's words; *I don't mix business with pleasure* and how much fun I'm going to have convincing her that she should.

The next day, I'm lying under the crusher when I hear Lulu shout, "Jack?"

"In here," I reply, without moving. I'm on my back underneath the huge machine, both hands on a wrench as I attempt to loosen the pump tap, which is probably clogged with so much shit I'm going to spend the whole afternoon cleaning it out.

I'm not sure which brainiac though jamming a broken crusher with more fruit was a good idea, but if Lulu doesn't have words with them, I sure as fuck will.

It's not only a waste of fruit, it's fucked up my machine too.

"What are you doing?" comes her voice, closer now.

I look over and see her long, tanned legs, her hands on her hips as she stands there presumably watching me, the upper half of her body hidden from view.

"Yoga," I reply sarcastically.

Even though I can't see her face. I know she rolls her eyes at me. "Ha ha smart ass," she says. "Do you think..."

"FUCK!" I suddenly shout, cutting her off as the relief valve finally gives and liters of rancid, week-old red grape juice gushes out of the crusher and all over me.

Almost immediately, Lulu starts pissing herself laughing, great heaving laughs that have her doubled over at the waist, hands on her knees.

Cursing, I yank on the wrench, shutting off the flow before dragging myself out from underneath the crusher. I'm fucking drenched and now purple thanks to all the shit in the tank.

Reaching for the nearby hose, I turn on the water so I can wash my face, all the while Lulu continues to laugh her arse off at me.

"You find this funny?" I ask as I scrub a hand over my face, flicking off the random stems that have somehow made it through the filter and contributed to the problem.

Lulu nods, barely able to speaks as she gets out a "Fuck yes," between laughs.

I grin, stepping closer. "Oh, is that so?" I ask.

She nods, wiping away the tears from her cheeks. "Serves you right after what you did to me when we were kids," she says, still hung up about me tackling her into the mud.

"What *I* did to *you*?" I ask, taking another step toward her.

"Uh huh," she replies, hiccupping a little as her laughs start up again. "Karma's a real bitch, isn't it, Jack? Although to be fair, this is way better than mud," she adds. "You're fucking purple!"

She gestures toward my formerly white t-shirt as she once more dissolves into hysterical laughter. Grinning, I take another step closer.

"Speaking of karma," I say and then before she has a chance to say anything more or even register what I'm about to do, I point the nozzle of the hose at her and turn the water back on, immediately soaking her in a blast of barely warm water.

"JACK!" she screams, her voice high and her hands up as though that will somehow protect her or stop me.

Now it's me laughing, giving her another dose of the spray so she's properly drenched.

"Ahhh," comes her scream as she jumps to the side, eyes closed as she scrambles to get past me.

"Not so fast, Lulu," I say, grinning as I grab her arm and pull her close, turning the water on once again.

"Jack," she shouts again in protest, her eyes scrunched closed as water falls over her and now drips from her hair, down her shoulders and over her tank top. The black material is stuck to her body, highlighting every single curve as a result.

I can't help but admire her, especially as the cold water has had a very sexy effect on her breasts too.

"What?" I ask, as though I have no idea what she's talking about.

"You little shit," she says, grabbing the hose from my hand and turning the water back on me now.

I burst out laughing, reaching for her again, but this time grabbing her wrist and hauling her against me. Her body crashes against mine, the hose still spraying us both with water.

"That's a mighty fine view, Lulu," I say, as my other hand moves to her waist and my eyes drop to her breasts.

"Jack," she repeats, the word catching in her throat as she drops the hose. I watch as her eyes move to my chest and the wet t-shirt that's now plastered to my skin.

"What?" I whisper, stepping even closer so our chests are almost touching. "Don't tell me you aren't admiring the view too?"

She swallows hard. "Let me go," she murmurs, even as she makes no attempt to pull away.

I grin, licking my lips as I stare at her mouth. "You gonna apologize?"

Her eyes meet mine and she shakes her head.

"No?" I ask, cocking my head to the side.

"No," she repeats, the word barely audible.

My grin widens. "Okay then," I say before lowering my head to hers, my eyes focused squarely on those parted full lips of hers.

"Aunt Lauren!" comes Oliva's high-pitched voice, causing Lulu to immediately jump backward before my lips have a chance to reach hers.

I watch as she steps away from me, her hands running over her hips as though she's somehow trying to straighten herself out, leaving me standing in the middle of the room wondering if that was really about to happen.

"Aunt Lauren?" comes Oliva's voice again, closer this time.

"In here," she calls out, her voice shaky.

Oliva walks in and stops when she sees both of us, soaking wet and me half purple.

"You look like Barney," she says, pointing at me.

I chuckle, even as internally, my body is going haywire at the thought that I very nearly kissed Lulu.

"Yeah, I think I might need a shower," I say, walking toward her.

As I do, I brush past Lu, ours arms touching as my fingers skim across the inside of her wrist, making her shudder.

"What do you think, Oliva?" I ask, arms out as I turn in a slow circle in front of her.

She crosses her arms over her chest as she stares up at me, her face solemn as she nods. "Definitely."

Grinning, I step closer and slide both my hands over Oliva's ears before looking back at Lu. "Just remember, Lu, you're welcome to come join me," I say, winking before removing my hands and walking out of the shed.

Chapter Eight

Lauren

Olivia is staring up at me wide-eyed and grinning as my heart races in my chest, my words trapped in my throat. I feel like there's an electric current running though my body and every single nerve is on fire.

I almost kissed Jack and fuck me if it wouldn't have been amazing.

I scrub my hands over my face trying to clear my head and stop myself from running after Jack. I've never wanted someone to kiss me as badly as I wanted Jack to just now. The way his body looked all muscled and tan, his t-shirt wet and clinging to him, accentuating every single part of his chest.

Hell, maybe Ellen is right? Maybe I do need a rebound? And who better to do that with than Jack. He's not sticking around, and the likelihood of me getting attached is pretty much non-existent. Or at least that's what I'm telling myself. I won't find myself in the same situation I did before.

"Mommy's looking for you," Olivia says, tugging on the bottom of my wet tank top. "Was Jack flirting with you again?" Her hands are on her hips now and her self-taught bitch face is in full effect.

Looking down at her, I can't help but laugh as she glares at Jack's back as he walks away.

She learned from the best of them and right now she looks exactly like me. Ellen is constantly reminding me to stop letting my face say what I'm thinking, but I fail miserably at it. Turns out it must be hereditary because Olivia is my soul mate when it comes to maintaining a solid chronic bitch face.

"Take it easy, killer," I say teasingly, giving her braid a little pull as I reach for her hand and walk out of the shed with her to find Ellen.

I walk the property for a few minutes with Olivia and since we can't find her immediately we start goofing around. If I'm being honest, I'm still avoiding Ellen and it's not just because of her incessant teasing. I know the conversation is coming; the one where she reminds me to stop being so closed off and bitter, her words not mine.

After about thirty minutes of playing avoidance hide and seek with Olivia my phone chimes out with a text.

Ellen: Where are you?

Me: Out in the fields with Olivia.

Ellen: Meet me in your office?

Me: K

Ellen is sitting at my desk when I walk in, sorting through some papers and I'm sure squaring away payroll. She keeps that part of our business organized and running smoothly. Numbers have always been her strong suit and without her, this place wouldn't run as smoothly.

"Hey, what's going on?" I say to her as I walk in, keeping things casual and hoping she wants to discuss payroll or purchasing or something other than Jack.

"Hey, I'm sorry about the other day," she says abruptly and I have no idea what she's talking about. Guessing the look on my face indicates that because she continues. "I'm sorry I said you weren't single by choice. I shouldn't have brought it up."

"It's okay."

"No, it's not," Ellen snaps back and I'm not sure what to say. "We do this thing where we joke about it and it shouldn't be a joke. He fucked you up and you know it. It's why you haven't let anyone get close to you. It's why you're shutting Jack out."

"I'm not shutting Jack out," I defend. "I'm not interested in Jack." The lie falls from my mouth so easily like a hot knife through butter.

Ellen nods her head, but the look on her face says she doesn't believe me. I don't even believe myself anymore.

"I'm just saying you should give him a chance. He's not..." Ellen trails off, not wanting to say his name.

It's become commonplace for neither of us to say it. In the beginning I just cried when anyone mentioned him. Then my sadness turned to anger, me snapping at anyone who talked about a wedding, getting married and anything to do with marriage. Weddings at the vineyard are still on hiatus.

"I hear you, Ellen, but..."

"You're lonely," she says, interrupting me.

"Just because I'm alone doesn't mean I'm lonely."

"Whatever you say," Ellen says, shrugging her shoulders. "I just want you to be happy and I know you're not that."

She's right. I haven't been happy in a long time, but I'm pretty certain I'm allowed to be unhappy. I don't think there's a hard and fast rule on when you get over being stood up at your own wedding.

"I know and I'll get there," I say, reassuring her and myself.

It's Jack's accent that cuts through our conversation. He's back in the adjoining tasting room, and back at it with my customers and Penny.

I roll my eyes and Ellen laughs.

"See, you really think I'd be interested in that? He's out there flirting with Penny now. It's just what he does." My hand flits at the door and Ellen laughs again.

"He's flirting with Penny to get your attention."

"Oh my god, you sound just like Mom."

Ellen and I walk out of my office just as Tommy is walking up. Stopping us, he begins to fill us in on a few issues that have arisen with one our crushers being down. Production is behind and we only have a few more weeks before we run out of the cabernet we produce on the property. While this isn't a huge disaster, it's enough to put us a little on edge.

Tourist season is almost in full swing and what kind of winery are we if we run out of one of our biggest sellers? The whole process usually takes us at least twelve weeks and with our main machine down, we need to come up with plan B.

"Off-site?" Ellen suggests and it's really our only option.

We use an off-site co-packer to produce some of our cheaper wines and until this crusher is fixed it looks like this is it. The quality won't be nearly as good, but it'll sell.

Ellen heads back into my office to make some calls and see if our co-packer even has the capacity or the room to add another wine to our production schedule.

I turn, my eyes catching Jack through the window of the tasting room. He's behind the counter with Penny and they're laughing and chatting with customers.

"Lauren?" Tommy calls despite me standing next to him. He's obviously been calling my name.

"Yeah?" I respond, turning back toward Tommy.

"You okay?" The sympathy is in his eyes. He was there when it all went to shit. It was Tommy's sister who filled in for me when I couldn't get out of bed. He's been a part of this company since Ellen and I took over and he's as loyal as they come. But even more than being loyal he watched me fall apart and he was there to pick up the pieces. Without Tommy this place would've gone under when my life was at its lowest point.

"Yeah, I'm fine," I respond, trying not to let it show that I'm bothered by Jack's friendliness toward Penny.

Tommy rests his hands on my shoulders, his eyes looking directly into mine. "Don't let anyone change the progress you've made. Things are good. You're good."

I nod my head unable to speak, a lump forming in my throat at the kindness in his words. I fight back the tears that form in my eyes, blinking hard as I hear Jack call out my name.

"This guy giving you a hard time, Lu?" Jack calls as he approaches, a stern look on his face. He slips his arm around my waist and I shy away, that feeling of tears suddenly returning.

"No Jack. Tommy and I were just discussing some production issues." My voice sounds hollow and right now I'd give anything to be back in the shed with Jack, the hose drenching both of us. It's better than feeling like this.

"I gotta get back to work," Tommy says, his glare staring deeply at Jack.

"Good call, mate," Jack quips, and I turn to look at him, my lips pursed as I swat at his arm.

"Mind your business, Jack," I warn, walking away to finally change out of these wet clothes.

"Need some help?" Jack calls after me, jogging a bit catch up. "I've had me a shower, but I'm happy to help you out." He nudges me with his shoulder and it's hard to not find his blatant comes-ons kind of charming.

"While I appreciate your help, I think I can take care of this myself."

"Well, I guess I'll see you later, Lu," Jack says, giving up far easier than he usually does and the stupid part of me can't help but read into it. Maybe he is interested in Penny? Maybe I've played hard to get for a little too long? "Hey, Lu?"

"Yeah?"

"You're lucky Olivia caught us because that kiss was about to be fucking epic."

And just like that he draws me back in.

The night comes quickly, but sleep doesn't. I'm three wines deep, but still wide awake and my thoughts are swirling with everything that Ellen, Tommy and Jack said today. I turn off the TV even though I know I'm not going to fall asleep.

I slide my feet into my boots and grab a flashlight this time, but when I look out the window, there isn't a light on in the cottage Jack is currently occupying. Guess I don't really need to worry about him sneaking up on me.

The flashlight is unnecessary. I know the path in the darkness. I'd know it with my eyes closed. It's something I'll never be able to erase from my memory.

It only takes me about five minutes to walk there, my key slipping into the lock of the small shed set a little farther back.

I turn the light on and find the fuse box, flipping the dozen or so labeled switches and I take a deep breath before I walk out.

My eyes are closed when I step out the door, and for a second, I rethink my actions. It's been awhile since I've done this and I should probably just head back to my house.

But I don't stop myself from opening my eyes and taking in the hundreds of trees and grapevines covered in tiny white lights. The trellis' flowers are now blooming and they practically glow under the sparkling white lights that are wrapped around it.

This is where I was supposed to get married, and while the chairs are missing and the people are gone, I can still picture it like it was yesterday.

The flowers on the trellis were planted a year in advance, pale pink Eden roses, because I needed them to be in bloom on that day. They've been growing ever since, even when I don't water them, even though I couldn't care less if they die.

I stand under the trellis for a few seconds before my gaze falls on the Weeping Willow's trunk wrapped in lights; the swing still tied with thick rope to one of its branches.

I remember watching weddings take place here as a kid and being mesmerized by its beauty, and I knew then that this would be the place where I would get married. I'd sit on the swing in my white dress, the backdrop of the vineyard and the lights. It would be as perfect as all the weddings I'd seen play out here.

But now it's all ruined.

I hate that he was able to take my happiness with him, but I hate that he ruined all the wonderful memories I have of this place.

I walk over to the swing, tugging on the rope, wondering if it will hold me. It's been unused for some time now. There have been no pictures of brides or grooms on it for months.

I'm certain Oscar and Olivia haven't used it either, especially after I yelled at them on a particularly bad day. Telling them to get off it and never come back here again.

Olivia had cried and called me mean. It broke my heart and still does, but Ellen constantly reminds me that they are resilient. They forgive easily and they love with all their heart.

This vineyard is as much their sanctuary as it is mine and I ruined a part of it for them just like he did for me.

Because I am bitter.

Because I am lonely.

I sit down on the swing, my feet pushing off the ground to get it moving and it picks up speed, my head falls back, letting the wind blow through my hair.

With each pass of the swing, I feel lighter, like the weight I've carried today is disappearing, and I try to take myself back to that moment in the shed with Jack. His lips nearly touching mine, the happiness I felt being near him. It was the first time in a long time that I can remember laughing, like truly laughing.

It wasn't forced. I wasn't reminding myself to laugh. It just came naturally as does my attraction to Jack. There's something about him that calms me, but also makes me feel alive.

My eyes are closed as I swing, my hair blowing wildly and when I open my eyes, the vineyard is lit up like a single ship on an empty ocean. Everything around it is dark, pitch-black except the millions of twinkling lights.

I often wonder if it can be seen from the sky, a beacon of light in an otherwise black existence.

One thing I do know, if you're anywhere on the property at night, you can see the glow radiating from this part of the fields.

Chapter Nine

Jack

My phone ringing is what wakes me and for a second I think I must be back in Australia because no one has called me since I got to the States. I reach for it just as the ringing stops and when I see the name on the screen, I'm glad I missed the call.

"Fucks sake, Mel," I mutter to myself.

It's bad enough all the emails she keeps flooding my inbox with, but to now start calling me. I'd thought I'd made it pretty obvious the last time I saw her that I never wanted to speak to her again.

Clearly, she isn't getting the message.

There'd been a heap more emails when I finished up with work yesterday, only this time I'd actually opened a couple, only to immediately delete them when I saw all the bullshit they contained.

It had totally killed any ideas I'd had of heading over to Lu's house and trying to pick back up with that almost kiss we'd had earlier in the day too. Instead, I'd sat on the couch nursing a beer in the darkness, my eyes blankly watching a TV show that I wasn't following, before I eventually dragged myself to bed.

My phone chimes out to let me know she's left a voicemail. Groaning, I drag myself from bed, pulling on a pair of track pants before wandering into the kitchen to make some coffee.

I most definitely need caffeine to hear this, probably laced with alcohol if I'm being honest.

I switch on the machine and while it does its thing, I take a deep breath and listen to the message I really should just ignore and delete.

"Jack, hi, it's me, Mel," she starts, as though I can't possibly work out that the voice belongs to the woman who ruined my life. "Look, I don't know where you are or what's going on here, but we really need to talk. Can you please answer my emails or better yet, return this phone call? Please, Jack, I..." she pauses and already my body is bracing for what I think she's going to say, the words that are nothing but lies. "I miss you, okay and I..."

The message cuts off before she has a chance to say anymore and I'm grateful. Throwing my phone on the counter, I turn and grab my coffee just as a knock sounds at the front door.

Walking over, I nearly drop my cup when I see who it is.

"Lu, hey," I say, grinning at her, the voicemail now a distant memory.

"Hi," she says, her eyes flicking to my bare chest.

I watch as she licks her lips and swallows hard and I can't resist saying, "You here to finally take me up on my offer?"

Lu immediately rolls her eyes, shaking her head as she pushes past me and walks into the house. I follow her into the kitchen, chuckling a little while also using the opportunity to check her out. She's wearing some sort of summer dress that's nothing more than a piece of material that stops just above her knees, thin straps on the shoulders that I'm already itching to pull down.

"No, smart ass," she says as she walks in and pours a coffee for herself.

"No?" I repeat.

Lu shakes her head as she grabs her mug.

"Ok, so what are you here for?" I ask. "I mean aside from the whole you can't stop thinking about me thing, obviously."

Lu rolls her eyes again. "Oh boy," she mutters. "Even though I'm already regretting this, I'm actually here to see if you want to take your rental car back. It must be costing you a fortune hanging on to it and you can use ones of ours. I was going to suggest I follow you into town so you can return it. Maybe, ahh, maybe see if you wanted to grab lunch or something before we come back?"

My grin widens as I stand watching her, hip against the kitchen bench, coffee in hand.

"What?" she asks defensively.

I laugh. "Oh nothing," I say, shaking my head a little as I finish my coffee.

"No really, what?" she repeats, frustrated. "What are you thinking right now?"

I shake my head. "Nothing, Lulu, nothing at all," I tease. "I'm just gonna take a quick shower before we go though," I add on my way out of the kitchen. "Did you want to…" I pause, gesturing first to her and then in the direction of the bathroom.

"Go," she says, throwing a tea towel at me.

When I walk back into the kitchen, Lu is perched at the kitchen bench, another mug of coffee in front of her, alongside what is now a half empty packet of Tim Tams.

"I thought we were going for lunch?" I ask, grabbing the packet from her.

She swallows, groaning a little. "It is seriously criminal that you keep all of these in here, you know," she says, licking her lips. "You can eat them anytime you want, you really should just give them to me."

I chuckle, grabbing my wallet, sunnies and keys. "Is that so?" I ask, gesturing toward the front door.

"Yes," she nods as we head out to the cars.

"Tell you what," I say, half way into my hire car. "How about I give you a packet for every time you're nice to me?"

Lu stares across the roof of her car at me, a small smile tugging at her mouth. "Well in that case," she says, smirking. "I'll just grab the rest of the packets when we get back then, won't I." Then she hops into her car, slamming the door as she gestures through the front window for me to do the same.

The drive into Napa takes about thirty minutes and as I follow Lu, I can't stop thinking about what's brought all this on today. I'll admit, I'm intrigued, but more than that, I'm happy she's actively choosing to spend time with me.

I'd never mentioned anything about ditching this car, even though I clearly didn't need it and hanging onto it was costing me money. But for some reason, not only has Lu thought to save me a few bucks by lending me one of the work cars, she's also volunteered to be the one to help me out.

Obviously, I am starting to have an effect on her; a thought that has my mind racing with possibilities and a grin plastered on my face the whole drive into town.

After we've ditched my hire car, I slide into the passenger seat of Lu's SUV.

"So where to?" I ask.

She smiles. "You remember much of this place?" she asks, gesturing out the window.

I glance around, nothing much coming to mind as I shake my head. "Not really."

She nods before pulling out of the car park and heading back toward downtown. Eventually she pulls into a spot in front of a bar and grill specializing in American food.

I grin. "Wow, this place is still here."

"Uh huh," she says as we both get out of the car.

"I loved this place," I say, half to myself as we make our way to the front door. Lu's family had taken my dad and me here the first day I'd arrived in the US for my summer holidays. I remember being amazed by it, how it was so different to any restaurant we had in Australia and instead, exactly like the restaurants you saw in American movies and TV shows.

"I remember," she says, holding the door open for me.

I can't help but grin at her, pausing to say, "Check you out, all reminiscing and shit." I run a finger down her nose and then walk inside before she can say anything.

Lu steps in behind me and as soon as what looks like the manager sees her, she comes over.

"Lauren, hey," she says, leaning in to kiss her cheek. "It's been ages."

"Hi Carey," Lu replies. "I know, sorry, I've just been so busy and all."

Carey is nodding, even as she glances at me, her brow furrowing as though she's trying to work out where she's seen me before. "Is that…?" she trails off, not finishing her question.

Lu nods once. "Yep, it is," she says. "Back to fix some stuff for us and, you know," she adds, waving a hand in the air as though this will explain things.

"Is that so?" Carey asks, smiling a little as she blatantly runs her eyes all over me.

I shoot Lu a glance, but she ignores me, instead rolling her eyes at Carey as she adds, "No, not that."

Carey's grin widens as she turns back to Lu and says, "Uh huh, you keep telling yourself that."

She reaches for some menus now, her hand out motioning to the large French doors that lead to an outdoor patio that overlooks the river running through the middle of downtown.

We follow her outside, taking a seat at a corner table under a huge sun umbrella. Lu orders us a bottle of wine and Carey runs through some specials that I pay zero attention to, before finally walking off and leaving us to decide what we want.

"Ok," I say, as soon as she leaves, my arms resting on the table as I lean closer to her. "What was *that* all about?"

"What?" she asks, her eyes on the menu.

"Ah, that," I say, reaching over and lowering her menu so she's forced to look at me. When she finally does, I flick my eyes inside as if to emphasize what I'm talking about.

Lu shakes her head, eyes back on her menu as she says, "I don't know what you're talking about."

I shake my head at her explanation, a smile tugging at my mouth as I see Carey heading toward us again, bottle of wine and two glasses in her hands. "I see," I say, turning to grin at Carey now. "Sorry, Lu didn't introduce us before." I extend a hand out to her. "I'm Jack."

Carey places the glasses on the table before shaking my hand, giggling a little as she says, "I know."

I cock my head to the side. "You do?" I ask, shooting a quick look back at Lu, who's now studying her menu like her life depends on it. "Have we met before or something?"

Carey sighs a little as she murmurs something that sounds like *that accent* before she opens the wine and pours a taste into my glass. I gesture to both glasses, trusting Lu's choice as Carey continues. "You were here like fifteen years ago, right?"

"Yeah."

She nods. "You came to our school dance, the winter one."

I look at Lu now, who's shaking her head, a look on her face that suggests she wants the balcony to open up and dump her into the river below.

"Ohhhh," I say. "You guys went to school together?"

Carey nods. "Yep."

"And you remember me from that night?" I ask, grinning. This is fucking fantastic.

Carey smiles back at me. "Oh, we all do," she says, her smile widening.

"Okay, I'm having a burger with everything, he'll have the same only extra pickles," Lu suddenly says, interrupting our walk down memory lane as she grabs my menu and shoves both of them at Carey. "Thanks, Care."

Carey looks at Lu, who avoids her gaze now as she reaches for her wine glass. I pick up mine, holding it out in a toast toward her as Carey finally walks off.

"Everyone remembers me, huh?" I say, grinning as I hold my glass out to hers.

Lu rolls her eyes, clinking her glass against mine as she takes a long sip. I do the same, swirling the buttery chardonnay in my mouth before swallowing. It's good wine.

"How do they all remember me, Lu?" I ask, nudging her with my foot under the table.

Lu puts her glass down, sitting up a little straighter as she meets my stare. "Don't get too excited," she says, tucking a strand of hair behind her ear. "It was just the winter dance I was forced to take you to, that's all."

I chuckle. "Forced? From memory, I thought I actually saved you that night, taking you when you didn't have a date."

She rolls her eyes at me, reaching for her glass. "Pfft, whatever," she says, taking another sip. "You were just some novelty to a bunch of bored teenagers," she adds, trying to act like this isn't a big deal. "The tall, mysterious foreign guy with the hot accent, whoopee," she adds, shrugging. "If anything, you were great for my rep because all the girls were swooning and all the guys were jealous as hell." She waves a hand in dismissal as though none of this is a big deal.

I burst out laughing. "Lulu," I say in mock scolding. "You never told me any of this."

Lu scoffs. "Like your ego needed anymore stroking, Jack."

I grin at her, as she sits across from me, trying to fight the smile I know she wants to give me. I watch as she bites her bottom lip, lowering her sunglasses to her eyes as though it's the glare and not the reminiscing that's bothering her.

Reaching across the table, I slide my fingers over hers as they fiddle with her wine glass.

"Tall, mysterious foreign guy, huh?" I say, pulling her fingers from the stem. "Hot accent?"

Lu blushes now as she murmurs, "Mmmm."

I chuckle, turning her hand over as I brush my thumb across the inside of her wrist. I open my mouth to speak just as Carey reappears to drop off some appetizers, compliments of the house.

Lu pulls her hand from mine, reaching for her napkin now as she busies herself with pretending to eat. I let the moment go, even though there are so many things I want to ask her.

The rest of our lunch passes by with no further discussion about the school dance or what it might mean that her friends all still know about me.

Eventually, after we finish off the bottle of wine and decline dessert, I head inside to fix up the bill while Lu hits up the bathroom.

"On the house," Carey says, grinning at me.

"No, I can't let you do that," I say. "Please, let me pay."

Carey shakes her head. "Nope," she says.

"Okay, fine," I say, pulling a fifty from my wallet anyway and sliding it into the tip jar by the cash register. "Thank you. The food was great, just as I remember it."

"You're welcome," Carey says, grinning. She looks over my shoulder as though checking for something before turning back to me. "She never forgot you, you know?" she says, her voice a whisper as though she doesn't want anyone to hear what she's telling me.

"What?"

"Lauren," she says, eyes flicking behind me again. "She..."

But her words are cut off as Lu materializes beside me. "Ready to go?" Her question stopping any further discussion.

"Was great to see you again," Carey says, hugging her. "Don't leave it so long next time."

We say our goodbyes and head back out to the car, but I can't resist glancing backward as I hold the door open for Lu. Carey is watching us, a strange smile on her face as she meets my stare quickly before turning away.

The drive back to *Somerville's* is quiet, the only noise the songs coming from the radio and the gentle breeze that blows in through Lu's half open window.

I watch as her loose hair blows around her, her fingers constantly tucking it behind her ears every time it gets in her face. I have an urge to reach out and do it for her. To run my fingers through her long blonde strands, wrap them around my hand as I pull her close to me.

By the time we pull back into the vineyard, my mind and body are going crazy with lust, fueled by everything I learned today and every kilometer I sat silently watching her on the way home.

Lu parks in front of her house and we both get out of the car. I wait as she walks around toward me, reaching for her hand as she stops beside me.

"Thank you for lunch," I say, my eyes locked onto hers.

"You're welcome," she says, swallowing.

"I," I start, pausing as I try to work out the right words. "I ahh,"

"Aunt Lulu!" comes Oscar's voice as he comes tearing out of her house, the front door slamming and totally killing the moment.

I glance over, see him staring at us, arms crossed over his chest. When I turn back to Lu though, her eyes are still on me, watching.

Knowing this isn't the right moment, I grin as I lean down and put my mouth against her ear. "That hot accent," I whisper, my eyes closing as I breathe in the scent of her. "You should hear me talk dirty in it."

And then before I give in and do all the things I've only dreamed about, I let go of her hand, turn and give Oscar a wave, before heading inside my house.

Chapter Ten

Lauren

He's growing on me.

Or maybe he's just always had a place in my heart.

I'm still smiling as Jack walks away and with Oscar looking up at me, I'm beginning to wonder if these kids are catching on.

They seem to have impeccable timing, but maybe that's good. It's keeping me from jumping into something with Jack that I might not be ready for.

"Where've you been?" Oscar asks, his excitement about seeing me has now turned accusing. He narrows his eyes and waits for my answer.

"Why?" I ask, teasing him as I mimic his face back.

"Ollie tells me you've got some old grapes you need to throw away."

"Ollie?" I question, my nose wrinkling up as I cock an eyebrow at him. "Who's Ollie and why are they worried about my old grapes."

Oscar lets out a long sigh, his annoyance with my questioning wearing thin.

"Olivia," he replies like I'm a total idiot for even asking. "Jack calls her Ollie so now I call her Ollie."

"Should've known," I mutter in mock annoyance, but I'm anything but bothered. I love that Jack has taken an active interest in them. They're probably the coolest kids I've ever met and I'm loving that he's noticed too.

"So..." Oscar leads waiting for me to tell him he and Olivia can have my old grapes.

"Let's go," I say, holding out my fist and he bumps his against it and then screams for Olivia as he runs for the shed.

The two of them are impatiently waiting for my slow ass to arrive in the shed and they act like they've been there for a decade. As soon as Olivia sees me, she begins jumping up and down and screaming.

I'm laughing before I even reach them, because the last time we did this, they swore it was the best day of their lives.

It's not often that we waste grapes or that I have the time to stop and fuck around with them, but today seems like a great day for it. I can't remember the last time I just stopped and enjoyed the day.

My lunch with Jack was the perfect start, and now I'll end my day having a grape war with the kiddos.

I walk into the shed and Olivia and Oscar are gathered by the buckets of grapes, but when I take in what's there, I could've sworn we had more than just four buckets full.

The amount of grapes that came out of that machine was insane; a total waste and I recall feeling sick to my stomach at the thought of throwing them all away. I know they were going out into our compost areas, but I didn't realize Tommy had worked so quickly clearing the place out. He had a ton of other stuff on his plate this week.

"Okay, grab a bucket," I say to the two of them and they both examine the buckets trying to decide which one has the most. Because like everything in their lives, they want more than the other one and that's when the argument ensues.

"I want that one!" Olivia shrieks, her hand clutching the handle of the bucket and Oscar practically throws his entire body on top of the same bucket.

"It's mine," Oscar hisses at her, and as frustrating as their arguing can be, it's also comical. They can go from best friends to worst enemies in no time flat.

"There are three other buckets," I say, knowing it doesn't matter and that all logical reasoning has been thrown out the window. "Come on, guys. We aren't going to be able to do this if you can't..."

No one is listening to me and the arguing has kicked into high gear with Olivia now screeching at the top of her lungs as the fake tears pour down her cheeks.

It's her go-to when she wants to win, but Oscar is immune to it now and he has no qualms about using brute force to get his way.

Just as he's about to shove her out of the way, Jack appears in the doorway. He slips past me and grabs Oscar around the waist. He hauls him into his arms and spins him around until I swear Oscar is going to puke.

He's dizzy as hell, but laughing so hard he can hardly speak. And when Jack finally sets him down, he doesn't get a break.

"My turn!" Olivia yells, running right up to Jack and holding her arms up at him.

"You've gotta tell me what's going on in here first," Jack states, his hands on his hips.

"Oscar was trying to take my bucket," Olivia wails, really turning on the drama for Jack's sake.

"We were about to have a grape war," I add, knowing the drama will continue to overshadow the fun we were going to have if I don't cut in.

"A grape war?" Jack questions, now intrigued by what that means. "Fill me in here, Ollie."

The flow of huge crocodile tears cease immediately and Olivia begins talking so fast that I'm certain Jack misses ninety percent of it.

But that doesn't stop him from shouting an enthusiastic, "I'm in," and then he begins to name teams. "I've got Ollie," he says, high fiving her and shooting a glare in my direction. "You're going down, Lu."

"Oh, you think? Oscar and I get the launcher!" I call running for the buckets and grabbing two of them before darting out into the fields.

Most of our fields are closed to the public and that's a good thing, because something tells me we are going to make a huge mess.

Before I can even reach the launcher the kids and I made last summer, Jack has nailed me in the back with a handful of mushy grapes.

I drop the buckets where I stand and Oscar and I dig in, launching loads of smashed and rotten grapes in the direction of Jack and Olivia.

The kids are laughing wildly as grapes fly through the air. My face is covered making it hard to see and I'm caught off guard when Jack grabs me around the waist. He holds me in place and yells for the kids to attack.

It's a set up; they've ambushed me and I'm being pelted with grapes as I thrash around trying to escape Jack's grasp.

"Oh my god! You're cheaters!" I scream, laughing so hard tears stream down my cheeks.

When I finally escape from Jack, I grab a nearly empty bucket and attempt to dump it on him. But he's stronger than me and most of it ends up on my head, remnants splattering on Jack and the kids as they cling to him.

It only takes us ten minutes to exhaust all the grapes, but in that short amount of time, we're all thoroughly covered, including Jack.

"This was the best day ever!" Oscar cheers, throwing his arms around my waist and then doing the same to Jack.

Olivia is still hanging on to Jack, smiling up at him and he picks her up, lifting her onto his shoulders.

"We gotta go get cleaned up," I say, being the one to ruin the fun. "We're having dinner with your mom and dad tonight and she's going to kill me if we show up at my house covered in grapes."

I lead everyone back to one of the sheds that has a shower and a clean-up station for the employees. It's not just grape wars that cause people on the property to become covered in grapes.

Jack drops Olivia off his shoulders and I shove her and Oscar under the water. They both dance around rinsing off as I grab for Olivia, Jack reaches for Oscar and we begin washing their hair. This isn't going to get them totally clean, but it'll be enough for me to sneak them back to my house, put them in the bath and get them clean clothes before Ellen makes it back there.

They're both wiggling around and it's like trying to wrangle a greased pig, and once again they have Jack and I laughing. I look up at him as Olivia manages to slip away from me and the smile that is plastered on his face makes my heart race.

I feel my stomach flutter, the feeling of butterflies rising up into my chest.

I'm suddenly overcome with a dream of what my life would be like if Jack and I were in a relationship. This is what I imagine every day to be like. That I wake up feeling happy, that seeing him brings a smile to my face.

It's something I long for. It's something I've never experienced, and I realize now that had I gotten married, I would've sold myself short, because days like this should be the norm and they never were.

Jack steps toward me, his fingers swiping at the grapes that are stuck to my face.

"You okay?" he asks, his head tilted to the side and I wonder what the look on my face is telling him.

"Yeah, I'm great." For once in the last year I actually mean it.

We leave Jack in the shed while I rush Oscar and Olivia back to my house to get cleaned up. We make it just before Ellen and Will walk in the door and Ellen's pleasantly surprised when she finds them clean and already in their pajamas.

"Wow, look at that. Aunt Lulu being all responsible," she jokes, giving a wink to the kids as they watch an episode of *Teen Titans Go* barely noticing the arrival of their parents.

"I'm always responsible," I retort back, also winking at the kids. "And I even made dinner."

Ellen follows me into the kitchen, the table already set with plates, salad and wine, and while it's by no means gourmet, I did manage to make a couple of frozen pizzas. It won't impress Ellen, but it would if she knew I threw this all together in ten minutes and managed to scrub her children clean.

Will is much easier to please, giving me a quick smile and simple hug as he takes in the pizza.

"Nice work, Lauren. Nothing like coming home to a nice home cooked meal," he says, winking at me because he knows what a pain in the ass Ellen can be.

We eat and chat, but we only make it about ten minutes before Olivia rats me out and confesses that we spent the afternoon covered in grapes.

Both her and Oscar are so animated and excited as they tell Ellen and Will about our afternoon. They leave no detail out, and as much as I know Ellen isn't a fan of me wasting grapes and teaching her kids to chuck them at each other, she takes in their every word.

The night ends with Ellen and Will carrying the kids out to the car since they both passed out on the couch, exhausted from their day. I follow them out, opening the car doors so they can slip the kids in.

"Later, guys," I say, waving to them as I walk back to the house.

"Lauren," Ellen calls and I turn back toward her finding Will already in the driver's seat and her waiting outside the passenger's side. Thinking she's going to make some snarky comment about me letting her kids get dirty I almost roll my eyes. "Happiness looks good on you. It's been a while," she says.

I smile a thank you, but say nothing more.

She's right. I haven't felt this free, this happy in so long. My whole body feels different, almost healthier and as much as I should confess this to her, I keep it to myself, wanting to enjoy it a little longer.

I walk back into my house and grab a beer from the fridge. It's a beautiful night of clear skies and stars and warm breezes as I take a seat on my front porch. I hit play on my phone and the music comes through the Bluetooth speakers, playing softly.

Only a few seconds later Jack walks up. He's clean, but his clothes are still stained from earlier today, like he hadn't gone back to change.

"What are you doing out here?" I ask, stepping off the porch, meeting Jack at the bottom of the stairs.

"I was fixing the gutters on one of your outbuildings," he says, tossing his head in the direction of where he just came from. "Damn gutter was all clogged up and wasn't draining properly."

"You didn't have to do that Jack. I'll make sure that Ellen pays you for your time."

"I didn't tell you because I expect you to pay me. I'm telling you because it's something that needs to be done regularly and it seems like it hasn't been."

I swallow hard; even though there's nothing in Jack's words or the way he speaks that indicates that he thinks I've done something wrong. I know I've slacked on things and playing catch up is more difficult than I thought.

"I know it needs to be done regularly," I say nodding my head in agreement. "Things just got a little…" I trail off not finishing my thought because I don't want to get into it with Jack right now. He doesn't need to know that when I fell apart, I practically took the business down with me.

I change the subject quickly. "So, Ollie, huh?"

Jack shrugs his shoulders, but that cheeky grin is written on his face. "She liked that I call you Lulu. Thought I'd give her a nickname too."

"She loves it. She adores you, you know? They both do."

Even in the dim porch light I swear I see a small bit of blush creep onto Jack's cheeks and it makes my heart skip a beat.

"They're cool kids." Jack laughs a little and steps closer to me. "You know what's funny, Lu?"

"What's that, Jack?"

"I thought they were your kids when I first got here." We both chuckle a little at his words. "Crazy thing, it kinda got me right here," Jack says, his hand over his heart and now I'm laughing even more at his dramatics, shaking my head at him. But what he says next makes my breath catch in my throat. "I always hoped you'd wait for me." His tone now serious and all humor is gone.

There's a stillness between us now, a silence as his words hang heavy in the air, and there's no joking passing between us at this point.

I don't know what comes over me, but in the quiet of the night I murmur, "Maybe I still am."

Now it's my words that float around, a comforting silence, but the charge in the air between us sends sparks throughout my body.

"You want a beer?" I ask, my voice shaky, and I swallow back the lump that has formed in my throat.

"Yeah, that'd be great."

When I step out the door, Jack's beer in hand, he takes it from me, setting it down on the small table between the two chairs.

"Dance with me?" he asks, his hands sliding over my hips as Miranda Lambert's "Vice" starts playing in the background.

I don't say yes, I just lean into him, my arm wrapping around his neck, my fingers threading into his as we sway to the music slowly.

Jack's lips are next to my ear; his warm breath causes goose bumps to raise up on my skin and when he begins to whisper the lyrics I nearly melt in his arms.

"Another vice, another town. Where my past can't run me down..."

My lips brush his neck, and my body is wired with want and need and nervousness. I can feel my heart racing in my chest, slamming hard and fast against my ribs. I wonder if Jack feels it. I wonder if he's having the same response.

I'm trembling despite the warm evening; my hand shakes in his and he tightens his grip.

And when the song ends, neither of us moves.

Chapter Eleven

Jack

My heart is pounding.

Pounding hard against my ribcage, against her as she stands in my arms, her body against mine.

My eyes close as her lips brush against my neck, her breath warm against my skin. My hand at the small of her back tightens, urging her closer, our bodies fitting together so easily it's as though they were always meant to.

I've lost count of how many times I've thought about doing this. Since I came back here, since I was a kid, all the years in between.

Time and distance haven't changed how much I want her, they've magnified it and fuck me, I want her so bad right now.

"Lu," I whisper against her ear just as a new song starts playing, the music masking the hard beat of my heart.

She lifts her head and my hand slides up her spine, cupping the back of her neck as she stares up at me, our eyes locked together in the darkness of her front porch.

She swallows hard and I feel the movement of her throat, watch as she licks her lips, not moving closer, but not pulling away either.

Our other hands are still linked and I lift them to my mouth, my eyes never leaving hers as I press a kiss to her knuckles. She whimpers at the touch and my knees nearly give way at the sound. As I realize this is it.

This is the moment I've been dreaming about since I walked into her kitchen a week ago and saw her for the first time in fourteen years. Since I walked away from her all those years ago.

This is fucking it.

I let go of her hand now, sliding my arm around her waist and pulling her closer. Her hand falls to my chest, her fingers curling into the fabric of my t-shirt as she holds onto me, her other hand still around my neck. Her thumb brushes against my skin, sending a jolt of electricity straight down my spine.

The air hums between us, charged with so much intensity and heat, that it's almost unbearable, the tension wound so tight that it's almost impossible to resist.

And then I stop trying.

Lowering my head, I gently touch my lips to hers, the low moan she lets out nearly undoing me. Her lips part and I press my mouth harder as I slowly slide my tongue against hers, both of us groaning now.

I feel her hand at the back of my neck pulling me closer, her tongue as it slips into my mouth, teasing me, tasting. My body feels wired, loaded with an energy that's all lust and heat and want.

Desire for her.

"Lu," I murmur against her lips, pulling her against me so there isn't a single bit of space between us. Our bodies meld together as my arm wraps around her waist, the hand at the back of her neck sliding down to her shoulders.

Her skin is warm beneath mine, and I feel goose bumps rise beneath my touch as my fingers gently brush against the bare skin of her shoulder, against the tiny straps I imagined pulling down this morning.

We kiss and kiss, never stopping, never coming up for air as we breathe each other in instead. My lips move slowly against hers, tongues touching. Everything about this moment feels intense and amazing and a million times better than I ever could have imagined it to be.

I don't ever want it to end.

When the song ends though, we both pull back, far enough that our lips part, but close enough to still share a breath. I rest my forehead against hers, my eyes closed as I try to calm the craziness inside my head and my heart.

They are warring against me, against each other. One of them telling me to stop, to take this slow because I don't want to fuck it up and I don't want to get burnt. The other telling me to ignore all that shit and drag her inside, take this further, where we both want it to go.

Where there's no turning back.

"Jack," she breathes out, my name nothing more than a quiet whisper between us, but still with a tiny trace of hesitation that makes up my mind.

"I don't want to stop," I whisper, my forehead still against hers, eyes closed. "But I'm going to."

I feel her fingers, which are still twisted in my t-shirt, tighten.

"I don't want to, Lu," I tell her, my voice husky. "But tonight, I will."

"Jack," she repeats and I open my eyes, find hers already open, watching me.

Pulling back a little, I smile at her, brush a thumb across her cheekbone. "Goodnight, Lulu," I whisper, leaning in to press one last kiss against her lips.

Then I uncurl my arms from her body and before I can question whether this is the right thing to do, I turn and walk down the steps, across the lawn to my place and go inside.

I wake with the sun, my body wired from too little sleep and from everything else that happened yesterday.

I'd thought Lu showing up at my house to take me to lunch was going to be the best part of my day. Had thought the grape war with her and the kids was an added bonus. But fuck me if that kiss last night didn't blow everything else out of the water.

"God," I groan, shoving a hand through my hair as I drag myself from bed.

I pull on some running clothes, knowing this is going to be the only way I can work all this excess energy off. I should be exhausted, I barely slept after I came inside, but instead, I'm on edge, my body hyped and unable to stay still.

After a couple of half-arsed stretches, I head out the front door, glancing across to Lu's place because I can't stop myself.

It's quiet and still and I imagine her inside, asleep in her bed. Images of me lying beside her, of waking her and working all this energy off in a very different way flood my brain. Groaning again, I force myself to look away, to get moving and run as hard as I can, pushing my body to exhaustion.

I do eight laps before I finally stop and my legs protest any more movement and I have to give in before I collapse.

When I get back to my house, everything looks the same as when I left, no sign of movement at Lu's. Reluctantly, I drag myself inside, take a long, barely warm shower before dressing and making some coffee, all the time wondering what's going to happen when we finally see each other today.

Will things be different between us? How could they not be? After that kiss, everything's changed.

Everything.

I've been in the shed for two hours by the time Oscar wanders in.

"Hey little dude," I call out, as I empty the last of the crushed juice from the smaller crusher Lu has. "What's going on?"

Oscar takes us through our complicated handshake routine before taking in what I'm doing. Shooting me a sideways glance, he says, "What's happening here?"

I grin. "A secret," I tell him. "So, zip it, alright?" I say, as I drag my fingers across my mouth in the universal action for shut the hell up.

Oscar grins at me, arms crossed over his chest as he rocks on his heels. "Yeah, and what's in it for me?"

I chuckle, ruffling up his hair as I drag the tank I was filling out to a back room, Oscar following close behind me. He watches wordlessly as I pump the juice into an old oak barrel, checking the acidity and sugar levels before putting a stopper in the top and jamming it in with the mallet.

Turning, I see him still watching me, a wary look on his face. "Well?" he prompts.

Now it's me crossing my arms over my chest. "What do you want?" I ask, raising an eyebrow.

Oscar's hand goes to his chin as he contemplates my offer, a serious look on his face because this is clearly serious business to him.

"Come on," I prompt. "Time's a ticking and I don't have all day."

He nods his head once. "You have to come over and have dinner with us," he starts. "And then build Legos and then watch a movie. That's what I want."

"That's it?" I ask, smiling.

"Yep," he says, nodding.

"Okay," I say. "And who else is joining us?"

"Well, there's you and me, obviously," he says, shooting me a look as he counts this off on his fingers. "Maybe Mom and

Dad, probably Aunt Lulu and I guess we should ask Ollie, too, although she'll only be a pain in the butt."

I chuckle. "Your sister's not a pain the butt."

"Oh yeah," he says, hands on his hips. "You try living with her."

I laugh harder as I put a hand on his shoulder and steer him out of the back room and into the main part of the shed. "So, when's this big get together happening?"

He shrugs. "Dunno, I'll have to ask," he says.

"Okay, you do that," I tell him. "In the meantime though, this is our little secret, right?"

He nods as he glances back over his shoulder. "So, what are you doing?"

I ruffle his hair. "I'm making something."

"For Aunt Lulu?" he immediately asks.

I cock my head at him. "Why would you think that?"

"Duh," he says, hands out in front of him as though it's obvious. "You totally like her," he says. "Who else would you be making it for?"

I laugh at his seriousness, even if it does surprise me how much he sees, how much he notices around here. "Hmmm," I say. "And what if I am making it for her?" I ask, glancing down at him. "What would you think about that?"

"That'd be cool," he replies. "It's okay that you like her."

I burst out laughing. "Thanks man, I'm glad I've got your approval. Where is your aunt, anyway?"

"I dunno," he mutters, walking over to the broken crusher. He picks up a wrench, turning it over in his hands as though he's contemplating just how much destruction he could wreak with it. I pull it from his hands, shaking my head when he huffs.

"You don't know?"

He shrugs. "I don't know, I think she went to town or something, errands. Who knows," he says as though it's no big deal. "Can we go do something?"

I chuckle, as I throw the wrench back in the toolbox. "I gotta work, dude."

Oscar rolls his eyes. "Well that's lame."

"That's life, my friend," I tell him.

"Come on," he says. "Aunt Lulu won't mind."

I shake my head. "Even if she didn't," I tell him. "I still gotta do it."

"Okay, whatever," he says, waving his hand in dismissal. "I can see I'm getting nowhere here. Later."

I laugh. "Laters, little dude," I say. "Let me know about that dinner," I call just as he walks out the door.

After Oscar leaves, I spend a couple more hours pulling the crusher apart. It's still a couple more weeks until the parts get here, but I figure it's the perfect time to give the whole machine a good overhaul and cleaning.

Judging by how clogged up the thing was, I'm gonna guess it hasn't been done for a long time. Kind of like the gutters on the outbuilding and a couple of other things I've noticed around the place.

And as much as I know Lu is a professional who takes pride in her work and would never ruin the reputation her family has spent generations building, it makes me think that maybe she needs an extra pair of hands around the place.

That maybe I could be the person to help her out with things and what that would mean if I did.

Could I really leave my life in Australia behind?

When I boarded that plane in Sydney, I'd thought this would be a couple of months in the States that would allow me to escape the shit fight my personal life had become at home.

An opportunity to look up the girl I've never forgotten about, despite all the years that had passed.

I'd been an idiot not to keep in contact with her when I left, but I was also a guy, a teenage boy that didn't know what the fuck to do when it came to women.

And even though I've grown up a lot since then, I can't help but wonder if I should have done something sooner. Should have come and found her years ago, before I had the chance to make the million other mistakes I've made.

What would my life have been like?

What could my life be like now?

As weird as it was that I'd admitted those things last night, things about her having kids and how much that bothered me, I knew I'd never take those words back.

Knew I meant it when I had said them to her.

At lunchtime, I finally take a break and wander down to the main office, looking for Lu. But she's not there, instead I'm greeted by Ellen.

"Hey," I say, standing in the doorway, feeling weirdly nervous.

Ellen looks up. "Hi," she says, a strange smile on her face.

"Is, ah, is Lu around?" I ask, glancing around the obviously empty except for us office.

Ellen chuckles as she sits back in the chair, crossing her arms over her chest in a move that is eerily reminiscent of her son. "No," she says, still smiling. "She's gone to see one of our co-packers," she says. "She'll be back later. How are you?" she adds, head cocked to the side as she watches me.

I shrug. "Fine," I say.

"Just fine?"

I narrow my gaze at her. "Yeah," I say cautiously.

"Not great, or fantastic or un-fucking-believable?" she asks.

"Um," I say, scrubbing a hand across my jaw. "I guess."

Ellen nods, the smile still on her face as she uncrosses her arms and goes back to whatever she was doing when I walked in. “Alright then,” she says. “I’ll be sure to tell Lauren you’re looking for her,” she adds, chuckling to herself a little.

“Okay,” I say, as I turn and walk out.

I don’t know what the fuck that was all about, but something tells me that Ellen is more like Oscar than I realized.

And I get the feeling she just might know about that kiss last night too.

Chapter Twelve

Lauren

I walk into my office and Ellen occupies my chair as she feverishly works on the books. She knows there's a possibility we may not be selling as much of our bestselling wine as we usually do.

I know she's currently working on cutting costs because that's what she does best. If necessary she can save us money without cutting jobs and without the tourists realizing we've changed our vegetable supplier when they eat at the restaurant.

"Hey," I say as I walk in and Ellen's head whips up and looks at me, flashing me a quick smile before returning to what she was doing.

Without looking up again, she says, "What do you think about hiring Jack for the maintenance position we have open?" She starts punching numbers into a calculator acting like she didn't just send me into a tailspin.

She can't possibly know that Jack and I kissed last night!

"Why would we hire Jack?" I ask, my voice abnormally high-pitched and I curse inwardly at myself for being so damn transparent.

Ever since Jack and I kissed, my body has been buzzing, a low hum that has me wired and on edge.

Our paths have yet to cross, and that's partially because I'm avoiding him, but when they do I feel like it's going to be totally awkward. He just walked away, left me standing on my porch in silence, yet I never said a word to him either. I just stood there like a damn fool.

"Um, because he's been doing most of the stuff anyway," she says nonchalantly like I should've realized that myself.

I want to tell her that I can't think clearly because my head is a fucked up mess of wondering what would have happened if I had just invited Jack inside after that kiss.

That kiss.

Fuck me. Just the thought of it has me reeling all over again

"You're the one who told me to pay him for cleaning out the gutters and I figured it would give him something to do while he waits for the parts to arrive."

I nod my head, but I've barely heard her. Each mention of Jack has me picturing him shirtless and tanned and muscled, fixing roof tiles and weeding, his body sweaty and hot. I picture him in my shower, his dirty blonde hair wet as water droplets run in rivulets over his amazingly chiseled abs.

Oh my god this isn't a fucking porno.

What is wrong with me?

It was one kiss, one simple kiss. I must be really lonely because I've turned a PG kiss into an X-Rated wet dream.

"It would be some extra money in addition to his daily rate we're paying to retain him to fix the crusher," Ellen drones on. She's still fucking talking and she has no idea that I'm not even listening. "Obviously we'll still have to hire someone once he's gone."

And there's what pulls me out of this hazy daydream I've been floating around in all day.

Once he's gone.

"Lauren!" Ellen snaps and I practically scream out loud, startled and shocked at the realization that I can't possibly start a relationship with Jack. He's going to leave.

He's going to leave me.

It was just a kiss. Who am I to think it would even lead to more? He's been here for a week and judging by his looks he isn't used to going that long without female contact. I'm just another girl in a long list of girls he's played.

"Are you even listening to me?"

"Yeah, yeah, um..."

"So, what do you say? You wanna talk to him about it?"

"He's not going to be interested, Ellen," I snip back at her, letting my thoughts run wild, making me crabby. I'm taking it out on her because she's here. "And he's not a maintenance man. He's a wine maker and really good one at that. Again, he's not going to be interested."

"Really?" she questions, her eyebrow rising as she points out the window.

I look and find Jack hauling a ridiculous amount of broken branches and twigs, his flexed arms showing off just exactly how qualified he is for the maintenance job we have open.

"And I think he's interested in more than just helping out around here," she adds, elbowing me in the side as she stops to stand next to me.

I roll my eyes prepared to defend myself against Ellen's constant teasing when she pounds on the window and calls Jack's name.

"Oh my god! What are you doing?" I screech, practically falling flat on the ground to hide from him as he looks over at us. I didn't think she meant she wanted me to ask him now. I'm not prepared to have this impromptu conversation with him especially after what happened last night.

"Asking Jack if he wants the job," she responds swinging open the door and calling to him again. "Settle down. I won't ask him if he wants you too, because that's obvious."

"Jack!" Ellen shouts across the open field to him and flags him over with her hand. She's waiting in the doorway when he walks up and she steps aside to let him in.

He's breathing heavy and his chest moves with each breath he takes, stopping me from thinking about anything but him naked. I memorize every part of him as he stands there; the small scar that hits right above where his jeans are slung low on his hips, the shape of his collarbone and how my head fit there perfectly when we were dancing, and his hands, his calloused, strong hands that I'd give anything to feel on my body again.

I've never felt such a mix of emotions in my life. My heart is racing, my stomach fluttering, a pent up mess of anxiety and nervousness; worried that I'm going to say something idiotic or that I've assumed something that isn't even there.

"Hey, Lu," Jack says, and Ellen smirks at me.

She cuts right to the chase, no small talk, no making sure I'm not being super fucking weird.

"Lauren and I were wondering if you'd be interested taking on a few other jobs around here. Obviously we'd pay you and you're kinda already doing them."

"Maintenance work?" Jack asks and I nod my head. "Yeah sure. Don't have much else going on until the parts come in and it looks like you could use an extra hand around here."

Jack winks at me and clearly he isn't at all affected by what happened last night. He's back to his arrogant self and assuming every woman in the world is into him, including me. He'll probably run off after this to flirt with Penny.

"Check in with Lauren tomorrow and she'll set you up with what needs to be done. Sound good?" she asks, looking between Jack and me, giving us both a nod.

"Always happy to check in with Lu," Jack says, smiling at me and shooting me a flirting glance that doesn't go unnoticed by Ellen.

"One more thing," she says catching Jack before he walks out the door and turning to face me. "Can you watch the kids tonight? Will and I want to actually have a quiet dinner alone."

"Of course I can. They can stay the night too," I tell her and she thanks me, but the look on her face tells me that this isn't the only thing she needs to say.

Ellen bites her bottom lip and lets out a slow breath. "Any chance you're free too, Jack?" she asks, her nose scrunched and her teeth pressed together like she's willing him to give her the answer she's hoping for.

For fuck's sake my sister is trying to set me up.

"Oscar's really hoping you'll be there," she adds, using her kid as her excuse. "Not that they're not excited about seeing you, Lauren, but you know." She shrugs her shoulders, but she doesn't say anymore knowing I realize Jack is a novelty, something new.

"Nothing going on," Jack says. "If it's okay with Lu..."

"It's okay with Lu," Ellen says and I roll my eyes, but she gives a quick raise of her eyebrows and tight-lipped smile that tells me to shut up and just go with it.

So I do.

Several hours later Ellen has wrangled up the kids and shoved them through my front door, shouting a thank you to me as she climbs into her car before I even have a chance to greet her.

"She needs a night out," Oscar comments, flopping down on the couch dramatically. "Jack coming over?"

"He is," I answer as I go into the kitchen to finish making dinner.

I can hear Olivia and Oscar whispering in the other room and I know they're up to something, possibly something their mother has helped them set up. I'm interested to see how this evening plays out.

Jack knocks on the door just as I'm putting the grilled cheeses on plates. Nothing fancy but the kids aren't too particular. Hopefully Jack isn't either.

They're both screaming and jumping on him when I walk into the room with the food. One of their favorite parts about staying with me is watching a movie and eating in front of the TV.

I set the plates down on the coffee table, but Olivia shakes her head and simply states that we must eat in the kitchen. This is an interesting turn of events, so I move everything back to the kitchen, setting the plates on the island.

Once everyone has convened around the island, Oscar grabs a bottle of wine from the rack and sets it down in the center.

"Having wine tonight?" he asks, looking from me to Jack and back. "Does this pair well with grilled cheese?"

I cover my mouth with my hand to hide the fact that I'm about to burst out laughing. The tears are pooling in the corners of my eyes and the smile on Jack's face is stretched so wide.

"Absolutely," Jack says, jumping in and saving me from the laugh that I'm trying to keep trapped. "Thanks for taking care of it, dude."

"So tell me," Olivia says very astutely, her grilled cheese in her hand, "do you keep your promises, Jack?"

I cough, my hand again covering my mouth as I nearly choke on the mouthful of wine Jack just poured us.

"Um, well, I would say yes, Ollie, I do."

"Good, good," she responds nodding her head and I watch her give Oscar a side-eye.

"Aunt Lulu only likes guys who keep their promises," Oscar interjects, and he looks over at me and tries to wink several times but fails and it's taking everything in me not to crack up laughing.

These two obviously have an agenda here, and as much as I want to stop them, I'm really getting a kick out of this whole thing.

"She also likes guys who are funny," Oscar continues. "Like really funny. Not the boring kind of adult funny."

"Okay," Jack says, taking in everything they say in complete seriousness.

"Like this one time Mom made Aunt Lulu laugh so hard rice came out her nose. Can you make rice come out her nose?" Olivia questions and she's dead serious, but the way she asks it makes it sound like she's asking if Jack can pull a rabbit out of a hat.

"Well, I'm not sure. We aren't eating rice tonight, but next time I'll give it a try."

I can't get over how sincerely Jack is taking everything. Not once has he cracked a smile since they've started this conversation.

Their questioning goes on for the rest of our dinner with Jack answering everything they throw at him and not once does he tell them to stop or seem annoyed by any of it.

I watch him with the kids and how they respond to him and how he treats them, and there's something about it that's comforting, and it makes my heart clench in my chest. He's so good to them and they adore him.

By the time we're done, the kids are exhausted and they're sprawled out on the couch with Jack while I clean up the kitchen.

When I walk into the living room, the TV playing quietly, Olivia jumps up off the couch and throws her arms around me.

"You sit next to Jack," she says, grabbing my hand and tugging me toward the couch. I sit down next to him, but we're both sitting stiffly, my hands folded in my lap.

Neither of us has looked at each other, hell we've barely spoken, and that tension between us is back. It's buzzing in the room and I thank fuck that we're here with two kids who are back to being oblivious.

Olivia is practically asleep and Oscar is on his way out, and they don't notice when Jack excuses himself to go to the bathroom.

My leg begins to bounce on its own accord and I can't let it continue like this. This weirdness that has now settled between us is far worse than the lead-up to our kiss.

Maybe the kiss ruined things, but I can't take it back now.

I look over, checking to make sure both Olivia and Oscar are asleep, and then I tiptoe down the hallway and stalkerishly pace outside the bathroom door.

The door swings open and Jack jumps back, startled to find me hovering outside the door, but before he can say anything I whisper-shout, "Why are you being so weird?"

"Me?" he replies, affronted. "You're the one being weird. You avoided me all day."

"I did not," I lie, and he smirks at me.

"You've always been a terrible liar. It's written all over your face."

His grin is cheeky and I bite my bottom lip as I feel the room begin to swirl with the desire that blanketed us last night on my porch.

"Why are you avoiding me, Lu?" he asks, and his voice is low and sexy, the words spilling from his lips like warm honey, sweet and seductive.

My breath catches in my throat, a quiet rasp, but something about it, something about his words and this night together urges me on.

"Because I want to kiss you again," I murmur and my voice doesn't sound like my own. It's a soft whisper of desire that grows to a yell as my body calls out to reach for him and that's exactly what I do.

I don't know who makes the first move, but suddenly we're flush against each other, the warmth of our bodies heating my already sensitive skin. Jack backs me up against the wall behind us and my heart begins beating so hard I'm practically certain it will rip through my chest.

I had no idea that a second kiss could elicit this response, that it could possibly be even better than the first. The lead up is intense and all consuming, and we're suspended in nothing, like we're the only people in the world.

"Jack? What are you doing? I ask, my words coming out breathy and hoarse.

"Exactly what you want," he whispers against my mouth as he clutches the back of my neck and pulls my mouth to his.

My lips part and I run the tip of my tongue along his bottom lip and Jack moans into my mouth. Grabbing the hem of his shirt, I pull him closer to me until there isn't a centimeter of breathing room between us.

My hands trail under his shirt, exploring every inch of hard muscle until I reach the fast rhythm of his heartbeat, and I let my hand rest over it.

He slides his knee between my thighs as I slip my tongue into his mouth, tasting him; the taste of red wine and mixed with the way he smells makes me lose myself in our kiss.

He consumes me until the patter of little feet cuts through like a gunshot in a silent room.

And then comes "Aunt Lulu," muttered by the sleepy voice of a seven-year-old.

Chapter Thirteen

Jack

Lu and I both freeze.

I've got one hand on the back of her neck and one hand on her hip, holding her against me. She's got both hands under my shirt and I swear if we were alone right now, neither of us would be wearing clothes anymore.

She pulls back a little, turning her head toward Ollie, so her ear is now against my mouth. "I think we're busted," I whisper. Short of being naked, we're in a pretty compromising position right now.

"What's up, Ollie," she says, pulling her hands from under my shirt, her fingers trailing over my skin and sending shivers up my spine.

"I'm sleepy," she replies, rubbing her eyes.

I take a step back and Lu crouches down to face her niece. "You want me to put you to bed?" she asks.

Ollie shakes her head. "Jack," she mumbles, pointing up at me.

I grin, bending down to pick her up. "Come on, Ollie," I say, pressing a kiss to the top of her head, before glancing at Lu.

"Spare room," she says, pointing toward a closed door.

I nod before carrying Ollie in there and gently putting her to bed.

"What were you and Aunt Lulu doing?" she asks, even as she rolls over, her eyes closing.

I ruffle her hair a little as I pull the blankets up. "Just talking, Ol," I whisper. "Go to sleep."

When I walk out, I find Lu draping a blanket over Oscar as he lies fast asleep on the couch.

"Want me to carry him to bed too?" I ask, standing in the doorway.

She looks up and shakes her head. "He can stay here," she whispers.

I nod and we stare wordlessly at each other as though neither of us wants to suggest what happens next. I know I can't stay though, not when the kids are here and from the look on Lu's face, she knows that too.

"I should probably go," I eventually say.

Lu nods and stands, walking around the couch and following me to the front door. We both step out onto the porch, the coolness of the evening doing nothing to calm the heat that's still raging through my body. Lulu motions to the door with her thumb out.

"I guess I'll..."

I turn, cutting her off as I press my mouth against hers in a hard kiss. Lu moans, her body folding into mine as I slide my arms around her back and pull her against me. Our mouths fuse together, tongues entwined, our lips and teeth hungry for more, neither of us wanting to stop what we started back in the hall outside the bathroom.

"Your niece and nephew are great," I murmur between kisses. "But their timing really sucks."

"I'm sorry," she breathes out, pulling back a little, her fingers digging into my back.

"Don't be," I murmur. "But have dinner with me tomorrow night?" I whisper, my forehead against hers. "Just you and me?"

Lu nods, biting her bottom lip as her eyes find mine and she understands the full implication of everything I'm saying to her, all the unspoken things that we both know could happen the second we find ourselves alone again.

At this point it feels inevitable and something we both want to happen. God knows, it's hard enough controlling myself now, but I know when it finally does, I want there to be zero chance of interruption—from anyone.

I grin, pressing my lips against hers in a soft kiss before murmuring, "Goodnight, beautiful," and turning and walking down the stairs.

The next morning, I head up to the shed early and continue to work on cleaning out the crusher while I wait for Lu to appear. By mid-morning, there's no sign of her so I wander over to her office.

I find her standing over her desk, her back to the door as she studies something intently. She doesn't hear me as I walk in, doesn't sense me behind her as I press a kiss to the back of her neck and slide one hand over her hip and across her stomach.

"Shit," she says, jumping as she turns to face me.

I grin. "You being weird again, Lu?" I ask, kissing the end of her nose.

Her eyes dart around the room as though she's terrified of someone seeing us. "No," she finally says, still not looking at me.

I duck down, slide two fingers under her chin and tilt it up so she's forced to look at me. "Yeah, you are," I say grinning.

She swallows hard, her tongue slipping out to lick her lips and it's enough that I can't stop myself as I lean in and suck her bottom lip into my mouth.

"Jack," she whispers, hands on my chest as though to push me away. She doesn't though and I smile against her mouth as I deepen the kiss.

She pushes me away now though, her eyes wide as a slight flush rises over her cheeks. I slide my fingers up her neck, brushing them across her jaw as I move my hand from her stomach and slip it into the pocket of her jeans and pull her closer.

"Aunt Lulu," comes Oscar's voice as he strolls into the office.

"Fuuuck," I mutter, stepping backward. "Hey, little dude," I say, turning to grin at him as I offer him my hand.

He eyes us warily, his gaze flicking from me to Lu and back to me again. Eventually he holds out his hand and takes us through our routine before he says, "What's happening?"

"Nothing, Oscar," Lu cuts in, her voice shaky. "Jack was just here to pick up the list of jobs that I need done," she says, scrambling for a piece of paper on her desk. "These are the priorities," she says, handing it to me. "Let me know if you need anything."

My smile widens, as I look back at her, watching as that flush now deepens. "Oh, I will, Lu," I murmur, winking at her. "I will."

Then I turn, and placing a hand on Oscar's shoulder, I say. "Come on dude, you're with me," before we walk out.

I spend the rest of the day doing random jobs around the property, Oscar occasionally trying to help out, but more often than not, wandering off when he gets bored.

There's more than enough work to keep me occupied for several weeks, if not longer, and even though it's not wine making, which is my true passion, I find myself not minding. I like the idea of helping Lu out and as I spend several hours restringing a row of grape vines, my thoughts consumed with wondering what it would be like to do this indefinitely.

I don't want to give up wine making, but this is a vineyard, so it's not like I'd have to. I'd even keep doing odd jobs around the place to help out if Lu would give me a shot at making some of their wines.

I know the current guy she uses and while I think he's more than capable of continuing to produce the stuff they are known for, I also know there's more potential they could tap into.

And maybe I'm the person to show her that.

Eventually, I finish up and head over to the restaurant to organize some things for tonight before heading back home to take a run. Before I go, I send a quick text.

Me: I'll pick you up at 7

I wait a few seconds, but she doesn't reply, so I plug in my earphones and head out to burn off some excess energy so I don't jump her as soon as we're alone. Halfway through my run, my phone vibrates with a new message.

Lu: ok...is it weird that I'm nervous?

I grin, slowing to a jog so I can type out a reply.

Me: don't be nervous, it's just me and I promise I'll be on my best behavior ☺

Lu: you're NEVER well behaved!

I burst out laughing, glancing around as though I half expect to find her out here watching me.

Me: I'm mortally offended by your suggestion that I'm some sort of bad boy...and at the idea that you don't like bad boys???

Lu: ☺ I never said I didn't like them...

I shake my head now, grinning as I abandon the rest of my run.

Me: is that right???

Lu: ☺

I chuckle, sliding my phone into my pocket as I jog the rest of the way back home.

At one minute past seven, I'm knocking on Lu's door. When she opens it, she's dressed in a long black dress, bare feet with her hair loose and hanging around her shoulders and fuck me if she isn't the most beautiful thing I've ever seen.

"Hey," she says, a shy smile on her face. "Let me just grab some shoes."

"No need," I say, grabbing her hand. I pull her toward me, my other hand sliding onto her cheek as I press a soft kiss to her mouth. "You ready?"

She swallows hard, a flustered look on her face as she nods, grabs her phone and keys and follows me down the steps and across the lawn to my place. Taking her hand, I lead her around the side of the house to the back lawn, which overlooks fields of grape vines and large tress in the distance.

In the middle of the grass is a blanket, surrounded by lanterns. To the side is a basket of food that I had the restaurant arrange for me, along with a couple of bottles of wine.

"Dinner," I say, indicating to the blanket.

Lu looks at me, then back at the blanket, before looking back at me again.

I chuckle. "Not what you were expecting?" I ask.

She shrugs. "I don't know what I was expecting," she admits.

I grin. "Come on," I say, pulling her toward the set up.

I hand her a bottle to open while I pull the food from the basket. The chef has put together a huge platter of meats and cheeses, fruit and chocolate, all perfect accompaniments to the wine I've brought.

"Another one of yours?" Lu asks as she hands me a glass.

"Yep."

She takes a smell, swirling the red liquid in her glass before lifting it to her lips. I watch as she sips the wine, moving it around her mouth before swallowing. The whole thing is fucking mesmerizing and it's taking every bit of self-control I have to not just say fuck it and pull her down onto the blanket so I can kiss her entire body.

"Shit, Jack," she murmurs. "This is really good."

"Thanks," I say, taking a sip of my wine.

"You should seriously be doing this for your own place," she says. "Not other vineyards."

I shrug. "Maybe," I say. "But I choose who I work with too, I don't make wine for just anyone."

Lu takes another sip, her eyes closing as she swallows and savors the flavor. God, it's almost impossible to keep my eyes off her as she sits beside me, her whole body practically glowing in the slowly disappearing sunlight.

"I could make some for you, if you want," I say.

She turns to me, her eyes wide as she meets my stare. "Really?"

I shrug, trying to act casual. "Sure," I tell her. "This is a great winery, a great brand, I'd be proud to have my name associated with it."

Her eyes lock with mine as she takes in everything I've just said. "We, ah…we have all our fruit locked in for this year," she says quietly, biting her bottom lip.

I shrug, trying for casual as I say, "Maybe next season then?" before looking away, reaching for some cheese.

Lu says nothing at my suggestion and I wonder if I've said too much, pushed too far. What she doesn't know is that I'm already doing something for her, something with the grapes she thought she'd lose when the crusher failed.

When I turn back to her, she's staring at me still. "You'd come back?" she asks, her words barely audible.

I nod. "Sure," I tell her, smiling a little. "I love it here."

What I don't say, what I find myself wanting to say, is that I don't want to leave here. That if she asked me to stay right now, I think I would. I have no idea where this is all suddenly coming from. I've only been here a week and it's not as though anything serious is happening between us that could give me reason to stay.

But regardless of how quick this all feels, I find myself wanting to know what *could* happen. When I left Oz, my brain was a mess, my heart broken at what I'd discovered had been happening behind my back for god knows how long.

Coming over here hadn't just felt like an escape though, it's had felt like coming back home, to something familiar, to memories I had never let go of despite how many years had passed.

And of course there was Lu.

The girl I'd never stopped thinking about, the girl who was always there in the back of my mind, regardless of what girl was right in front of me.

We eat in silence now, as though my admission has left us both unsure about what to say. I refill our wine glasses and watch as Lu curls her legs beneath her, her eyes on the fields in the distance.

"Do you remember," she eventually says, smiling to herself, "when you tricked me into eating that disgusting vegemite stuff?"

I chuckle. "Oh yeah."

Lu turns to look at me now, a small smile on her face. "You told me it was chocolate flavored."

I grin, shrugging as I say, "You were being stubborn. I had to get you to try it somehow."

"Yeah, but it was disgusting," she says, laughing a little.

"But you never would have known that until you tried it."

Lu shakes her head, still smiling as she says, "And then you smeared it all over my face because you were pissed I didn't like it."

I laugh. "Mmmm, maybe."

"Maybe?" she asks, confused.

I stare back at her, her deep blue eyes now pools of blackness in the rapidly fading light. "Maybe I did that for other reasons," I admit, my words a whisper.

Lu swallows hard as she stares back at me. "What reasons?"

I put my wine down, take hers from her hand and do the same. "This," I say, pulling her toward me as I fall backward onto the blanket.

Lu's body falls onto mine, her long hair falling around us as she looks down at me. I slide my hands up her back, one hand slipping into her hair, gathering it in my hand and winding it around my fingers at the base of her neck.

Slowly, with our eyes still locked together, I urge her closer until her lips are brushing against mine, the barest of touches. Lu exhales against me, her breath sweet like the wine she's just been drinking. I feel her hands as they slide up the sides of my body, slipping under my t-shirt so her fingers are brushing against my skin. I groan at the touch as a thousand goose bumps ripple over my skin.

"God, Lu," I murmur, pulling her closer as I kiss her now, my tongue slipping between her parted lips.

All around us, the air hums with electricity, the quietness of the night broken by our low moans and deep breaths. Still holding her hair in one hand, I slide my other around her waist, pulling her closer so her body now lies flush against mine, my leg slipping between hers.

She groans in response, pressing closer as her nails dig into my skin.

"God, fuck I want you, Lu," I whisper, my mouth at her jaw, her ear, her neck, kissing and nipping at her skin.

"Jack," she breathes out, finding my mouth again.

My hand at her back grabs at her dress, pulling the material higher. Just as I'm about to suggest we go inside, the moment is shattered by the sound of her phone ringing.

"Shit," she mutters, her mouth leaving mine as she turns to glare at her phone. She slips a hand from my t-shirt, silencing the noise before turning back to me, a small smile tugging at her mouth as she lowers it back to mine.

Her phone rings out again, the loud noise killing the moment.

"Sounds like someone's trying to get hold of you," I say, my fingers loosening against her dress.

"Sorry," she says, sliding off me. "Let me just see who it is."

She reaches for her phone, lying on her stomach. I roll onto my side, prop myself up on an elbow beside her.

"Hello?" she says.

Someone speaks, but the words aren't loud enough for me to make out. I feel Lu's body stiffen beside me, a strange look on her face as she looks up at me.

"Shit, okay, thanks, I'm on my way," she says before hanging up the call.

"What's wrong, is everything okay?"

Lu shakes her head, standing now as she brushes her hands down the front of her dress, not looking at me.

"Lu, what is it?"

She exhales hard, finally lifting her eyes to mine. "One of the security alarms is going off," she says. "It's coming from the offices. I need to go check it out."

I nod, standing. "I'll come with you."

She shakes her head. "It's okay, Jack," she says. "I'll..."

"Lu," I say, reaching for her hand and squeezing it. "I'll come with you."

Chapter Fourteen

Lauren

My hand is still in Jack's when I reach my office, the sound of the alarm blaring through the quiet of the night, and this is one of those times that I'm grateful no one lives nearby. The sound is practically deafening and we haven't even entered the building.

The keys are in my hand and before I can slip the key into the lock, Jack reaches for them.

"I'll do it," he says, his tone firm and I smile a little at his sudden need to protect me.

"The alarm goes off from time to time," I respond, shaking my head and attempting to sound unconcerned, but that doesn't mean my heart isn't hammering against my chest like a jackhammer.

It has nothing to do with the alarm and everything to do with Jack and his words and his lips and his hot body and this insane desire to hop in the sack with him.

"I don't want you going in there on your own."

I'm about to roll my eyes, but I catch myself. It's been a long time since I've had someone worry about me, and I realize I shouldn't dismiss it.

"Thanks, Jack," I say, but my sentiment is lost in the sound of the alarm as he opens the door.

I follow him in; punching the code in, the alarm falls silent, yet it still rings in my ears.

Jack moves through every one of the small offices and then heads into the tasting room that's adjacent to my office. I'm certain he won't find anything, but I indulge his need to be sure.

He comes back, a hand running through his hair as he announces that all is safe and clear.

"Does it go off frequently?" Jack questions. "Your alarm system seems a little outdated."

He's right, it is, but rewiring the place is a huge expense and an even bigger undertaking. We added cameras a couple of years back and it's been working out all right.

"Every couple of months or so," I tell him shrugging my shoulders. "We can watch the video from the cameras if you want to see if you can figure out why it went off."

"I feel a little better knowing you have cameras, but..."

"Jack," I say, interrupting him, because I don't think I want to hear where's he's going to go with this conversation. It's weird having someone interested in my safety, in addition to taking an active interest in the winery. "It was probably just a bobcat or a fat raccoon. The motion detectors are a little sensitive. They pick up things through the windows sometimes."

"If you say so," he replies conceding, but I don't see this being the last of the conversation.

We walk back to the cottages in silence, neither one of us wanting to bring up what was about to happen between us. We both know had we not been interrupted we'd be in Jack's bed right now.

I'm not one to believe in signs or fate or anything else like that, but it's hard to push it from my mind. Jack showing up here after all these years, still harboring those unrequited feelings he admitted to, and me, while not admitting it out loud, completely agreeing that there was something between us fourteen years ago.

Looking back on it now, I may have claimed to hate Jack and all his teasing, but I remember finding myself strangely jealous as girls threw themselves at him at our school dance. That feeling tightening deep in my stomach and pushing its way into my chest as my heart clenched in response.

We were just kids and at fifteen years old neither one of us knew what it was we were feeling or even how to act on something like that. Jack teased me mercilessly and in response, I claimed to despise him.

I did hate it then, and I looked at him as immature and childish, but I was no better. Stomping around, huffing and puffing, rolling my eyes at everything he said and did. Not wanting him around and being far more dramatic than necessary when I was asked to entertain him.

The thing is, when he finally left, I missed the hell out of him. Whenever friends from school would bring him up, a lump would form in my throat, strangling my words and I'd dismiss their conversations. I couldn't bring myself to talk about him.

I moped around the vineyard for weeks after he left and my mom even suggested I write to him. That was also the first time I met Will when Ellen brought him home to me our family. He agreed with my mom and suggested the same thing. But that would mean I had to admit my feelings for Jack.

At fifteen, having that conversation with your mother is mortifying and there was no possible way I was going to give up on the ruse I had stuck with.

Jack was annoying back then, and actually still is, but as always, there was something endearing and sweet about him, and that was the part I missed.

We stop just between our two cottages, and while we both know the moment has passed, that spark between us is still lingering. It's something I imagine won't ever be extinguished, because if it can last fourteen years, it can last a lifetime.

"It's late," I say, breaking the silence. "I should be getting to bed. I have to be up early tomorrow."

"Me too," Jack replies, but he's smirking at me. "My boss is a real hard ass and I don't want to ruin this good thing we've got going on. She might fire me."

"You're ridiculous." I give Jack a little shove and let my hand slide down his arm, giving his hand a squeeze before I walk away. "Good night, Jack," I call, looking over my shoulder at him, a smile on my face that just won't seem to fade.

"Night, Lu."

I'm up with the sun and spend most of the morning clarifying and transferring wine into barrels with Tommy's help. It's a long and tedious process, but something that is necessary if we want our wine to taste well. After about five hours, both Tommy and I call it quits, getting in our cardio for the day, moving barrels and climbing ladders, driving forklifts and walking the length of the massive storage building.

I haven't seen Jack yet, but I know he's up and working his ass off too. I heard the sound of a nail gun echoing across the vast openness, so I know he's fixing the loose boards on the side of one of the sheds. I'm guessing he's working his way through the list I gave him the other day and there's something about that that I find comforting.

I wash up and head to my office, needing to finish up a few things in there. After my evening with Jack there's an email that needs to be answered. It's been sitting in my inbox for a few days and I've been avoiding it. But my time with Jack has given me the clarity I need to get back into things.

I need to stop putting my past ahead of what is best for the business, and this newfound happiness I have with Jack around has made me want to move on more than ever.

I flop down in my desk chair and pull up the email. I'm not sure why this woman's inquiry is any different than the ones I've received in the past, but something is different.

Something about me is different, and I owe it to Jack.

I send off the email, a smile still lingering on my face when Ellen walks through the door.

"I booked a wedding for August," I announce, proud of myself for finally getting past the hurdle and the association of weddings with the collapse of my own. I give Ellen a curt nod of my head, but she doesn't say anything.

I thought she'd be thrilled knowing this is a huge moneymaker for us, but instead of responding with excitement she says, "I ran into Nate today."

And maybe what I thought the universe was trying to tell me was wrong. Maybe it's reminding me that I'm a damn fool.

I close my eyes and scrub my hands over my face. Not entirely certain how to respond to Ellen's words.

"Boy, you know how to start a conversation, don't you?" I say, my tone clipped and any happiness I had has now faded like the logo of an old t-shirt.

"Did you want me not to tell you?" Ellen responds back, her hands on her hips. "He asked about you."

"I'm sure he did." I roll my eyes, wondering when this fucking game with Nate will ever end. It's like he has this radar on me, and just when I start to feel settled, it alerts him and he resurfaces like black mold, disgusting, clingy and hazardous to my health.

"If it's any consolation, Olivia hissed at him when she saw him," Ellen adds smiling at me a little.

"That helps," I mutter, feeling this weight pressing down on my chest. "What did he say?" I ask the question even though I know I shouldn't. He gave up the right to ask questions about my life when he bailed on our wedding.

"He asked if you were seeing anyone."

"Why would he ask that?" I practically scream at Ellen, an annoyed look blanketing my face. I'm standing now, rage burning inside of me over the fact that just the mention of his name can ruin my day.

"Because he heard you were. News travels fast in the wine world," she says, trying to lighten the mood.

"He's not even involved in the wine world," I say, air quoting the words *wine world* back to her. "And I'm not seeing anyone."

"You are if you ask anyone who's seen you with Jack."

I want to argue with Ellen, insist that I'm not seeing Jack, but even I know it's a fruitless argument.

When I don't respond Ellen adds, "He's toxic, Lauren. Jack isn't. Please don't let this ruin the progress you've made. Things are good."

I nod, but the damage is done.

"Why did you tell me then?"

"Did you want me to lie to you? Keep it a secret and then have you find out later? You would've been furious if it played out like that."

She's right. Had I found out later that she ran into Nate and didn't tell me, I would be angry. But that doesn't mean it doesn't sting to hear his name, to know he's asking about me.

"You're right," I concede, trying to shake off this heavy feeling.

"Jack is good for you. He gave me back my sister…"

Ellen tries to continue, but I talk over her. "Jack's going to leave too, Ellen, but at least this time I know it's coming."

"You don't know that."

"Um, what's he going to do?" I ask, my voice dripping with cynicism. "Stay here and be our maintenance man? He's far too talented for that and I'm sure he has a life back in Australia."

"Something brought him back here and it wasn't just our broken crusher."

"I'm done, Ellen," I snap, my ass hitting the chair hard as I begin to scroll through the few emails that have come through in the last few minutes.

"Do you want to talk about the wedding?"

"My wedding!? I practically yell. "Fuck no!"

"The wedding you booked," she says, wide-eyed at my over the top response.

"I'm cancelling it."

Ellen lets out a long sigh and runs her hand through her hair. "You're not cancelling it." Her tone is harsh and firm and before I can continue this argument she walks out the door.

The entire rest of my day is spent attempting to complete the most mundane tasks but being completely distracted.

I've once again allowed Nate to consume my thoughts and weasel his way back into my life.

It's not like I have any attraction to him anymore or that I want him back. He's just a reminder of how blindsided I was by manipulation and years of letting someone control me.

Him not showing up at our wedding was the biggest embarrassment of my life, but it was also the best thing that ever happened to me.

It's like looking back at pictures from high school and wondering what the hell you were wearing, but then coming across that one where you still look amazing.

Nate is tube tops and self-cut bangs and silver eyeliner. Things that are humiliating to look at, but gratifying to know you survived.

But it's also a reminder that I never want to go back, that I can't let someone get so close that I'm hurt again. That's exactly what will happen if this thing with Jack goes any further.

I'm about to get in the shower when my front door opens and Jack steps in.

"I came looking for you at lunch but I couldn't find you," he says, his eyes shining as he walks over to me.

When he reaches for me, I shy away and confusion washes over his face. I watch as his demeanor changes, his shoulders fall and he shakes his head slightly.

"What's the matter?"

"Nothing."

"Bullshit, Lu. You just pulled away from me. I thought we were past this being weird shit."

"What are we doing here?" I ask, but the words fall from my lips with a bite to them and a harshness to my tone. I gesture between us, and Jack steps closer to me.

"I thought we were starting a relationship, but I guess I was wrong." He sounds affronted and I don't blame him given my reaction to him.

"Why? So you can fuck off back to Australia and leave me?"

"Whoa, Lu," he says, hands up defensively. "I'm not sure when the argument started, but I need to catch up."

"There's no argument," I hiss back, knowing I've left him far behind and confused by my behavior. "You'll leave and I'll be here looking stupid. It is what it is."

Jack is silent, his eyes taking me in, his lips parted slightly as if he wants to say something but words fail him.

"Good bye, Jack," I spit out, walking down the hallway that leads to my bedroom and into my bathroom. I slam the door behind me, and the knot that had formed in my stomach, tight and nauseating, slowly begins to uncoil.

I take a deep breath, start the shower and strip off my clothes, but before I can take off my bra and underwear, the door to my bathroom flies open.

"Jack, what the..." I shout, as he forces me against the glass wall of the shower, the length of his body pressing into mine.

"You don't get to walk away when we argue," he asserts. "And I'm not going to fuck off back to Australia and leave you."

He's looking down at me, his deep blue eyes serious and it makes it hard to form a coherent sentence. I hear the truth in his words and I want to believe him. I swallow hard and suck in a ragged breath.

He places his hands on either side of my face and I close my eyes because there's no way he's still here after the fit I just threw. He's supposed to leave.

His lips brush against mine in the smallest, softest movement causing my entire body to shudder, chills rushing down my spine.

He kisses his way along my jaw until he reaches my neck, sucking and biting at me. His hands slide over my breasts, the lightest touch of his fingertips trailing over the bare skin of my stomach.

"Jack..." I start, breathless and needy, but he cuts me off murmuring, "Don't ruin it, Lu."

Chapter Fifteen

Jack

My hands grip her hips, pushing her backward into the shower stall as I follow her in, my lips never leaving her skin as I kiss my way back to her mouth. The water falls around us, my clothes now soaked and clinging to my skin as I slide my hands up her back to her bra strap.

"Jack," she murmurs, her hands moving to the waistband of my jeans.

My fingers pause on the strap as I pull back a little. Lu stares up at me, her lips slightly parted as though she isn't sure what to say. "I'll stop if you want me to, Lu," I tell her. "But I really don't want to stop and I don't think you want me to either."

Lu swallows hard, her bottom lip between her teeth as she continues to look up at me. Just when I think she's about to say yes, stop, her fingers slide into the top of my jeans and she pulls me back to her.

"Don't stop," she whispers against my mouth.

Groaning, my fingers fumble with the strap, undoing her bra before I pull the straps down her arms and it falls to the floor. Lu's fingers fumble with the buttons of my jeans, her hands shoving the wet material down my hips when she finally gets them undone.

I let go of her long enough to pull my t-shirt over my head before throwing it in the corner of the shower stall. Sliding my hands around her back, I pull her closer, so we're chest to chest, her skin against mine as I lower my mouth to hers once more.

I feel her hands on my hips again, pushing my briefs down before she does the same with her own panties so there is no longer anything between us.

"God, Lu," I murmur against her mouth as I back her up against the wall. I kiss a trail down her neck, sucking on her collarbone before I lower my mouth to her breast.

When I suck her nipple into my mouth, she moans, low and sexy as her head falls back and her body bows into mine. My arms tighten around her waist, holding her as I move lower, my teeth grazing against her hip before kissing a trail across her stomach to her other hip.

"Jack," she groans and it sounds so fucking sexy I nearly lose it. As I drop to my knees, I feel her fingers slide into my hair, my hands gripping her hips as I pull her closer, pull her against my mouth.

"Oh jesus christ," she murmurs, her legs buckling a little as I tease her with my tongue, my hands holding her up. Her moans echo in the shower stall, even as the water continues to fall around us.

I take my time, teasing her, pushing her closer and closer to the edge only to stop just when I think she's about to let go. Every time I do, her fingers tighten in my hair, urging me back to her, her low murmurs begging me to keep going. I open my eyes, stare up her body, the water falling down over her skin. Her eyes are closed, her whole body leaning back against the wall, bottom lip between her teeth.

She looks fucking incredible.

I hook one of her legs over my shoulder, trailing my fingers up the inside of her thigh. She groans again, hands in my hair holding me against her and this time I give her what she wants, pushing her harder and harder until eventually she lets go, calling out my name as she comes, her voice husky with desire.

Standing, I pull her into my arms, reaching behind her to turn the water off.

"Come with me," I whisper.

We both step out of the shower, my mouth finding hers again as I walk her back into her bedroom, neither of us bothering to dry off. When we reach her bed, I gently push her on to it until she's lying naked in front of me.

I lean forward, my hands on either side of her shoulders as I brush my lips against hers. "You are so beautiful," I whisper, lowering my body onto hers.

Lu's hands slide around my back, the water still dripping from both of us as she pulls me against her, her legs wrapping around my hips.

"You want me to stop?" I whisper, smiling as I pull back so I can see her.

Lu's deep blue eyes lock with mine as she slowly shakes her head, a smile tugging at her mouth.

My smile widens as I lower my head and kiss her. She arches beneath me now, her hips moving up to meet mine as her hands slide down my back to my arse, pulling me closer.

When I slide inside her, we both groan. "God, you feel fucking amazing," I whisper between kisses.

"Jack," is all she says and then both of us stop talking.

We move together, our bodies so in sync it's like we've been doing this forever. She fits perfectly against me, her bones and muscles all moving to accommodate mine, her fingers digging into me, nails scoring my skin, marking me as I move against her.

My body feels like it's on fire, my skin hot against hers as electricity courses between us. We kiss constantly, both of us pushing each other harder and harder, hands and lips everywhere.

Eventually, neither of us can hold back any longer and as she arches beneath me, calling out my name again, I push deep inside her one more time as my body shatters against hers.

I collapse against her, our bodies now covered in sweat as we lie together, both of us breathing hard. My heart pounds in my chest as I press soft, gentle kisses, slowly brushing my lips against hers.

"That was amazing," she whispers.

I smile. "Fucking fantastic," I murmur. "God, I've dreamed about this, Lulu."

"You have?" she asks, eyes opening.

I grin down at her. "Yes," I say, pressing another kiss to her lips. "Many, many times," I tell her. She giggles now and it's fucking adorable. I roll over, keeping her with me so she's now lying on top of me. "I've had a crush on you since I was kid, Lu," I confess, brushing her hair back. "It's never gone away. And it's only intensified since I got back here."

Lu stares down at me, a shocked look on her face as she takes in my words, my admission to her. It's all true, everything I've just said. Back when I was a kid, I'd thought it was just a teenage crush, the kind of crush that would disappear as soon as I went back home to Oz and forgot all about the skinny little blonde girl who I couldn't seem to stop tormenting.

But it hadn't and even though I hadn't seen her for fourteen years, it didn't mean I didn't miss her, didn't wish that maybe I'd kept in contact with her. That I hadn't been so mean to her all those times I teased and tormented her. And even though it hadn't been all bad between us, plenty of good memories too, a part of me wished I'd done things differently.

God, I even looked her up on Facebook once or twice, just to see what she was doing. I'd thought maybe I could drop her a message, see how she was, but instead all I'd seen was photos of her and some other guy, which were enough to stop me from reaching out.

"Does that scare you?" I ask her, skimming my thumb across her cheek.

"Maybe," she whispers.

I lean up and kiss her again. "So, does that have something to do with whatever that was earlier?"

Lu shakes her head, sliding off me a little so she's half lying on me, her head now resting on my shoulder. She smooths a hand over my chest, down my stomach to my hip, her fingers tracing the scar that's there.

"Lu," I say, titling her face to mine. "I meant what I said, okay? I'm not leaving you."

"But you are going to go back to Australia," she finally says, her words barely audible.

I exhale because I know she's right. I *am* going back, I have to, for so many reasons. But that doesn't mean I don't want to do this, don't want to find a way to make it work.

"But I'm not leaving *you*," I tell her again. "We've only just gotten started, Lu," I try, desperate to find a way to explain this so she doesn't give up on us before we even have a chance to begin. "We can find a way to make this work."

She lets out a long breath, leaning her forehead on my chest. I feel her lips against my skin, her breath warm as I trail my fingers up her spine. Eventually she lifts her head, her eyes meeting mine as she offers me a small smile. I smile back at her, my fingers brushing against her cheek.

"Don't give up on us," I whisper.

She leans forward, her lips meeting mine as she whispers, "Okay."

The next morning, I wake with Lu naked and asleep in my arms. Every single part of me wants to wake her up with my mouth, make her moan and call my name again like she did so many times last night.

I don't though, reluctantly easing her off me as I slide out of bed. Even though it's early, I know Ollie and Oscar are coming over today and I don't want to risk them finding us like this. It's bad enough Ollie busted us kissing the other night and I'm sure it's only a matter of time before she's announcing that nugget of information to the world.

My clothes are all still on the floor of the shower, soaking wet. I grab them and a towel, which I wrap around my waist before walking back into the bedroom. Lu is lying on her side as she half opens her eyes, a sleepy smile on her face.

I lean down and press a kiss to her shoulder. "I gotta go and get some dry clothes before work," I whisper, nuzzling at her neck.

"Mmmm," she murmurs, her hand sliding out from under the covers as she reaches for the towel. "Stay."

I grin, kissing my way up to her ear. "I wish I could, beautiful," I whisper. "But I gotta get to work."

"Hard ass boss?" she says, smiling.

Her fingers brush against my skin before slipping beneath the towel. It takes everything I have in me to still her hand, stop her from pulling at the towel when it's exactly what I want her to do.

"Nah," I say, nibbling the skin just below her ear. "She likes to think she is, but I know she's a total softie underneath."

Lu rolls onto her back now, the sheet slipping a little. I can't stop the groan that falls from my mouth as I move my lips down her neck and across her now uncovered chest. "God, you make it impossible," I murmur against her skin.

"Stay," she repeats, her hand finding the towel again.

This time I don't stop her, my wet clothes joining the towel on the floor as I crawl onto the bed, pushing the sheet completely out of the way so it's my body that's now covering her instead. Lu leans up, her mouth finding mine in a hungry kiss that leaves me breathless and my hands sliding down her ribcage, over her hip to her thigh, which I hitch around my hip.

"Aunt Lulu!?"

We both freeze.

"Aunt Lulu," Ollie calls again. "Where are you?"

"Fuck," Lu says, shoving me off her. I can't help but laugh as she scrambles from the bed, grabbing a robe from the back of the door, which she quickly shuts. She pulls it on, wrapping it tightly around her before she turns back to me.

"Go," I tell her, smiling. "I'll sneak out the back."

"I'm sorry," she says, shaking her head.

I get out of bed and walk over to her. "It's okay," I whisper, my mouth at her ear. "We can pick this back up tonight," I add, before opening the door and pushing her out.

The truck is pulling up as I reach the shed, Tommy and another guy are both standing there waiting. It had taken nearly thirty minutes for me to get out of the house, as I listened through the door to Lu trying to convince Ollie and Oscar to stay in the living room and watch TV.

In the end, I'd managed to sneak out the back, legging it across the lawn to my place in nothing but a bath towel, my wet clothes still on the floor in Lu's bedroom.

Totally worth it though.

"Morning," I say.

The other guy, who I think is called Greg, returns the greeting, but Tommy just nods, his face stony as he stands with his arms crossed over his chest. Not sure what the fuck his problem is.

The delivery driver gets out, his eyes scanning his clipboard before he looks up and says, "Jack?"

"That'd be me," I say, stepping forward. Tommy mirrors the action, standing beside me as he watches the driver and I share a look.

"Okay," the delivery guy eventually says. "Sign here." He indicates on the form and I do as requested before all the parts for the crusher are unloaded.

When the truck's empty, the guy leaves and I take in all the boxes, mentally checking them off with the list in my head.

"Everything here?" Greg asks.

"No," I say, shaking my head as I skim over the invoice in my hands. "Two parts are missing."

"You forgot to order them?" Tommy asks.

My head shoots up. "Of course I fucking didn't," I say.

Tommy shrugs. "Well, looks like you did," he says before turning and walking into the shed.

I glance at Greg, who puts his hands up as if to say *don't ask me*. I shove the invoice at him asking him to check everything over before walking into the shed.

"Tommy!" I call out.

He stops, looks up at me.

"What the fuck was that about?" I ask, walking over to him.

"What?" he asks as though he's got no idea.

I roll my eyes. "Out there, the order?"

He shrugs. "Well, someone forgot to order the parts."

"Right," I say, crossing my arms over my chest. "And you just assume that person was me."

He raises an eyebrow as if to say who else would it be and I immediately want to punch the guy in the face. Instead, I pull my phone from my pocket, scrolling through to the company's contact details and hitting the green dial button.

Tommy stares at me as I explain the situation, the woman on the other end looking up the order before she finally explains that two parts are still on back-order and won't be shipped for another four weeks. Thanking her, I hang up the phone, sliding it back into my pocket and turning back to Tommy.

"So, as I said, I didn't forget."

He shrugs again, before turning back to whatever he was doing.

"What the fuck is your problem with me?" I ask.

"What are you talking about?"

"The attitude," I say, motioning to him. "The bullshit about me not knowing what I ordered."

Tommy glances around, shaking his head as though he has no idea what I'm talking about.

"You hate the fact I'm here, don't you?" I tell him.

"No," he says, a little too defensively.

I nod. "Yeah, you do," I say. "And I think you really hate the fact that Lu and I are close."

Tommy stiffens now, taking a step toward me as he says in a low voice, "You hurt her and I will hurt you." I laugh at his words, but he gets right in my face and continues. "I mean it, Jack," he says. "She doesn't need any more shit, okay?"

I've got no idea what the hell he's talking about, but I'll be damned if he's gonna tell me what I can and can't do, especially when he thinks one of those things is hurting Lu.

"Lu and me is none of your business," I say. "So stay the fuck out of it."

Then I turn and walk out of the shed, forcing myself to calm down as I head down to the office so I can tell Lu about the delay with the parts.

Chapter Sixteen

Lauren

Jack comes storming into my office, his face flushed and his hands clenched in fists at his side. He practically whips the door off its hinges as he lets out a mumbled string of swear words.

I stop and look up from my computer, a pen between my teeth as I watch Jack drag a hand through his already disheveled blonde hair and exhale hard.

"You okay?" I ask, chewing on the pen cap.

"So two of the parts for the crusher are delayed and you know what, that dick Tommy tried to blame me. Claimed I didn't order them."

I smirk at him, the pen still between my teeth as I shake my head a little. "You're here to tattle on Tommy?"

"No," Jack snaps, his tone defensive as he looks at me with his hands on his hips.

I stand up and walk over to where Jack is standing, hooking my finger into the front of his jeans and pulling him toward me.

"What's got you so worked up?" I ask, smiling against his mouth as I press small kisses to his lips. "The fact that the parts are delayed or that someone questioned your competency?"

I slide my hands under his t-shirt, feeling his body relax against mine as I kiss my way along his jawline until I reach his ear. "I wouldn't worry too much," I murmur in his ear. "You're...

"Lauren!" I hear Penny call as her feet plod against the floor toward my office.

I shove Jack away and lean against my desk awkwardly, trying to look natural. Jack's face is still flushed but this time for a different reason. We look guilty as hell.

Penny walks in without knocking, not like she ever would've knocked in the past, and starts talking immediately.

"We're running really low on the cab so I pulled it from the tasting menu and I'm going to talk with..." She doesn't finish her thought as she takes in my awkwardness and Jack's presence.

"You okay?" she asks, her forehead wrinkling up at her question as she looks at me and then at Jack and back again.

"Mmmhmm," I mumble, nodding my head.

"Just letting Lu know some of the parts are going to be arriving later than planned," Jack says seemingly out of nowhere, his voice cutting through the silence I've left floating in the room.

"Then I'll definitely let the restaurant know to pull the cab from the menu there too," Penny says, smiling at Jack, but her smile screams that she knows something is up. "I'll be going now, so whatever it was that was going on here," she flits a hand between us, "can continue."

She closes the door behind her and as soon as she does Jack is on me like white on rice.

"What's the big secret, Lulu?" he asks, his mouth now close to my lips, smiling and sending a wave of shivers up my spine.

"No secret."

"You're lying, but that's okay. I'm kinda enjoying this cheeky sneaking around thing. But I get it, you gotta keep up the *I hate Jack* persona you've taken so long to expertly cultivate."

I laugh, putting my hands on his chest and shoving him a little, but he grabs my wrists and pulls me closer.

"I'm glad the parts are on the slow boat from Oz," I comment back, and Jack laughs.

"Slow boat?"

"Your shipping systems suck. It's slow as hell. Anytime we order stuff from there we have to give like six weeks for it to get here. But in this case, the longer it takes to get here, the longer you have to stay."

I smile up at him, his blue eyes look down at me, but he doesn't return my smile and I pull back slightly.

"That's not the only reason I'm still here," Jack says, his tone now serious. "Anyone could install these parts and you know that. I'm here because I want to be with you."

"Okay," I respond, but it's not what he's looking for. It's only been a few weeks since his arrival, but I understand what he's saying. The connection between us is even stronger than it was when we were kids. It's intense and consuming and I do wonder if that's only because we know this whole thing has an end date.

"I'm serious, Lu," he asserts and I nod my head. I want to tell him I feel the same way, that I understand he'd be here regardless, but the words won't come.

"I know, Jack." I put my hands on either side of his face and kiss him, because maybe the feelings in my kiss will explain everything I can't say out loud.

Jack spends the day working through his to-do list, our paths crossing every so often, but most of the time Oscar or Olivia are stuck to him like glue. I don't think I'm the only one who is enjoying Jack's time here.

My heart tightens in my chest. Australia is a long way from California, fourteen and a half hours by plane to be exact, and that's just to Sydney. I'm not going to be the only one with a broken heart when he finally leaves.

By the time the evening arrives, I've spent most of the day trying to arrange deliveries with our co-packer, hoping to get as many bottles of our cab in by the time tourist season is in full swing in August. It's still early June, but a good wine can't be rushed. Unfortunately, in this case, it will have to be rushed.

Ellen and I are discussing the likelihood of our customers realizing the change when Will walks into my house with the twins.

They're all here for dinner since Ellen ended up working late and we've got pizzas ordered.

"Where's Jack?" Olivia asks, looking around the room, her hands on her hips, like he's become a staple in my house.

"I don't know," I reply back, reaching over and flipping her ponytail as she hugs me tightly, squeezing my waist.

"Why don't you invite him over?" Ellen suggests. "We have plenty of pizza and I'm sure he'd rather not spend the evening alone."

"I'll go ask him," Oscar offers, and before I can say anything, he's scampering out the door and across the grass to the cottage next door.

Moments later Oscar returns with Jack in tow, but Jack looks a little sheepish as he follows Oscar in.

"My mate here invited me for dinner, but I wasn't sure if it was him inviting me or…" Jack trails off when he sees everyone in my kitchen staring back at him.

"Of course you're welcome," Ellen says without missing a beat. "Jack, this is my husband Will. Will, this is Jack. He's the guy I've been telling you about. He's finally going to fix our crusher." Ellen gives Will a funny look that suggests this isn't the only thing she's been telling him.

And from the look on Will's face, I'm guessing he knows exactly who Jack is too. The first time I ever met Will was just after Jack had left, he knows exactly who he is.

Will shakes Jack's hand and makes some small talk about the vineyard and Jack's experience, as front gate bell rings alerting us the pizza is here.

One of the shit things about living on a massive vineyard is that pizza delivery doesn't come to your front door. I literally have to get in the car and drive to the front gate to pick it up.

When I return with the pizza Ellen has plates set out on the patio, wine is poured and Jack has fit right in with Will and the two are still talking.

As we take our seats, Olivia and Oscar begin to argue about who will sit next to Jack. He's still high on their list of awesome people, the novelty not growing thin in the least.

Ellen steps in, taking both of them by the hand and moving them away from Jack before the two of them start swinging.

"Why don't we let Aunt Lauren sit next to Jack?"

"Don't be silly, Ellen. They can both sit next to him," I say, placating the kids and giving Jack a grateful smile as he pulls out the chairs on either side of him.

"You sure you don't want to sit next to Jack?" she asks, but her tone is full of insinuation and I'm getting real tired of everyone assuming there's something going on between Jack and me.

Even if there is.

I don't acknowledge her comment; I just take a seat at the end of the table so Ellen and Will can sit next to each other.

"How are you liking it here?" Will asks, his question directed at Jack. "The kids really seem to like having you around."

"It's been good. I was keen to get back to the States. I haven't been here since I was kid and even better that I was able to return to *Somerville's*."

"Yeah, this place is great. Ellen and Lauren have done an amazing job," Will compliments as he puts an arm around Ellen's shoulders. "We lived here in this cottage until the twins got a little older. We ended up moving off property a few years ago. Bought a bigger house in a neighborhood because we thought it would be nice for the kids to have other kids to play with. But it turns out they love it here."

Will can talk to anyone and right now I'm totally okay with his non-stop talking because it takes the heat off me and keeps Ellen from making her teasing backhanded comments about Jack and me.

The conversation continues and it's light and casual. The kids are filling Jack in on their upcoming vacation to Disneyland, which they invite him to join them on, but he politely declines.

I can't remember a time when things were this simple, this easy. Nate never wanted to have dinner with my sister and Will. He never would've allowed the kids to dominate a conversation, but more than any of this, he never supported anything I did here at the vineyard.

Even if this thing with Jack amounts to nothing in the end, it's taught me that this is what normal looks and feels like.

There's a lull in the conversation and as if it comes out of nowhere, Olivia announces to the table, "I saw Jack kissing Aunt Lulu!"

I feel the flush creep heavily across my face and I had no idea that armpits could produce so much sweat in a matter of seconds. My hands instinctively cover my face and Jack nearly chokes on the sip of wine he's just taken.

Coughing and sputtering, I slide my hands down over my face and watch as Jack wipes at his mouth with a napkin.

I can't bring myself to make eye contact with anyone at the table other than Jack. Leave it to the kids to sell me out. I should've seen this coming because they can't keep anything a secret.

"Of course I was kissing Aunt Lulu," Jack replies nonchalantly. "That's how we greet people in Australia."

My eyes are still locked with his and I can't even figure out why he's lying for me. I know he would prefer to have this whole thing out in the open.

"I thought that was France?" Oscar questions doubtfully, as he considers Jack's words, his little brain searching to see if there's any truth in what he's said.

"Well, Australia is part of the Commonwealth of Britain and Britain is near France, so we've taken to kissing people as a way of greeting."

By now I'm covering my mouth with my hand to keep from laughing and I know I'm not the only one finding humor in this conversation. I scan the table quickly as I watch Will and Ellen give each other a side eye. It's not going to be long before we can't keep this whole thing hidden, but it looks like we're riding this lie train until the end.

Jack loses Oscar right around the time that he starts to explain how Australia separated from the British Monarchy and both kids leave the table without pressing the idea that Olivia saw us kissing.

Totally unlike Ellen and her constant nosiness, she rises from the table and takes Will with her, saying, "I think we'll get going. Thanks for dinner and you guys enjoy the rest of your night."

She shuffles the kids out the door in record time, and when the door closes behind them I feel my shoulders sag with relief.

I have no idea why I'm hiding the fact that I'm hooking up with Jack. It's not just the fact that as kids I pretended to despise him, but a part of me wonders if I'm trying to protect everyone around me from what I know is coming too.

But maybe their hearts are stronger than mine.

"Well, that was interesting," Jack says, chuckling a little as he slips his arm around my waist. "Those kids don't miss a thing, do they?"

"Nope, they don't. They're like little detectives, but evil ones. They store up information and drop it when you least expect it."

We're both laughing as we make our way over to the couch with Jack sitting down and me lying down and resting my head in his lap.

"I'm pretty sure they all know we're hooking up now after your elaborate story about Australian's greeting people with kisses."

"Is that all we're doing here, Lu? Hooking up?" Jack questions, but there's something in his words that suggest that he's not okay with that label.

"I don't know, Jack. Is it?" I ask, turning the question back to him as I sit up so I'm facing him now.

He can't possibly think this will materialize into anything more, even if that's exactly what I want it to do. I'm logical enough to know that the Pacific Ocean is a pretty big wall that will set itself up right in the middle of our relationship.

I straddle Jack's hips so I'm now face to face with him. His hands slide over my thighs and up to my waist.

"I like having you here with me," I admit, but I can't bring myself to ask him to stay.

Chapter Seventeen

Jack

"I like being here with you, Lu," I stay, staring up at her. "This is more than just hooking up for me. You know that right?"

Lu nods, her bottom lip between her teeth as she stares down at me. "It is for me too," she whispers.

My fingers at her waist slip under her shirt, grazing her warm skin. "But you're still holding something back," I say, not taking my eyes off her. "Like you're scared or something."

Lu exhales, her hands resting on my chest now. "I just don't see how this can work," she says, looking down. "Not when you live in Australia and I live here."

I sit up a little, so we are closer. Close enough for me to press a kiss against her lips. "But I'm here now," I whisper.

Lu's forehead rests against mine, her eyes closed. "But for how long?" she asks.

I brush my lips against hers again. "For as long as you want me here," I admit, even though I know it's not as easy or simple as that. I have commitments and obligations back home, a house and a heap of shit I can't just walk away from, even if none of it seems important right now. "I meant what I said, Lu," I continue, needing to get this all out. "I've wanted you since we were kids and nothing about that has changed. It's only gotten stronger and if I had one regret it would be that I didn't do something sooner."

"Jack," she whispers, pressing her mouth against mine in a hard kiss.

I groan, deepening the kiss as my tongue slips between her lips, my arms pulling her closer against me. Lu's arms slide around my neck now, holding me close as she straddles my lap and feels everything this is doing to me.

"You gonna finish what you started this morning?" I whisper between kisses.

"Mmmm," she murmurs, hands sliding down my body as she lifts my t-shirt over my head and throws it on the floor. Her hands move to my jeans next, unbuttoning them quickly before she awkwardly shoves them down my hips.

I lower my hands, sliding them up her legs and under her skirt this time, my thumbs grazing the soft skin of her thighs.

"Lu," I whisper, kissing my way along her jaw. "I know this is kinda a little too late, but I have condoms in my pocket." I don't know why I say this, especially after all the times we were together last night without ever using them. In the cold light of day, it had seemed like a dick move on my part though, to not even consider asking her if she wanted me to wear one. To not just stop and put one on anyway. At the time, everything between us had just seemed too intense, too wild and hot for either of us to stop and ask.

Lu's head falls back even as she laughs a little. "I'd say it's very late actually," she says, smoothing her hands down my chest and sending a shiver all through me. "But it's okay, I'm on the pill."

I exhale against her neck, sucking at her pulse. "I'm, you know…clean."

She nods, lifting her head and finding my mouth with hers. "I know, I trust you, Jack," she whispers as her hands trail down my stomach to my boxers.

I lift my hips this time as she pushes them down, her hands moving to my dick, fingers circling around it as she slowly starts to stroke me.

"Fuck," I whisper, sliding my hands higher where I brush my fingers lightly against her panties before pulling them to the side, my finger brushing against her and making her moan. Slipping one hand round to her hip, I urge her up before slowly lowering her onto me, both of us groaning as I bury myself deep inside her.

"God you feel amazing," I whisper against her mouth.

"So do you," she says as she slowly starts to move.

Both of my hands circle her hips now, guiding her as she rocks against me. She kisses me constantly, her arms around my neck as she holds me against her. I need to feel her skin though, so I lift off her shirt, before moving my hands to her bra, pulling it off her where it joins the rest of our clothes on the floor.

Lowering my head, I kiss a path down her neck to her breast, before sucking a nipple into my mouth. Lu groans as her head falls backward, never stopping her hips as she continues to slowly ride me.

I tease her with my teeth, alternating between nibbling and sucking, as I slip a hand back under her skirt to where we are joined and gently start to work my thumb against her.

"Oh jesus christ, Jack," she moans. "Fuck, that feels so good."

I switch to her other breast as I press my thumb harder, rubbing a little faster. Lu moans again, her hips moving faster against me now as I slide in and out of her.

"God, I'm so close," she says, nails digging into my back.

I work her harder as I kiss my way up her neck, nibbling at her jaw before finding her mouth again. "Tell me," I whisper.

She lets out a loud groan, her nails digging in even more as my name falls from her lips.

"Tell me, Lu," I repeat.

"God, I'm coming," she whispers, kissing me harder as she works herself against me, our hips grinding together. "God, Jack, yes...yes."

And then I feel her, clenching around me so tight that I can no longer hold back, pushing up into her one last time as I come with her.

She collapses against me, her pounding heart against my chest mirroring what's going on with my own heart. I always knew this would be intense between us, that if Lu even felt half as much as what I feel, that it would be crazy hot when we finally got naked together. But even this blows my mind, far exceeding any of the millions of fantasies I've had about being with her.

"Can I make a confession?" she suddenly says, her mouth against my neck.

"Okay," I say, a little warily.

She lifts her head so she can look at me. Her cheeks are flushed, her lips swollen and red from all of our kisses. "I don't really hate you," she says.

I burst out laughing, kissing the end of her nose as I say, "Beautiful, if this is you hating me, then I'm all for it."

She giggles. "Also," she adds, her cheeks flushing a little more. "I did actually miss you after you left," she admits, brushing a hand across my cheek as I raise an eyebrow in surprise. "I even wrote to you."

"What?" I ask, shocked. "I never got any letters."

"I never sent them."

I grin, leaning close to kiss her. "Right, the *I hate Jack* factor, I get it."

She smiles at me. "Mmmm," the only thing she admits to.

I laugh. "So what sort of things did you write to me about, aside from admitting you liked me of course?"

"Well," she says, head cocked to the side. "I can show you?"

"You still have them?"

She nods. "Yep, in a box under my bed."

"Well," I whisper, leaning in to kiss her lips. "Your bed is where we're gonna end up anyway, so this seems like as good an excuse as any."

She giggles again, her laugh punctuated by a low groan as I lift her off me. Standing, she holds out a hand, pulling me up off the couch. I kick off my jeans and boxers, leave them lying on the living room floor as I follow her back to her bedroom.

Lu ditches the rest of her clothes before joining me on the bed. I watch her, lying on her stomach, as she leans over and pulls a box from underneath it, shuffling through a pile of folded papers until she finds one.

"Here," she says, handing it back to me.

I roll onto my side, prop myself up on an elbow as I run my hand down her spine. "Read it to me."

Lu looks back over her shoulder at me, a heated look in her eyes as she considers my request. Not taking my eyes off hers, I lean in and press a kiss to her shoulder before gently biting it, loving the mark I leave on her.

She swallows hard and looks away, unfolding the paper. "Dear Jack," she starts, groaning as I run my fingers down her spine again, before dipping them between her legs.

"I like the start of this already," I whisper, sucking on her neck.

"Jack," she says, her warning tone lost in the husky moan she lets out.

"What?" I ask, feigning innocence.

"You're distracting me," she murmurs.

"Sorry," I lie, running my fingers back up her spine. "Continue."

She shakes her head a little before turning back to the letter. "Dear Jack," she repeats. "I hope you made it back to

Australia okay. It's been very quiet and peaceful here since you left."

I can't help but chuckle, scooting closer so my body is pressed against hers. "So much animosity," I whisper, sucking on her ear lobe.

Lu moans again, low and sexy, even as she tries to continue. "I still haven't forgiven you for the mud thing," she adds, making me laugh against her skin even as I kiss my way down her spine this time. "Or the million other things you did to annoy me while you were here."

I slip my hand back between her legs, my mouth lingering at the base of her spine where I press a soft kiss to her arse before gently biting it. Lu sighs, her legs widening a little as though to encourage me.

"Nobody here misses you, in case you were wondering," she continues, her words breathless and husky as I slide a finger inside her. "I hope your friends in Australia were at least happy to see you again," she adds, pushing herself against me. "Anyway, feel free to write back, if you want. From Lauren."

I run my tongue up her spine now, smiling as her head falls onto the pillow. "So obvious you fancied me," I whisper, my mouth at her ear.

Lu groans, turning her head toward mine. "Is that right?" she says. "You want me to read another one?"

I smile against her mouth. "Nah," I murmur, rolling my body onto hers. "I think I've got a better idea."

The next morning, Lu and I wake early, fooling around for an hour or so without any interruptions from the kids this time. Everything about it, sharing her bed, waking up with her or just having coffee together in her kitchen feels so perfectly normal, I know that the longer I stay, the harder it's going to be to leave.

Once again, I'm plagued with conflicted thoughts on what I'm going to do with my life. With wanting to keep this thing between us going, but confused with how the hell I'm going to find a way to stay when I have so many things going on back in Oz that I can't just simply walk away from.

"What's on the agenda for today?" Lu asks, half reading my mind.

I smile at her, sitting across from me at the kitchen island, her wet hair pulled into a messy bun on the top of her head. "I'm going to sort out the barrel room," I say, taking a sip of coffee. "Make sure the rotation is correct, check all the barrels are still useable."

Lu smiles at me, lowering her mug. "I really appreciate you helping us out like this," she says. "I know it's not really your job."

I return the smile. "It's all good, Lu," I tell her. "I like helping you out, seriously."

She swallows. "Well, I was wondering..."

Her words are cut off by the front door flying open and Oscar and Oliva running inside, their chorus of, "Aunt Lulu," echoing down the hall to the kitchen.

I grin, even as Lu shakes her head and mutters something about needing to keep her front door locked. The sound of pounding feet comes at us and before long, both kids materialize in the kitchen, their wide eyes looking from Lu to me and back to Lu again.

"Morning," I say, lifting my mug in salute.

"What are you doing here?" Ollie asks, hands on her hips.

I chuckle, shooting Lu a quick glance before turning back to Ollie. "And what are you, the Spanish Inquisition?"

"The what?" she says, head cocked to the side.

"Jack and I are having breakfast together, Ollie," Lu says, jumping in. "Is that alright with you?"

Ollie's head flicks between us again before turning to her brother where they share a secret look before turning back to us. "Yeah, that's alright with us," she says, nodding.

I laugh, pushing out my stool and standing. "Well, thank god for that," I say, rinsing out my mug and leaving it on the draining board. "I would hate to think we didn't have your approval," I add, walking over to them.

Oscar stands silent, hands on his hips as he gives me a once over.

"What?" I ask, mirroring his action.

"Aren't these the same clothes you were wearing last night?" he asks, flicking his hand at me.

I laugh, shaking my head as I reach forward and pick him up, slinging him over my shoulder. "Enough with the interrogation little man, you're with me," I say, before turning to Lu. "I'll see you later," I add, winking at her.

"Wait a minute!" Ollie shouts and I pause, halfway out of the kitchen. "Aren't you forgetting something?"

I glance at Lu, see the confused look on her face. "What?" I ask her niece.

Ollie gives me a straight up WTF look as she stands, hands out and says, "A kiss goodbye? Isn't that what the French do?"

I burst out laughing. Fuck me these kids don't forget anything. Lowering Oscar to the floor, I walk toward Ollie, grabbing her tiny face in my hands as I press a bunch of kisses all over her cheeks and forehead. "Bye, Ollie," I say.

When I step back, I can't help but laugh at her flushed cheeks, the embarrassed smile she tries to hide. Glancing at Lu, I see her watching us, a strange look on her face. Unable to stop myself, I step to her next, leaning in and pressing a lingering kiss to her cheek. "Laters, beautiful," I whisper, before turning, grabbing Oscar and heading outside.

Oscar heads toward the drive, but I call out a, "Hold up," before running back to my place to grab some shoes. When I come back out Oscar is sitting on my front steps.

"So, no shoes?" he asks, as though prompting me to explain.

I grin, pulling him up, before crouching down to offer him a piggy back. "It's an Aussie thing," I tell him. "We hardly ever wear shoes."

"Right," he says, arms around my neck as I stand and start walking toward the sheds that house the barrel rooms. "So are you and Aunt Lulu like a thing now?" he asks.

I chuckle. "What exactly is a thing, Oscar?" I ask, stalling.

"You know," he says, his hand flitting out in front of me. "Like boyfriend and girlfriend," he explains. "Someone you get all smoochy about."

I burst out laughing. "Is that what you and your girlfriend do then?"

"Pfft," he scoffs. "I don't have a girlfriend," he says, in a disgusted tone.

"Really?" I ask. "Cause you seem to know an awful lot about boyfriends and girlfriends," I add, teasing him.

"I just know things," he says, as though this explains it.

"I see," I add, offering nothing further in response to his questions.

We walk in silence until we reach the sheds. Oscar jumps from my back and heads inside, me close behind. I grab the clipboard that lists all the barrels Lu keeps and the dates and stock of what they've been used for. Just as I'm about to get started, Oscar surprises me with one more nugget of information.

"Well, I like you better than Aunt Lulu's other boyfriend," he says, before wandering off toward the back of the shed leaving me to contemplate just who this previous boyfriend was.

Chapter Eighteen

Lauren

It's pretty hard to keep something a secret in this family, especially when you've allowed them access to your entire life. When my wedding failed to materialize I needed them more than I ever thought I would and I certainly can't tell them to shove off now.

Not that I think I'm fooling anyone because it's clear that Jack and I are spending a substantial amount of time together. I guess I could chalk that up to the fact that I live alone on a vineyard and there's finally someone to spend time with. Yet Jack and I know it's far more than that.

Jack and I were supposed to get together for dinner, but he's running a little behind; texting me about an hour ago to let me know he's still working on something. He called it a little surprise and I didn't push for more information. It's kinda fun and cute the way he's been sneaking around working on something. I have yet to figure out what he's up to and I'm not sure I want to know. He's made surprises fun again.

Instead of quietly waiting for him I decide to do something fun in return. I had already opened a bottle of wine to have at dinner and it's currently sitting on the counter breathing.

I grab two glasses, filling them about half way and then proceed to set up my phone to capture what I'm about to do. As ridiculous as I know it is, Jack will get a kick out of it.

I strip off my t-shirt and bra, tossing them over the island trying to land them near my bedroom door. I grab the two glasses, position them in front of my boobs as I sit down on a stool at my island and then I hit the timer on the camera.

I'm poised and ready, a cheeky smile on my face as the camera starts to beep notifying me as to when it will snap the picture when Ellen's voice rings out loud and clear through my house.

"Hey! Oscar forgot his iPad," she calls out as the front door slams, and there's that damn iPad sitting just inches from where my supposedly sexy picture is about to be taken.

My house isn't big and it will take her maybe ten steps before she reaches my kitchen and my damn t-shirt and bra are a solid twenty steps from me.

Why the hell did I send them flying across the room like that?

I reach for the first thing I can get my hands on, a dishtowel that's draped over the sink to dry, and I slap it in front of my naked boobs just as Ellen walks into the kitchen.

She dead stops in her tracks to find me standing in my kitchen with no shirt on and a damp dishtowel covering me.

My eyes are wide as if I'm a deer caught in the headlights of a car heading straight for it. I can't move.

I'm the stupid deer.

Neither of us says anything until the damn camera clicks at the most inopportune time and my face feels like it did when I fell asleep in a tanning bed circa 2001 and burned like the fire of a thousand suns.

Right now I'm pretty sure I'd take the tanning bed burn over this any day.

"I don't even want to know," Ellen says, grabbing the iPad from the island and holding her other hand up as she turns her head away from me. “Back to whatever it is that you were doing. I’ll be going now.”

I listen for the front door to close and I collapse onto the counter, my arms covering my head, as I lay there mortified by what just happened and hoping the coolness of the quartz countertop will soothe my burning and humiliated ego.

I’ve gotta start locking my doors.

After I’ve recovered from the embarrassment, which I know will not fade as quickly I would like it to because Ellen will never let me live this down, I grab my phone and look at what my camera did capture.

It’s a beautiful shot of my belly button and the bottom of a dirty dishtowel. It’s definitely not what I was going for and there’s not a chance in hell I’m going to try to recreate it now.

I guess sexy wine-related pictures are not my thing.

I wake up the next morning with Jack’s warm body pressed against mine. Despite showering last night, he has this amazing sweet smell of grapes mixed with cedar and I press my lips to his bare chest.

I have no idea what time it is and I don’t bother looking. It’s a rare occurrence for me to sleep in and forego work, but I own the place and I need to start doing it more often. I hire people to make sure things go smoothly and I’m entitled to a morning off every now and then.

Jack stirs a little and lets out a low moan, sliding his hands down my body. I kiss my way down his chest, placing kisses on his well-defined muscular stomach as I lead my way down a little farther.

He’s more than ready and I wet my lips, my arousal as ready for him as he is for me. Jack pushes the sheets back and I look up at him as I slip my mouth around him. He moans and it makes me weak, I want him more than I’ve ever wanted anyone.

There's something between us, something unspoken and intense. I felt it the day he walked back into my life, something I mistook for hatred has built into a deep intense desire and need for each other.

"Lu," Jack moans, his words husky, his voice deep as he slips his fingers through my hair. "I need you." But I don't stop, my mouth sliding over him until his hands guide me back up his body.

It's now Jack who begins to explore my body as I lay stretched out on the bed, his mouth finding every sensitive spot, my body so responsive to his touch. It feels like every part of me is screaming for him to touch me, for him to be inside me.

He's slow and deliberate, his fingers finding me, working in and out until I feel like everything around me is going to shatter into a million pieces. I can't hold out any longer.

"Please, Jack," I beg, my words a desperate plea. "I need to feel you…" And before I can finish my sentence his hands cup my face and he slides inside me in one movement. Both of us gasping in unison at the sensation and he stops, holding perfectly still as we take each other in.

I need the moment of quiet, my body needing to get used to the feeling of having Jack inside me, something that is still so new no matter how many times it happens. I never want to forget what this feels like. The way my body feels like it's on fire, the way my mind commits his every movement to memory and the way my heart tightens, clenching hard in my chest as a reminder of what it feels like to fall for someone so fully.

My once shattered heart is slowly healing because of Jack.

My legs wrap around Jack's hips, pulling him closer and he begins to move, slow at first, knowing neither one of us wants this moment to end.

Our mouths are connected the way our bodies are, exploring and tasting each other as the need and want blooms heavy in both of us.

Desperation begins to take over and my nails are dragging down Jack's back, marking him as I moan his name, begging for him to fuck me as his hips grind hard against mine. His movements become erratic and less controlled, he's rough and needy.

It's only seconds before my body clenches around him, pulling an orgasm from each of us, along with the last pleading desires from our lips as we lie sated and breathing heavily on my bed.

I can't remember the last time I ever woke up like this. Honestly, I'm not certain I ever have. Nothing in my life has ever felt this right.

"Plans for today?" Jack asks, his fingers absentmindedly twirling a few strands of my hair around his finger.

"I have no idea," I respond still somewhat breathless and Jack laughs.

"I'm so good at this that I've blown your mind," Jack gloats and what once would've annoyed me, now has me smiling and teasing him right back.

"Oh, you'd like to think it's your amazing body that has this effect on me, huh?"

"I don't think it, I know it. The way you moan my name..." Jack starts, his lips once again trailing along my neck, "tells me that it's my dick that you want, always."

He wasn't kidding when he said dirty talk and that accent are a deadly combination, and I find myself moving against him again.

But that idea is short-lived because we are once again interrupted by the sound of a door slamming and small feet pounding on the wood floor.

"Aunt Lulu!" comes Olivia's singsong voice as she searches my house for any signs of me.

There are so many things I suddenly regret as I lay here naked in bed with Jack, but the biggest of them all was teaching those two how to find the house key I keep hidden under the doormat.

"Put some clothes on," I whisper-shout as I shove Jack out of the bed and I scramble for my robe. "And don't you dare come out of this room unless you want the firing squad out there to hit you with a million questions."

"Aunt Lulu!" Olivia screams louder this time, because like all kids she thinks if she screams louder it will suddenly make me appear. Which it actually does because I emerge from the bedroom to find Oscar and Olivia standing in my kitchen with Olivia wearing Jack's work boots.

"Where's Jack?" Oscar asks, looking around like he's going to appear out of nowhere. "He's not in the shed and it's late."

"He's not here," I defend immediately and Olivia gives me the stink eye.

"Why are his boots here?" she asks, shuffling her too small feet around in the clunky boots.

"I don't know," I respond, stumbling over my words and knowing they are totally on to me.

Damn, these two are good.

Both of them stand there eyeing me and knowing I'm lying through my teeth, but how the hell do you explain to two seven year olds that you've spent the night with someone and you don't mean a sleepover. The questions will be endless.

"Some more parts for the crusher just got delivered and I had the guy bring them to the shed," Oscar says like he's running the place. "And Mom wants to know where you are."

"Okay, thanks," I reply hoping it will send them on their way, but neither one of them budges.

"What's going on?" Oscar asks, his eyebrows up and the skepticism loud and clear in his question.

"Nothing, why? Just woke up late. Gotta get moving, right? You said Mom was looking for me."

"Woke up late?" Olivia scoffs as she clomps around the island in Jack's boots leaving little bits of dried mud in her wake. "You never wake up late."

"You sick?" Oscar asks. "One time when I threw up at school, I slept late too."

"No," I answer back, finding it hard to hold back the laughter that builds inside me.

These two are piece of work.

"You two need to head out of here so I can get dressed, got it?" I say, trying to be firm but struggling as I picture Jack hiding in my bedroom while these two badgers won't give up.

They don't move and I finally concede to them.

"Listen, yes, Jack is here," I say, letting out a long exhale, my hands on my hips. "He's probably just about to get in the shower because he spent the night."

"Did you watch a movie?" Olivia asks, the boots now gone from her feet with one left by the sink and the other by the entrance to my hall bathroom.

"Not exactly."

"Was it a date?" Oscar now asks.

"Sorta."

"Is he your boyfriend?" Olivia questions, her voice going up in a teasing way as she says the word boyfriend.

I pause for a moment, choosing my words wisely because whatever I say here will be brought back to Ellen and twisted in a way that only a seven-year-old can do.

"Yes. Jack is my boyfriend." I keep it short and simple. They understand boyfriends and girlfriends, not in the way that I was just shacking up with Jack, but rather in the way that they know I like him. I'm not sure how else to explain my relationship with Jack to them. I'm not certain that boyfriend is the right word, but for them it works. It's easy.

"Finally!" Oscar shouts, throwing his hands up in the air dramatically as he turns on his heel and walks over to the front door.

While the conversation with Oscar ends there, Olivia is a little more difficult.

"Are you going to get married? Can I call him Uncle Jack? Does he live at your house now? Why is he allowed to wear muddy boots in your house but I'm not?"

"Whoa, take it down a notch, sister," I tell her, my fingers twisting one of her pigtails into a bun. "Jack is still my friend. We just like to spend time together. That's all."

"I want you to marry him," Olivia states firmly before shrugging her shoulders and following the path her brother just took.

Now that the Spanish Inquisition has vacated my house I head back to the bedroom, but as I push the door open it nails Jack right in the side of the head.

"Shit, Lu, be careful," he says, rubbing the spot on his face where the door hit him.

He's standing there in his underwear, clearly not concerned about putting on some clothes as the kids questioned me in the kitchen. I can picture him with his ear pressed against the door trying to eavesdrop on every word of our conversation.

"Were you listening through the door?" I ask, giving him a teasing pinch to his side.

His hand closes around my wrist as I move it away, and Jack pulls me into his arms. The smile on his face is spread so wide and his eyes crinkle up in the corners. I can practically feel the happiness radiating off him.

"So, I'm your boyfriend, huh?"

Chapter Nineteen

Jack

"So, it's official now, is it?"

I look up and find Ellen standing just inside the shed, a huge shit-eating grin on her face as she looks at me.

"Jesus, word travels fast around here."

Ellen laughs, stepping toward me. "The beauty of working in a family business, Jack," she says. "Don't worry, you'll be married by lunch and have her knocked up by dinner."

I shake my head, unable to stop the smile. "Good to know," I tell her. "And for the record, those kids of yours would make fantastic interrogators."

Ellen laughs again. "Ugh, I know," she says. "But just so you know, I like this thing you've got going with Lauren," she adds, serious now. "Despite her protests, she does actually like you. You make her happy and it's good to see. She deserves it."

I nod. "Making her happy is all I wanna do," I tell her.

"I know," she says. "Just be kind to her, okay? She's been through a lot."

Our eyes meet but Ellen goes no further and as much as I want to ask, I don't, certain she's not going to tell me anyway. "I will," I say instead. "I'm not fucking about here."

Ellen nods. "So," she continues, her eyes never leaving mine because clearly, this isn't over yet. "What does this mean long-term?"

I shrug, trying for casual, as though the fact I live in Australia is somehow no big deal in all of this. "I don't know yet," I admit. "We haven't worked out the logistics."

"You know she'll never leave this place, don't you?"

I stare back at Ellen, wondering if she too doubts my intentions or the intensity of my feelings for her sister. I wasn't lying when I told Lu I wouldn't leave her, but I'd be lying now if I said I had everything worked out for how this whole thing was going to work.

I don't and to be honest, I'm not sure I even know where to begin with any of it.

"I know, Ellen," I say, running a hand through my hair. "I don't have all the answers yet, okay, but like I said, I'm not fucking about here."

Ellen nods once more, before smiling at me. "Okay, enough with the interrogation," she says.

I chuckle, relieved that I've passed her test, for now. "I can see where your kids get it from," I joke, just as my phone chimes out with a text.

Ellen waves a hand in dismissal before turning and walking out of the shed. I pull my phone from my pocket, smiling at the message on my screen.

Lu: you had your talking to from Ellen yet?

Me: just now ☺ word travels fast around here

Lu: ugh, those kids haven't shut up all morning…sorry…

Me: don't be, I like that people know we're boyfriend and girlfriend ☺ it's so retro

Lu: well I'm not certain ALL the staff know yet, but I'm sure it's just a matter of time.

This morning, after Lu had finally managed to get Oscar and Ollie out of the house, I'd confronted her about the fact she'd told them I was her boyfriend, effectively admitting this thing between us was really happening.

It was cute watching her get all embarrassed about it and even though I was totally on board for us being outted, I could understand how it might be awkward for her. After all, she's the boss and technically, I'm her employee. I can imagine that people will start talking and assuming I'm getting more than just sexual favors here.

Me: it's all good Lu, I'll see you later xx
Lu: x

I slide my phone back into my pocket and get back to work, but it chimes out with a new text. Pulling it from my pocket, my smile quickly fades though, when I see who it's from.

Mel: Jack, please stop ignoring me. We need to talk. PLEASE!

I shake my head, muttering a fuck's sake as I finally do what I should have done the second I discovered what was happening and block her number. No matter how much she might want to talk, I'm not interested because I don't see how anything she could say can excuse what she did.

I should block Matt's number too, but I don't, grateful at least that he seems to have given up on trying to contact me. I'm not sure I can ever actually forgive him, but we have longer history and somehow that stops me for cutting him out of my life permanently.

The rest of the day passes quickly, a couple of the workers giving me strange looks when we cross paths because I'm sure they've heard the rumors by now, but no one actually asking me about whether they're true.

After I finish up for the day, I head home for a quick shower, before going over to Lu's armed with Tim Tams and a bottle of wine.

"Hey," she says, smiling as I walk in through the back door.

I dump the wine and biscuits on the counter, pull her into my arms and plant a hard kiss on her mouth. "Hey yourself," I say and Lu smiles against my mouth as she slides her hands up under my t-shirt. "Yes," I murmur. "I like where this is going."

She pulls back, whacking me on the arse. "Dirty boy."

I grin, pulling her close again as I lower my mouth to her ear. "I thought you liked the dirty part," I whisper, nibbling on her neck. "Seemed to be working for you this morning."

She groans now, her body melting into mine as I kiss my way along her jaw to her mouth, my hands sliding down to her arse and pulling her hard against me. Lu deepens the kiss, her hands pushing my t-shirt up as though she wants to take it off me.

"Lulu Somerville," I say. "Are you just using me for sex?"

"Maybe," she murmurs.

I scoff, pulling back a little. "I feel so used," I tease, grinning at her.

She smiles up at me. "Yeah, but I bet you like it," she teases back.

I grin now, squeezing her arse before letting go. "You bet I do," I say. "But before you completely have your way with me, let's eat."

"Building up your stamina?" she asks.

I wink. "For ravishing you all night, you better believe it."

Lu giggles and I give her another quick kiss before releasing her and grabbing the bottle of wine. I pour us both a glass before opening her fridge to inspect the contents.

Lu jumps up on the kitchen bench, her legs swinging as she watches me move about her kitchen, a relaxed smile on her face.

"You okay if I make us some dinner?" I ask.

She nods. "Of course, want me to help?"

I shake my head. "Sit there and entertain me," I tell her. She cocks an eyebrow at me, a sexy smile tugging at her mouth that has me laughing and shaking my head at the same time. "Now who's the dirty one?"

Lu laughs. "Okay, fine," she says, pretending to be annoyed as she rolls her eyes dramatically at me. "Tell me about Australia then."

"What do you want to know?" I ask as I start to chop ingredients for a pasta.

Lu shrugs. "I don't know, where were you living before you came here?"

I shoot her a quick look, wondering if she intentionally used the past tense when she asked me that. "Adelaide," I say, deciding to let it go. "Been working at a place in the Barossa for almost a year."

"And you gave that up to come here?" she asks, taking a sip of wine.

I shake my head. "No, it kinda came to an end anyway," I say, even knowing that's not the whole truth of why I left. "Was time to move on and the job here happened to come up at the same time," I add, smiling at her. "Almost like it was meant to be."

Lu smiles, a tiny flush on her cheeks. "Does it bother you moving around all the time?"

I shrug. "No, not really," I admit. "It's good getting to experience different places and try new things."

"Must be hard to maintain relationships," she says, eyes on her lap now. "Never being in one place for very long."

I stop, putting the knife down before stepping between her legs. "Lu," I say quietly, my hands sliding onto her hips. "That's not what's happening here."

She stares back at me, a sad look in her eyes. "But it must affect things," she says, hooking her legs around my thighs. "I mean it must have ended other relationships for you."

I lean in and press a kiss to her lips. "No, not always," I say, even if moving wasn't the only issue my previous relationship faced.

"How did your last relationship end then?" she asks, fingers sliding into the belt loops of my jeans.

I swallow hard, my eyes never leaving hers. "She wasn't the person I thought she was," I say, knowing that's partly true at least.

"What do you mean?"

I smile now, kissing her again. "She wasn't you, Lulu," I whisper, before silencing any more questions.

Lu moans into my mouth, her fingers in my jeans pulling me closer as she tightens her legs around mine. "Jack," she says, the word low and husky. "How are we going to make this work?"

I pull back, brush my fingers over her cheek, before cupping her face. "We'll find a way, Lu," I say. "I promise, okay? I really want this with you."

She stares back at me, her eyes searching mine before she eventually nods, her whispered, "I want this too," floating between us.

Our conversation over dinner returns to the easygoing way we started the night. We eat out on her back deck, cracking a second bottle of wine as Lu attempts to mimic an Australia accent.

"Oh my god, woman," I say, laughing. "That is terrible!"

"What?" she asks, also laughing. "I sound just like you!"

I shake my head. "Ah no, you do not. You sound like a bogan American."

"Bogan?" she asks. "What the hell's a bogan?"

I grin. "Like your version of trailer park trash."

"Oh!" she says, standing as she starts to clear the table.

I push my chair out, grinning as I reach for her and pull her down so she's straddling my lap.

"I do not sound like trailer park trash," she scoffs.

I slide my hands up her thighs, my fingers slipping beneath her shorts. "Yeah you do," I tease. "But for the record, it is adorable."

Lu wraps her arms around my neck, wriggling closer and sending a spike of lust right through me. "I'll bet you can't talk like an American," she says, pressing quick kisses against my mouth.

I slide my hands higher, over her hips and under her t-shirt to her breasts. "I bet I can," I murmur, my fingers teasing her nipples through the lace of her bra.

Lu's eyes close as she leans slightly back, giving me better access to her chest, while at the same time pushing her body right against my dick.

"Go on then," she says, breathy and low.

I grin, leaning in to suck her neck as I say, "What do you want me to say?"

Lu groans, "Anything," as her hips grind against mine, turning me on so bad. "Tell me what you want right now?"

I move to the other side of her neck, nibbling her skin as my hands move to her back, unhooking her bra before slipping around to her breasts again. Lu lets out a low moan, her hands sliding into my hair as though to hold me against her.

Swallowing, I move my mouth to her ear and in my best American accent I say, "I really wanna fuck you out here."

The noise she makes nearly undoes me and without even waiting for permission, I move my hands to her waist, pulling her t-shirt up and over her head. Throwing it on the deck, I then move to her undone bra, sliding it down her arms before it joins her top.

"God, Jack," she whispers, finding my mouth. "We shouldn't, we…"

"Who's gonna see us?" I murmur between kisses. "Everyone's gone home."

She groans again, her eyes opening as she takes in our surrounds. The sun is low in the sky, casting long shadows and deep red light over her back lawn. It's silent though, the only noise, the soft music that comes from her phone.

I lower my head, take her breast in my mouth, teasing her nipple with my teeth.

"Where?" she breathes out and I can't help but grin, glancing up at her as I lick her skin.

With my hands on her hips, I push her up so she's standing in front of me, kissing her stomach quickly, before also standing. I pull my t-shirt over the back of my head, throwing it on my chair before walking toward her sun lounge, undoing my jeans at the same time.

When I've stripped off, I lie back, look up at Lu as I beckon her over with a finger. She smiles at me, biting her bottom lip as she quickly looks around again as if to check we really are alone, before undoing her shorts and slipping them and her panties down her legs.

"Come here," I say, my voice low.

She walks slowly over to me, pausing beside the sun lounge where I run a hand up her leg, my fingers dancing over the skin of her inner thigh. She smiles at me, her eyes flicking to my dick and my obvious arousal. Without saying a word, she straddles the lounge and slowly lowers herself onto me.

"Fuck," I breathe out, my hands moving to her hips.

Lu lifts her body from mine, before slowly taking me again, inch by painful inch.

"Lu," I moan, my fingers digging into her.

She grins down at me, her hands on my chest as she leans in and whispers, "That was the worst American accent I've ever heard," before repeating the move and leaving me unable to speak at all.

Chapter Twenty

Lauren

We're pushing four weeks since Jack's arrival and I'm trying not to focus on the fact that he will have to leave eventually. We're waiting on the last two parts for the crusher that are slated to arrive in the next four to six weeks, so that gives us a solid amount of time.

Time for me to prepare myself for him to leave or time for me to convince him that he wants to stay.

The pessimist versus the optimist.

But, if I've learned anything from my previous relationship, it's that you can't make anyone do anything.

When you've been burned that pessimist lives inside you; it screams louder, it pushes harder, and it reminds you that people suck.

I need Jack to not suck.

What I hate more than anything about that pessimist in me is that when she realizes I'm happy, she nags at the back of my mind, she whispers to me in my sleep and she reminds me that I've been left before.

I wake up covered in sweat, my heart hammering in my chest while Jack sleeps soundlessly beside me. I suck in a ragged breath and exhale slow and long as I try in vain not to wake Jack. My breathing is labored, hard and noisy in the silence of the room and I hold my breath when Jack shifts in his sleep.

If he wakes up, I'll have to explain everything to him, something I don't think I can do since I can't even explain it to myself.

It's been months since I've had the dream and I thought by now my subconscious would've moved on, but clearly it has other ideas.

It's not even really a dream, but more of a reminder of reality that creeps in when I'm sleeping.

He's going to leave.

The words float around in my head, but I push them away. It's not the same thing because I know Jack will leave, but he won't leave me.

I close my eyes as my breathing begins to settle and carefully slide myself back down in the bed, nestling my body against Jack's.

And I tell that voice inside my head that he's here now and that's what matters.

The morning comes and goes without Jack mentioning the minor meltdown I had while he was sleeping so I'm to assume he was none the wiser. I hate that I'm keeping this whole thing a secret from him, but I have no idea how to bring it up. I want Nate to be listed in that ex-boyfriend file, the one you gloss over, the one you shrug your shoulders at, like he was a poor choice in a long line of decent ones.

Ellen walks into my office, a smile on her face and looking like she's got a whole lot to say.

I haven't seen her since the kids unloaded Jack's and my news on her. I'm shocked that she hasn't been trying to hunt me down and harass me for all the details.

"I told Mom you and Jack are dating," Ellen announces, far more proud of herself than she should be. I swear she's been waiting for this moment since I was fifteen as payback for all those times I was terrible to her when we were kids.

"Oh my god, Ellen. Why would you do that?" I scrub my hand over my face knowing this is the perfect opportunity for our mother to shoot me with an I-told-you-so that she's been waiting to use for nearly fifteen years.

"It just slipped out," she says, lying through her teeth.

"Bullshit. Just like you didn't know it was Jack coming to fix our crusher when he showed up here a few weeks ago."

"Okay, that I didn't know. I promise. But look how well it turned out," Ellen brags, giving me a wink and a cheesy smile. "And speaking of how well it's turned out, do you and Jack wanna go to dinner tonight with Will and me? I finally got a babysitter that isn't you."

"Let me check with Jack," I reply, giving the idea much less thought than I would have in the past.

"You don't need to," Ellen says sheepishly. "I saw Jack a few minutes ago and mentioned it to him..."

"What did he say?" And I catch the nervousness in my tone. This isn't something that would be the norm. I've always had a relationship with Ellen that was entirely separate from my personal relationships.

And I get that since Jack is living on the property and working with me that we spend a substantial amount of time together so our relationship has accelerated faster than most, but I worry that a double date with Ellen is a little premature.

"He said yes," Ellen tells me with a look on her face that says I'm being stupid. "Why wouldn't he say yes?" she asks, looking for the answer that I've got buried inside my head. She knows I'm second-guessing everything.

"I don't know. It's kinda... soon?"

"It's not too soon. Jack is crazy about you and he has been forever." She shakes her head and shoots me a look that our mother perfected around the time that Ellen and I became teenagers. "He's not Nate, Lauren."

It's like she can read my thoughts, my transparency glaring and obvious.

"I know," I say trying to convince myself that this is a good idea. "Okay, what time?"

The smile that spreads across Ellen's face is large and beaming as she gives me the time and the restaurant and tells us to take an Uber because she plans on all of us getting drunk tonight.

It's several hours later and Will and Ellen are already at the restaurant when we arrive and from the looks of it, Ellen wasn't joking about that getting drunk thing.

There are two bottles of wine already on the table and Ellen is putting back what's left in her glass when we walk in.

"Yay!" she practically yells when we walk up, jumping up from her chair and hugging both Jack and me.

"Ellen doesn't get out often," Will says, jokingly smiling at us. "The kids were a little intense today with us leaving for vacation in a couple of days."

"You don't need to make excuses for Ellen's drunkenness. It's what she does best." I tease her as I pull out the chair next to her and sit down.

Jack pours us both a glass of wine in an attempt to catch up to Ellen who has obviously drunk more in a half hour than most people drink during an entire meal.

"Just catch up with me," Ellen says, her voice a touch louder than necessary and Will shakes his head, but smiles at her.

We order a few appetizers and another bottle of wine, and coax Ellen into drinking a little water so Will doesn't have to carry her out of here.

But it doesn't take us too long before we've caught up to her and the conversation begins to flow.

The vineyard dominates the conversation and even though Will doesn't work in the business, he knows it's something that has been front and center in our family.

"So, Jack," Ellen starts and I have no idea where she's going with this conversation. "Did you know that Lauren used to email me while I was away at school when you were visiting?"

"Oh, is that so," Jack plays back and he turns to smirk at me. "I'd love to hear what she said in those emails."

With her glass of wine in her hand, she's prepared to unload everything and I'm cringing inside. I can't for the life of me remember what I wrote to her in my annoyance-filled evenings with Jack.

"You kept her very busy," Ellen says, not giving anything away just yet. "An email practically every night. *I hate Jack. Jack's a jerk. Jack did this, Jack did that. Mom says he has a crush on me. Do you really think he like me?* She was relentless."

"Oh my god, Ellen. I was not relentless! And I never asked you if you thought he liked me!"

"Yes you did and I always told you he did like you. You made fun of Jack for having a big ego, but you were stringing Jack along because you loved the attention just as much."

"So you actually liked my attention, huh?" Jack says, wrapping his arm around my shoulder, a smug smile on his face.

"Stop," I say, shooting a look at Jack because he absolutely knows I liked him all those years ago. "And Ellen, you stop adding fuel to his fire."

"Fine, fine," Ellen concedes but not before adding, "I always knew you'd end up together. So glad Nate finally disappeared." She rolls her eyes dramatically, not even realizing what she's just said.

The conversation halts, the restaurant loud, but Ellen's words resound louder and my eyes widen giving away that what she said had an impact.

Will catches my eye and quickly flips the conversation away from Ellen's comment.

"Skeletons are meant to stay in the closet, El," Will, mutters, but I catch his words and force a smile at him. "I've heard you traveled around a lot, Jack," Will adds attempting to keep the conversation going without the awkward mention of my ex-fiancé.

Jack clears his throat, and I know he didn't miss Ellen's comment, but now is not the place to discuss it. He lets it go and begins to chat with Will about the places he's traveled because of his career. The list is pretty extensive and the two of them begin discussing their favorite places to visit since Will travels often for his job too.

"How did you and Ellen meet?" Jack asks, changing the direction of the conversation for the better as I pour everyone a little more wine. We might all be a little tipsy, but the more we drink the more likely it is that Jack will forget Ellen's little slip of the tongue.

"We met when I was a freshman and Will was a sophomore at the University of Michigan," Ellen says proudly and both Will and I let out a riotous laugh. This is the story she likes to tell and most people don't ask anything beyond this, but not tonight. Not after she sold me out and told Jack I liked him.

"Something tells me that isn't the whole story," Jack says, looking from Will to me and back again.

"Nope, not the whole story at all," Will says, pulling Ellen a little closer and pressing a kiss to her temple.

"Let's hear it," Jack demands, a teasing quality to his voice.

"Ellen and Will did meet at the University of Michigan, but it's not a simple story of meeting at a bar or being set up by friends," I begin and Will picks up where the story actually begins and I can see the flush creeping up onto Ellen's cheeks.

"Ellen was doing the walk of shame out to her car at about five a.m. in the parking lot of the apartment complex that I lived in," Will continues. "I was just making my way home from a friend's house where I had passed out on the couch and woke up because a blade of the ceiling fan had flown off and hit me in the head."

"This is already getting good," Jack says, nodding his head at the drunken antics of college kids.

"Oh, just wait. There's very little that can top this story," I say, leaning into Jack's side as I polish off the rest of my wine. Jack signals the waitress to bring us another bottle, because even he knows this story is going to need another drink.

"Turns out there was a skunk waiting silently under Ellen's car and when she opened the door to the car, she scared the hell out of the thing."

"Oh fuck," Jack says, despite not having skunks in Oz everyone knows the ramifications of startling a skunk.

"That stupid little fucker blasted me," Ellen says, seeking sympathy. "And so I started screaming."

"This is where I come in," Will says, trying to sound like the hero, but I know it's far from that. "I hear her screaming and I assume something horrible is happening. Girl in a dark parking lot screaming, you know. I run over and find Ellen smelling like death and puking next to her car. I'm still drunk from the night before and the sound of her puking makes me puke too."

"Such a hero, right?" Ellen says, giving Will a little push, but he pulls her closer. "Now you'd think the skunk spray and the puke would be the worst of it, right?"

Jack nods a little, but I look at him and shake my head.

"That fucking skunk got in my car!" Ellen yells and I start laughing as I remember the phone call to our parents the next day. "We spent a solid twenty minutes in that parking lot trying to get that damn skunk out of my car."

"How'd you get it out?" Jack asks, enthralled in this ridiculous story.

"Looking back now, we should've called the police or animal control or something, but we were both still semi-drunk and underage, our logical reasoning was not what it should've been," Will says defending his decision like every time he tells this story.

"So what'd you do?" Jack asks again.

"By that point, I was kinda crushing on smelly Ellen so I did what I thought would win her over. I grabbed the skunk with my bare hands, let it spray me like a million times as I pulled it from the backseat and tossed it into the field next to the parking lot."

The laughing at the table is crazy and I can't tell if it's because of the story, the wine or a combination of both.

"We puked a few more times, and then went up to Will's apartment and I showered fully clothed washing with Bloody Mary mix," Ellen adds like everything about this is totally normal.

"We had no tomato juice," Will says shrugging his shoulders. "My semi-drunk ass thought Bloody Mary mix would be the next best thing."

"And the rest is history," Ellen quips, leaning over and kissing Will.

"The story doesn't exactly end there. This is where Ellen likes to end it, but there's still more," I add, nodding my head and making Ellen roll her eyes again. "She then had to call home and explain what happened to our parents."

While I was only fifteen, I knew something about this whole thing was off as I listened on the other end with Ellen trying to explain what happened to our parents. The best part was when our father told her that the village had lost its idiot that day.

"The car was a total loss because they couldn't get rid of the smell. The insurance company just took our parents' word for it. No one came to look at it. They just towed it away and left a check in its place," I continue and we are all laughing despite how awful it really was because in the end Ellen and Will ended up together.

The night ends on that note, and Jack takes my hand in his and I lean against him as we leave the restaurant.

Chapter Twenty-One

Jack

"You're gonna ruin your Uber rating if you keep this up," I whisper, my mouth against Lu's ear, while her hand is half-way down the front of my jeans. Thankfully it's dark, the roads back to *Somerville's* barely lit as the car speeds along, the driver apparently oblivious to the soft porno that's going on in the back seat.

"Don't tell me you're suddenly shy," she teases, undoing the top button of my jeans, her body pressing mine into the corner of the seat.

I chuckle. "Never," I say nibbling the skin just below her ear. "Just didn't pick you for doing something like this."

Lu exhales hard against my neck, her breath warm against my skin, her sexy murmurs a low rumble in my ear as her fingers start to work another button of my jeans. She's drunk and it's making her both confident and horny, two things I like very much.

But I still reach for her hand, reluctantly stopping her even as the blood pulses in my veins, my dick throbs in my pants and my brain tells me to stop being a fucking idiot and just let her keep going.

"Why are you stopping?" she whines, low and greedy.

I smile against her jaw. “Because the last thing I need is to be arrested for public indecency and deported.”

Lu slings a leg over mine, her skirt riding up a little as though to entice me. “You’re no fun,” she protests, her fingers twisting in mine as she attempts to continue what she started the second we climbed into the car outside the restaurant in Napa.

I pull her hand from my crotch, lifting it to my mouth where I bite the heel of her palm. “Behave,” I warn. Lu pouts and it’s so adorable I can’t stop the laugh as I lean in and press a kiss to her lips. “I promise I’ll make it up to you when we get home,” I tell her, kissing her again before gently easing her off me.

Lu attempts and fails to behave herself for the rest of the trip home, her fingers trailing up my leg, refusing to stop every time I grab them. Despite my earlier protests, I don’t put up much of a fight though, my body humming with lust so that by the time we finally pull up outside her house, I’m ready to say fuck it and just have my way with her right on the front porch. The look the driver shoots me as we get out suggests he knows exactly what I’m thinking and what’s been going on in the back seat of his car too.

We tumble out of the car, a mix of arms and legs, hands everywhere, both of us laughing as the driver toots his horn a couple of times as he drives off.

“Yep, your rating is gonna be fucked,” I say, laughing against her mouth as I press a hard kiss to her lips.

“Jack,” she murmurs, her hands sliding back to the now half undone buttons of my jeans.

“What beautiful?” I whisper, walking her backward toward her house. Lu moans into my mouth, her fingers fumbling with my jeans. “Tell me what you want,” I say, hands sliding to her hips.

Lu pulls back a little, stares up at me with dark eyes that don't hide the desire she feels, despite how drunk we both are. "You," she whispers, smiling up at me.

I grin, hands sliding to her arse where I lift her, her legs wrapping around my hips as I walk us up the steps to her house and give her exactly what she asks for.

The next morning, I wake late and feeling a little dusty from last night. I'm in no rush to get up though, and it's made even better by the fact that it's Monday and the winery is closed today.

Lu lies asleep beside me, a leg flung across my thighs and her arm across my stomach. I lie on my back, my eyes closed as I replay the events of last night, the trail of sex that began at the front door the second we came inside, before moving through her house and all the way to her bedroom.

Our clothes are strewn everywhere, the duvet too and I smile as I remember the hunger and desire we both had for each other. It's only been a couple of weeks since this whole thing started, but it still doesn't feel like I'll ever get enough of her. I want her as much I did the first day I walked back into this place.

But last night had been about more than just the sex too. Hanging out with Lu and Ellen and Will had all just felt so easy and fun. Being an only child, I'd never had the closeness of a sibling to just hang out with. Maybe that's part of why I got so excited being over here as a teenager. Teasing Lu had been fun, not just because I could so easily provoke a reaction in her, but also because I'd so rarely had someone my own age around to do that stuff with.

"You awake?" comes Lu's muffled voice.

I grin, pushing her hand down, even as I keep my eyes closed. "What do you think?" I murmur.

She exhales hard when she discovers just how awake I am right now. “God, aren’t you hungover?”

I chuckle. “Never too hungover for this, Lulu.”

Lu groans, burying her face against my side even though she doesn’t move her hand, her fingers gently circling around my dick as she slowly starts to stroke me.

“You hungover too?” I ask, as my hand slides up her spine. She murmurs something that sounds like *fuck yes*, making me laugh. “You have fun last night at least?”

She nods against my side. “Yes, you?”

“I did,” I say, fingers sliding through her long hair, which lies tangled down her back. “Ellen and Will are great.”

“Hmmm.”

“You’re lucky.” I continue. “I always wanted a sister, growing up.”

Lu lifts her head a little, eyes half open as she tries to focus on me. “Why a sister?” she asks before resting her head on my shoulder.

I turn a little, press a kiss to her forehead. “Because she would have had a lot of girlfriends coming over all the time,” I say. “And you know, it would have…”

The rest of my words are cut off when Lu slides her hand off my dick and pinches me hard on the side. “Dirty perv,” she mutters.

“What?” I say, feigning innocence.

Her fingers slide across my skin, settling on my stomach. “Well, thank you for coming last night,” she adds. “I really appreciate it.”

“You don’t need to thank me,” I tell her. “I wanted to come, I want to spend time with you and your family.”

She mutters something now that I don’t catch.

“What did you say?”

“I said,” she exhales, pushing herself closer, face nuzzling my neck again. “I’d like to meet your family some day.”

I let out a long slow breath. "You will," I whisper, even though I have no idea how or when that meeting will take place. Right now my mum and dad are in Europe, travelling indefinitely. I've got no siblings back in Australia, only cousins and aunts and uncles that are spread all over the place.

"Maybe one day I'll take you back to Oz with me," I eventually say, lips against her forehead. "Show you where I grew up."

"I'd like that," she murmurs.

We lie in silence, neither of us saying anymore. A peaceful calmness fills the room and once again I find myself thinking about how easy this all is, how much like home this place already feels.

Despite Lu's reservations and my promises, we've still come no closer to finding a way to make this thing between us work when the time ultimately comes for me to head back to Australia.

I know I still have a month or so before the last of the parts turn up, but after that, I've got no idea. And even though I'd left a job to come here, it doesn't mean I don't have one to go home to.

Word travels fast in the Aussie wine world and as soon as it had got out that I'd finished up at my last place, the emails had come hard and fast. Job offers that no sane person could turn down, incentives that were off the charts.

I knew I'd be an idiot to not at the very least consider them, even if right now, it felt like here at *Somerville's* was the only place I wanted to be.

But I have no idea how that could work, what that could even look like. Because while I don't mind helping Lu out with random jobs now, that's not what I want to do for the rest of my life.

At the same time though, the idea of leaving Lu, of walking away, even temporarily, makes my chest ache. It's taken fourteen long years to finally find my way back to her and right now, I don't ever want to give that up.

Which makes me wonder about this Nate guy Ellen mentioned last night, the one who disappeared on her. Whoever he is, it's clear Lu didn't want to talk about it. But he must be somebody, if he provokes that sort of reaction and a part of me can't help but wonder about what sort of relationship he and Lu had...and who'd made the decision to end it.

"Lu," I eventually say, curiosity getting the better of me. "Who's this Nate guy Ellen mentioned last night?"

She doesn't answer though and when I look down at her, she's lying with her eyes closed, her lips slightly parted and her whole body relaxed against mine. Holding my breath, I hear the slow, steading breathing that tells me she's asleep again.

I must fall back to sleep too because when I next open my eyes, it's nearly noon, the room filled with sunshine from the half open blinds. Lu's still asleep beside me, but my now rumbling stomach forces me up and out of bed.

I pull on some sweats I've left at her place before walking out to the kitchen. Putting some coffee on to brew, I search her fridge for something that can take the edge off the last of our hangovers. Smiling, I pull bacon; eggs, tomatoes, and mushrooms out and start to get a late breakfast together.

"God something smells good."

I turn and see a still half-asleep Lu walk into the kitchen. She's wearing a t-shirt of mine, the hem stopping just below her arse. Grinning, I reach for her, pull her into my arms and press a kiss to her lips.

"Think you can stomach some food?" I ask, sliding a hand under the t-shirt and over her warm skin.

"Hmmm," she says, wrinkling her nose a little. "I think so," she adds. "I think I need to, anyway."

"Coffee?"

She nods, pulling herself from my arms as she walks to the pot and pours herself a cup. "How are you so okay this morning?" she asks, after taking a sip.

I smile. "Pfft, I'm Australian, baby, I can handle my alcohol."

She rolls her eyes at me. "Right," she says. "Bred tough down there, huh?"

I wink at her, reaching over to smack her on the arse with the spatula. "That's right."

She shakes her head as she perches on a stool and watches me finish making us breakfast. When I'm done, I slide a plate piled high with fried bacon and eggs, some sautéed mushrooms and grilled tomatoes toward her.

"Here, get this into you, it'll make you feel better, I promise."

"Thanks," she says, picking up a fork and tentatively trying some eggs.

"Okay?"

She nods and we both dig in, side by side at her kitchen island. We eat in silence, both of us apparently starving after a night of booze and sex. Eventually, Lu lays her knife and fork down and pushes her empty plate away, a contented sigh falling from her lips.

"Better?" I ask, doing the same before turning to face her.

"Hmmm, much," she says, licking her lips.

I grin, reaching forward, grabbing her around the waist and pulling her onto my lap, so she's straddling me. "Know what else cures a hangover?" I ask, kissing her greasy lips as I slide my hands under her t-shirt.

"Tim Tams?" she suggests, her hands trailing down my bare chest to my stomach.

I burst out laughing. "I was gonna say sex, actually."

Lu gives me a cheeky grin. "Of course you were," she says, wriggling closer as she locks her legs around the back of the stool. "How about you give me more Tim Tams and I give you more sex?" she suggests.

I chuckle. "You give it to me, huh?"

She nods, a wide smile on her face as she slips her fingers under the waistband of my sweats and brushes them against my dick. "Yep," she confirms. "Do we have a deal?"

My grin widens and I slip a hand up to her breast, cupping it as my thumb and finger pinch her nipple, my dick twitching at the gasp she lets out. "What happened to all those packets I brought over before?"

Lu's hand slips lower, fingers curling around my dick now as she slowly starts to stroke me. "I ate them," she says, as though this is hardly surprising.

"All of them?" I ask, swallowing as a wave of lust curls through me.

Lu shrugs. "Of course."

I chuckle. "What are you, like addicted to them or something?"

"Hmmm," she says, licking her lips as she leans in and kisses me. "I'm addicted to several things from Oz," she whispers, mouth against mine.

I groan, pulling her closer as I suck her bottom lip into my mouth and my other hand slides up to her breasts.

"But," she says, pulling back a little. "First, Tim Tams."

"Fuck the Tim Tams," I murmur, pulling her back to me.

Lu chuckles. "No, you can fuck *me*, after the Tim Tams," she says, sliding off my lap.

"Ugh," I groan, readjusting my now hard dick as I stand. "You, drive a hard bargain," I add, smacking her on the arse.

Lu laughs as she jumps away from me. "Hurry up, if you're lucky, maybe I'll decide to eat them off your body when you get back."

"Don't be wearing anything when I get back," I growl, heading for the front door.

I head over to my place, flying through the front door as I all but run into the kitchen. Grabbing a couple of packets, I head back outside just in time to see a car driving down the gravel road toward our houses. I pause, wondering who the hell it could be given the winery is shut today and it isn't Ellen's car.

I walk down the steps and cross over to Lu's porch as the car, which I can now see is driven by a guy, stops in front of her place.

He gets out, a strange look on his face as he watches me, standing half-dressed at Lu's front door. He's wearing jeans, which looked they've been fucking ironed and a polo shirt, tucked in but with the collar turned up so he looks like a total wanker.

"Can I help you?" I ask, blocking his path up Lu's steps.

He gives me a once over, not bothering to hide his distain. "I'm here to see Lauren," he says.

"Place is closed," I tell him, gesturing up the drive. "Didn't you see the sign?"

He stares back at me, a look on his face that suggests he doesn't give a shit that the winery is closed. Just as I'm about to tell him to fuck off, I hear the front door open behind me.

Turning, I see Lu, still half-dressed in my t-shirt, a look of fear and horror on her face as she stares not at me, but at this stranger who's just shown up at her house.

"Lauren," he says, taking a step up to the porch. I move to block his path, but before I can say anything, I hear Lu speak, her voice shaking as she says, "Nate, what are you doing here?"

Oh fuck.

Chapter Twenty-Two

Lauren

Watching him walk up pulls a knot so tight in the pit of my stomach that I'm certain I might throw up on the spot. There are very few people in the world who can provoke this sort of emotion in me, and Nate is top of that list.

Jack runs a close second, but for reasons far beyond what I feel for Nate. Nate is pure and utter hatred. I liked to believe I hated Jack, that what I felt for him wasn't lust or love or infatuation, but I know now that the feelings Jack evokes in me are on the opposite end of the spectrum.

"Nate, what are you doing here?" I ask, completely disregarding the fact that Jack is standing there staring at me wide-eyed and wondering who the hell this is. I don't have time for explanations or pleasantries.

"Hey Lauren. How's it going?" Nate asks casually like we're old friends. He smiles at me but all I see is the asshole who somehow convinced me that I wanted to marry him.

I want to punch him in the throat.

"What do you want?" I ask again, prefacing my question differently because he obviously isn't getting the point that he's not welcome. "Vineyard's closed," I add, my hands now on my hips, my eyes focused on him.

"Yeah, I know. Was just in the area and thought I'd stop by. See how you're doing."

Jack clears his throat, reminding me of his proximity to me and given the situation, my attention is focused solely on Nate.

I turn to him, trying not to sound like this man who is currently standing across from me is of any importance and say, "Can you give me a minute? I'll meet you inside." I tip my head in the direction of my house and Jack gives me a small nod but doesn't move.

"You good, Lu?" he questions, his eyes flicking to Nate, and I watch the curiosity mixed with jealousy spark in his eyes.

"Yes, I'm fine. I just need a minute."

This time Jack takes in my words and makes his way back to the house, letting himself in and closing the door behind him. I'm sure he's wondering what is going on, and after the comment Ellen made last night there's, no way he doesn't realize this is the same person she was talking about.

There's so much that goes into the explanation of who Nate is and why I despise him that laying it all out and letting Jack process it is going to really suck.

And not just for him.

"Who's that?" Nate asks and this time the jealously flares inside him. But he isn't jealous. He's controlling and that's what this whole visit is about.

"None of your business," I shoot back, the anger filling my words as the knot in my stomach loosens. My anxiety now replaced with rage.

Nate exhales hard and pulls a hand through his hair. I can tell by the look on his face that he's not interested in my lack of an answer.

"When's this cold shoulder thing gonna stop, Lauren?" he asks, his tone dripping with impatience.

"Never."

He chuckles a little but there's nothing comical about what I said or his laughter. I cut him off, shut him out of my life just one day after what was supposed to be our wedding. He didn't get it then and he still doesn't get it now.

"I've been trying to get in touch with you, but my calls won't go through and you don't answer my emails. Had to show up on a Monday so I could get past the gate attendant."

Everything he says should be a huge fucking clue that I want nothing to do with him, but he's oblivious. He can't understand why someone would turn him away. He's far too important and self-absorbed to rationalize it.

"Wow, you'd think after nearly a year of radio silence you'd get the point..."

Nate cuts me off, again his words laced with annoyance, "So you're still mad about that whole wedding thing, huh?"

"Nope," I reply, my tone clipped.

"What's the deal then?" he asks and now it's me who's laughing. I can't even believe I'm standing here having this conversation with him. "So how long until I'm back on your good graces?"

"Never, Nate, never, honestly. I wish I never even knew you."

He'll debate this all day with me and I know Jack is in my house wondering what is going on, left with a million unanswered questions.

The day after the wedding, Nate showed up like nothing had happened. Telling me he just wasn't ready to get married and that my life would always belong to the vineyard and my job. He wanted me to walk away from it all, leave it all to Ellen and get a job in what he dubbed "the real world".

This place is my real world and it always will be; something he could never appreciate or understand. He claimed he'd been having cold feet for months before the wedding but couldn't bring himself to tell me, so instead of growing a pair he found it wise to let all one hundred-fifty of our guests show up blissfully unaware.

It wasn't like a movie; there was nothing humorous or silly about it. It was just me waiting and eventually Ellen walked back to the small bridal suite to tell me that Nate's mom said he's not coming.

He didn't even have the common decency to tell me himself. He sent a text to his mom who was seated in the front row as clueless as everyone else.

I was the one who returned all the gifts, sent back all the checks, apologized to everyone in attendance, and I did it all without tears.

I saved those and the embarrassment that lingered for later.

"That's harsh, Lauren," Nate says, his hand over his heart like I'm supposed to feel sorry for him. There wasn't an ounce of sympathy given for what he did to me and as much as I'm not a vendetta kind of person, I owe him nothing. He gets nothing from me anymore, including my time.

"It's reality and if you show up here one more time, I'll call the police and report you for harassment."

He holds his hands up defensively but smirks at me like this is all one big joke. He steps closer and I shake my head, my lips set in a firm line.

"You know I don't give up that easily," Nate says, a smarmy smile on his face, my words not sinking in at all.

"Try me, Nate, just try me." I have no qualms about picking up my phone and hitting those three simple numbers to let him know I'm not playing around. I want nothing to do with him.

"You're being ridiculous, Lauren," he says condescendingly, this time trying to make me feel small and out of control, like my feelings don't matter.

"I'm going to ask you to leave one more time and then I'm calling the police," I answer back, my words firm and this time louder than I would like, because he doesn't get to control anything about me.

"Seriously..." Nate starts, but his words fall short and his eyes shoot to the doorway of my house.

"Hey, mate, I'm pretty sure she's asked you to leave," Jack says coming up behind me, but moving so he's now standing just slightly in front of me.

"I got this, Jack," I whisper, my hand sliding down his arm as I give his hand a little squeeze.

"I'm sure you do," he replies back, turning toward me and pressing a kiss to the side of my head. "Just in case," he adds, winking at me.

It only takes Nate a few seconds to catch up, watching Jack and me together before he walks back to his car without saying anything else.

Something tells me this won't be the last time I see him though.

Without missing a beat, and not that I blame him, Jack says, "Care to explain?"

"Honestly, no," I answer back, but knowing it's totally unfair of me to leave him in the dark.

Jack laughs a little when I smile at him, all jealousy from earlier is long gone and what's left is confusion.

I take in a deep breath and let it out slowly before starting. He's at least owed some semblance of an explanation.

"That's my ex. He's not of that much importance, but whenever he gets wind that I'm dating someone he comes back around. He doesn't want me, he has no interest in me, but..."

"But he doesn't want anyone else in your life either," Jack says, finishing my thought.

"Exactly." I nod my head, smiling at Jack thankful that he gets it and doesn't seem to be scared off by Nate and his ability to show up unannounced and unwelcome.

"What do you think about the whole thing?" Jack asks, pushing for my thoughts, because as much as he isn't one to pry, I get why he's feeling out the situation.

"I think I'd like him to disappear, and he will eventually," I say, trying to give off a nonplused vibe about the whole thing.

"If you want, I'd be more than happy to throw around some of this Aussie muscle and make sure he doesn't come back," Jack jokes, flexing his arm as he slips his other arm around my waist pulling me close.

"I'm pretty sure it wouldn't be a fair fight," I tease back knowing Jack would completely kick Nate's ass.

Even though there's a ton of stuff to get done here at the vineyard, Jack and I decide to take a drive into San Francisco and do some sightseeing while he's here. I can't remember the last time I just threw everything aside and spent the day away from here, but with Jack I want to.

"It's a lot colder near the bay," I warn Jack as we leave the vineyard with him dressed in shorts and a t-shirt.

"You think I'd miss an opportunity to wear shorts while on holiday?" he asks and I laugh at his lingo as I pull out onto the road.

"Suit yourself, but I refuse to be seen with you wearing an "I heart San Francisco" sweatshirt from an overpriced tourist stand. And I don't think I'd classify this as a holiday, you work for me, remember?"

"It's actually called a jumper not a sweatshirt," Jack says, teasing me as he twirls a few strands of my hair around his finger. "And would you be more inclined to not take the piss if I just called it a vacation?" He says the word vacation in his cheesy American accent and it makes me smile even more, but I'm laughing so hard I can barely get my next sentence out.

"Take a piss...what? Who is taking a piss where?" I ask, totally confused now by his obviously Australian comment.

Jack just laughs though, shaking his head as he leans over and presses a kiss to my cheek and whispers, "You're fucking adorable."

Traffic is light given it is a Monday and we've missed all the commuters by at least a few hours as we make our way into the city. I find a public lot and park the car figuring we can walk to pretty much anywhere.

It only takes about twenty minutes before Jack admits he's freezing, his ice-cold hands slipping under my shirt to the warm skin on my stomach.

"Someone may have mentioned this, but I guess I'll give you a pass since you are from the country where people can literally fry an egg on the ground."

We avoid the tourist shops and duck into a shopping mall so Jack can grab something that doesn't have San Francisco plastered all over it.

"You're lucky we found that mall because if we hadn't I planned on calling you "Alcatraz" the rest of the trip," I tease and Jack gives me a little push before pulling me back against him and kissing me.

We spend the entire day visiting every tourist spot in the San Francisco area and eating and drinking our way through lots of bars. We find ourselves laughing at the number of people taking a ridiculous amount of over posed selfies at all the prime locations: in front of the Golden Gate Bridge, outside the house from Full House, on Lombardo Street and a bunch of others.

It's not like Jack and I don't take pictures, we do, but we tried to live more in the moment and enjoy our time together.

Just because it isn't plastered on social media doesn't mean it didn't happen.

Our last stop is Alcatraz, something that if not booked in advance there isn't a chance of seeing it. Since this trip to the city was on a whim, we don't have tickets and there's none left for the day.

One of the perks about working in the tourist industry is that you make friends with a lot of people; people who can sneak you onto the boat to Alcatraz without a ticket.

I flag down Julie, a girl who worked for me hosting tours back a couple of years ago before she relocated to San Francisco and took a job as a tour operator on one of the boats that goes to Alcatraz.

She smiles at me when I catch her eye and she opens the rope that's keeping the waiting people from entering the boat before it's time.

"Hey Julie!" I call, as we make our way over to her. We hug and I introduce Jack as we make small talk. "Any chance you can get us on the boat?" I ask, a hopeful smile on my face.

"Sure, no problem. Let me print you a couple of tickets," she says, holding up one finger as she slips off to the side and into the ticket booth.

She returns a few seconds later and hands me the tickets.

"You're on the next boat," she announces, and I hear a few people behind us let out some muttered curse words.

"Thanks, we'll see you on board."

The day flies by and before I know it Jack and I are back in the car and heading back to *Somerville's* as the sun sets behind us.

"I had a great time with you today," I say, sliding my hand into Jack's. He lifts my hand, pressing a kiss to each of my fingers.

"Me too. There's no one I'd rather be with than you," Jack says back, and his words make my stomach flutter, a feeling of happiness settling in my chest.

Chapter Twenty-Three

Jack

The week passes quickly. There are no more surprise appearances from that wanker, Nate, and Lu and I don't talk anymore about it. Even though I know she was being kinda cagey with her explanation when I asked her about him, I didn't really want to push it with her.

And it had to have been pretty obvious to him that she and I are a thing. We'd both been half dressed when he'd shown up, for fuck's sake, so he'd have to be an idiot to not realize it was me who was now sharing her bed. Plus, Lu hadn't tried to hide the fact I was there either, so as much as I want to know more about exactly who he is and what happened between them, I'm okay with as much as she's given me for now.

"Jack?"

"In here," I call out, dragging myself out from under the crusher. I'm still waiting on two parts, but I'm taking the opportunity to make sure the whole thing is cleaned out and ready to be properly put back together when they finally get here.

Lu walks into the shed, Oscar hot on her heels. It's his last day before they head off on holidays to Disney and he's spent the past week trying to convince me that I should ditch the winery and come with them.

"Hey," I say, smiling as I take her hand in mine, pulling her closer for a kiss.

"Hi," she says, smiling back at me.

"Ugh, gross," Oscar says, rolling his eyes at both of us.

"What's gross?" I ask, glancing at him. "This?" I add before sliding an arm around Lu's back, dipping her backwards and planting a hard kiss on her lips, which given the low moan she lets out means it's one that's probably not entirely PG either.

"Ewwww," he says now, throwing his hands up in the air.

I can't stop the laugh, even as I pull Lu back up and against me, loving the breathy exhale she releases as she steadies herself against me. "Trust me, little dude, one day you'll get it."

"Right," he says, arms crossed over his chest as he gives me and Lu the stink eye. "Anyway, we've got a job for you."

I chuckle. "Is that right," I say, turning to Lu. "What's up?"

Lu pulls herself from my arms, swallowing hard as though she's trying to get herself under control. "A huge favor?" she finally says, eyes meeting mine.

"Oh yeah?" I say, grinning. "What sort of favor?"

Lu swats a hand at me as she gives me a cheeky grin. "Not that kind, filthy boy," she whispers.

I step closer, sliding a hand to her hip as I lean down and whisper, "You sure? We can ditch the kid, get some..."

"Ah hmm hmmm," Oscar says, clearing his throat. Lu and I both turn and find him watching us, arms still crossed as he glares up at us.

I chuckle, even as Lu steps backwards so we're no longer touching. "I've got one of our distributors coming in," she says, weirdly nervous. "But I've also got a tour starting soon, so would you…"

"Be able to do the tour?" I ask. "Course."

Lu exhales, reaching out to squeeze my arm. "Thank you," she says. "It's just the sheds and the whole wine making process, whatever you feel comfortable with is fine."

"Lu," I say, lifting her hand to my mouth. "It's all good, beautiful, I promise."

"I can run him through things," Oscar pipes up, taking a step toward us. "Show him the ropes and all."

"Oscar," Lu says at the same time as I laugh. "I'm sure you can, little dude. Come on, let's do this," I say, gesturing toward the shed doors.

Lu follows us out and walks us up to the main office, handing me some brochures to give out to the group as well as some vouchers for wine tasting and a discount in the restaurant. I have a vague recollection of tagging along on these tours as a kid, back when I spent the summer here, and I'm sure I'll be able to wing this one with no problems.

After Lu leaves, we wander over to meet the group, Oscar apparently deciding he's taking his wingman duties seriously as he runs through the introductions and explains how this whole thing's going to work. I don't miss the smiles a few of the guests have, the stifled laughs as the seven-year-old tour guide asks everyone to fall in and follow him down to the sheds.

"How about you let me handle it from here?" I ask, hand on his shoulder as we walk into the shed housing the broken crusher.

"You sure you got this?" he asks, deadly serious.

I wink at him. "Yep," I say. "But I'm happy to get your feedback on my performance when it's over. Deal?"

Oscar thinks for a few seconds before offering me his fist to bump. "Deal."

The tour goes well, the guests all seemingly loving the easy banter that Oscar and I share as I take them through the intricacies of wine making and the difference in grape varieties, including the whole Shiraz/Syrah story and why Aussies call it one thing and Americans call it another.

Oscar chimes in from time to time with a few random facts about oak casks and cellaring length, explaining to the guests how these affect the taste. It's funny to watch, particularly considering the kid isn't even old enough to drink wine. But I have to hand it to him, he knows his stuff, even the guests can see that.

After we're done, I take them all up to the tasting room and introduce them to Penny, who takes over. Oscar lingers, I'm sure hoping for a tip or two and so I wander back to the shed to finish what I was doing this morning.

By the time I'm done, it's late, so I fire off a quick text to see where Lu's at.

Lu: just finishing up...meet you back at my place?

I grin, as I type out a response. I don't think I've spent a single night at the house she gave to me since this thing between us started. And I really kinda like that.

Me: sounds good. C u soon x

When I get back to Lu's, I switch on my laptop and on a whim, log into skype. Almost immediately, I get a ping from my parents and I take a seat at the kitchen island as I wait for the call to connect.

"Hey!" my mum says as soon as it connects.

"Hey," I reply. "Where are you guys?"

My dad moves into the shot, waving at me as he takes a seat and says, "Bordeaux."

"Nice," I say, nodding in approval.

"Your father's drunk," Mum replies, patting him on the knee.

I chuckle. "No surprise there. What time is it?"

"Nearly three."

"In the morning?" I ask, shocked. I glance at the time on my laptop, mentally trying to work out the difference even though I suck at these conversions.

"Yep," Dad replies.

"What the hell are you doing on Skype then?" I ask, leaning in to get a better look at them. Mum's right, Dad does look a little drunk.

Mum shrugs. "It was your father's idea," she says as though this explains everything. "You know how he is."

I laugh, even as I'm nodding my head. "It's lucky you caught me," I say. "I just randomly thought I'd log on."

"Well, there was another reason," Mum adds as Dad sits silently beside her, his eyes half closing.

"Yeah?"

She swallows, glancing at Dad and nudging him awake before she turns back to me. "Mel contacted us."

"What?!" I half shout. "Are you fucking serious?"

Mum nods. "Yes," she says. "Apparently she's been trying to get hold of you and can't. Wants to know where you are."

I shake my head. "Fucking hell," I mutter. "She just can't take a hint. Did you tell her?" I ask, even as I hear Lu's front door open and I know I need to end this conversation right now.

"Well, yes and no," Mum says, looking a little sheepish.

"What does that mean?" I ask, even as I hear Lu call my name. "Hang on," I say, holding a hand up to the screen. "In here," I call to Lu. "Come and say hi," I add, reaching for her.

"To who?" she says, taking my hand.

I pull her closer and onto my lap as I gesture at the screen. "Mum and Dad," I say. "Dad, remember Lu, don't you?" I add.

"Oh my god," Lu breathes out at the same time a huge smile breaks out on my mum's face. She won't remember Lu because she didn't come to the states that time I did, but she'll definitely remember hearing about her, especially as my dad loved to give me so much shit about how much I liked her. Even more so when I told them both I was coming over here to work and planned on looking her up again.

"Lulu Somerville," my dad says, a huge smile on his face. "Look at you."

Lu blushes as she says, "Hi, Mr. Wilson."

Dad chuckles. "God, call me Tony, please," he says, suddenly more awake than he was two minutes ago.

"Dad's a little pissed," I say, kissing Lu on the cheek.

"He is?" she asks, turning to look at me. "What's he pissed at?"

I laugh, kissing her on the lips this time as I explain, "No, pissed as in drunk, not pissed *off*."

Lu shakes her head as she turns back to the screen murmuring, "You Aussies are so weird."

I see the huge smile on my mum's face as she watches us, clearly not missing the fact that something is going on here between Lu and me. I mean it's pretty obvious considering she's on my lap and I'm kissing her.

"So," Mum starts, gesturing toward us. "Is this a…" she asks, trailing off as though she isn't sure how to define it.

I chuckle. "Yeah, it is," I tell her. "Lulu finally admitted she fancies me," I add, squeezing Lu's hip as she pinches me. "It was always going to happen, obviously."

Lu shakes her head at me as Mum actually claps her hands and nudges my dad, a murmured, "I knew this would happen," still audible through the speakers.

I shake my head, even as I'm smiling at them both.

"So, you're staying a while then?" my dad asks.

I shrug. "Yeah, at the moment," I tell him, even as I feel Lu tense in my arms because an end date to my trip is something neither of us likes talking about. "Still waiting on some parts for that crusher anyway, so I'm here indefinitely at the moment."

"Maybe we should come over and visit," Mum says, her smile wide as she looks from me to Lu and back to me again.

I smile, relieved for the subject change. "You should," I tell them. "We'd like that."

The conversation continues for a few more minutes, but it's clear Dad's in desperate need of some sleep. After we tell them again that they should come and visit, we say our goodbyes and log off.

"Your dad hasn't changed a bit," Lu says, sliding off my lap as she walks around to grab some wine from the fridge.

I chuckle. "No, he kinda hasn't."

"And your mum is so nice," she continues, pouring us both a glass.

I grin, pulling her into my arms. "Mmmm," I murmur, leaning in to kiss the end of her nose. "This skype will have made her day."

"Really?" Lu asks, confused.

"Really," I repeat.

"Why?"

I laugh. "Seriously?" I ask her. Lu shrugs as though she doesn't understand what I'm talking about. "You, Lulu," I say, kissing her lips this time. "Seeing me with you will have made her day."

"Really?" she says again. "But she's never even met me."

I shrug. "I know."

Lu stares up at me, the confused look finally giving way to a smile as it dawns on her. "Oh my god," she says, swatting at my chest. "You totally told her all about me, didn't you?"

I laugh again, loving the look of smug satisfaction on her face. "Maybe," I tease.

Lu scoffs. "Bullshit maybe," she says. "Clearly I wasn't the only one who couldn't stop talking now, was I."

I pull her closer, wrapping both arms around her waist as I look down at her smiling face. It hits me in this moment, hard and right in the chest, just how much this woman means to me. How much I can't and don't ever want to let her go.

"You told her you fancied me too, didn't you," Lu continues when I don't say anything, her arms slipping around my neck as she smiles up at me.

I smile, even as I pull her closer. "Maybe I did."

Lu's smile widens as she pushes up on her toes and presses her mouth against mine. "I knew it," she says against my lips.

I chuckle. "What, that I fancied you?" I ask, kissing her again.

"Hmm hmm," she says.

I shake my head. "Yeah I'm pretty sure *everyone* knows I fancy you, Lulu," I tell her. "And I'm pretty damn glad about that too."

Now it's Lu laughing as she kisses me again. I tighten my arms around her, pulling her between my legs as I sit back on the kitchen stool, my hands sliding under her shirt and over her warm skin.

"I fancy you a whole lot, Lulu Somerville and I don't give a shit who knows that," I whisper, even as my brain tells me it's so much more than that.

Lu giggles as she leans her forehead against mine. "I fancy you too, Jack Wilson," she says, eyes locked onto mine.

I stare back at her, smiling. "Of course you do, baby," I say. "You always have," I add, winking at her.

Lu laughs again before kissing me once more. I pull her even closer, losing myself in how much I want and need this woman. How much I want to find a way to stay here with her.

But nagging at the back of my brain, like an annoying song you just can't get out of your head, is the knowledge that Mel has contacted my parents, trying to find me.

And that I still don't know exactly what they told her either.

Chapter Twenty-Four

Lauren

I loathe grocery shopping and one of the perks of having a job like mine is that I can avoid the masses and go at random times of the day.

I've got this shit down to a science. I avoid Tuesdays because that's senior discount day, and like hell if I move that slowly through the grocery store. I'm trying to break the *Guinness Book of World Records* for fastest shopper and those old peeps serpentine down the aisles like a drunken toddler. Obviously Saturdays and Sundays are out because that's when the rest of the world convenes in droves, and crowds and me just don't mix. Thursdays are five-dollar take and bake pizza day, and while I love pizza, I pretty much hate people more.

So that just leaves Monday and Wednesday, and I'm currently spending my Wednesday morning hauling ass down the aisles trying my damnedest to break my record of a full shop in forty minutes.

It all comes to a screeching halt when I hit the dairy section and there standing at the end of the aisle is Nate in his perfectly pressed polo and his oddly starched jeans.

What the fuck was I thinking?

I pause long enough to watch him dig through some cartons of yogurt, fucking up the whole lot of them before he finds the one with the latest expiration date.

Call it nosiness or fear or just plain stupidity, but whatever the reason is that I stopped, I stopped just long enough for him to notice me.

The gasp that falls from my lips is practically audible from where Nate stands as I hightail it around the corner and curse this stupid small town grocery store and myself.

"Lauren?" I hear Nate call and in my panic to get away from him, I take the corner a little too sharply colliding with an end cap filled with potato chips. I send about half the chips to the floor and then proceed to run the bags over with my cart.

Fuck my life. How and why does this shit happen to me?

I can hear Nate's feet jogging toward me and my chip debacle, and I do what any self-respecting woman avoiding her ex who left her at the alter would do. I ditch my cart full of groceries and beeline for the nearest aisle.

I nearly run until I reach the end and hide at the end cap on the opposite side, my heart racing and my breathing coming in hard pants as I realize I should really hit the gym more often. Not that I expected to be trying to outrun my ex in the grocery store today.

I'm spread out; my back against the shelving full of pickle jars with my legs wide, making sure the end cap hides my entire body. I look ridiculous and I know it, but I'm still standing like a boozy teenager hiding from the cops after an underage party bust.

I pull my phone from my purse and text Ellen. She's my voice of reason since clearly my voice was left back with the smashed bags of potato chips.

Me: OMFG!! Nate is in the grocery store and I'm hiding from him. What should I do????

Ellen: Um, wtf. Just leave.

Me: He's going to see me.

Ellen: So just walk out and don't acknowledge him. I'm about to get on the Matterhorn so figure this shit out.

Me: ELLEN!!!

This is the best advice I'm going to get so I guess I gotta go with it.

I peer around the corner in an attempt to be stealthy and ninja-like but I fail miserably because I come face to face with Nate.

Fuck my life once again.

Instead of acknowledging him, I turn on my heel and attempt to walk in the opposite direction, but he grabs my arm, stilling me.

"Lauren, where are you going?" he asks like we're friends and I'm the one being rude.

How dare he be here on my quiet shopping day! How dare he show up here when he doesn't even live in this town!

When I finally stop moving and make eye contact with him, he's smiling and I want to claw his eyes out. He still acts like he didn't try to ruin my life, that he didn't take control of something and make it all about him. He obviously thinks embarrassment fades faster than my pre-wedding spray on tan. He's wrong.

"What are you doing here?" I hiss, yanking my arm from his grasp.

"Shopping," he replies holding up his basket of perfectly selected cartons of yogurt.

"You don't live here!" I shout and a man walking by mutters something about people not living in grocery stores. I really want to tell him to mind his own damn business, but I'm distracted by Nate's ability to ruin everything.

"It's a grocery store, Lauren. It's open to the public..."

But I cut him off before he can say anything more. "You're here because of me and you fucking know it. Leave me alone."

Nate chuckles and shakes his head. "I'm here because I'm shopping and if I happened to run into you on a Wednesday morning, then great."

He had absolutely no interest in the things I did while we were engaged and the fact that he remembers my shopping schedule makes me irate.

"Listen, Nate. I have no interest in getting back together with you and I'm not just playing hard to get. I'm happy, happier than I ever was when we were together, so for the love of fuck, leave me alone."

Without letting him say anything more I do something I should've done the moment I saw him in here.

I walk away, but he can't take a hint and he follows me out to my car, calling my name as I ignore him.

"You going to tell me who the guy is?" he calls out and I roll my eyes knowing this is exactly what this is about. He has no interest in me, but rather his interest is in that someone else wants me.

"I blocked your number for a reason. Take a fucking hint," I shout back as I approach my car and climb in.

I will not let this turn into a screaming match in a parking lot. He will not knock on my window. He will not continue to embarrass me. I've done enough of that on my own today.

Right now all I want to do is get the hell out of here and get home to Jack. There's a safety in Jack that I've never had in anyone else, especially not with Nate. I find comfort in being with him, being near him and being able to be myself around him.

Now if I could only figure out a way to tell him I didn't just date Nate, but that we were supposed to be married.

The whole getting left thing really fucks with you. It says so much with one small act. It told me I wasn't enough, it said he wanted to do it in a way that I would remember forever, but more than all of that, he did it because it left him in control.

It also made me question why he couldn't have just told me before we got that far into it all.

I contemplate this whole idea more than I should, the idea that I could right now be married to Nate.

As much as I was devastated by the turn of events at our wedding, a part of me wonders if I would've been able to go through with it too. I wasn't so much embarrassed by the fact that he left me, but more by the fact that I made the mistake of thinking I really wanted to marry him.

Admitting it now is hard, but I went into it knowing I was marrying him for all the wrong reasons. I was alone, nearly thirty, far too dedicated to my job and wanting to have kids someday, but that someday was so far in the distance that it seemed it would never happen.

Desperate.

I guess that's the best word to describe me at that time. I met Nate on a dating app and it escalated quickly from there. The crazy thing is, on my first date with him as I walked through the vineyard toward the front gate, all I could picture was skinny, nerdy Jack Wilson with his mud-covered glasses and his sincere smile as he apologized for tackling me.

At the time I thought it was just loneliness and the memory of the last time I had felt anything for someone. But in the end it was more than that.

At fifteen any attention from a boy will give you butterflies, but I missed that feeling and I wouldn't feel it again until Jack walked back into my life.

Marrying some who can't give you that is a mistake and I almost made it. My mother always said that marriage should be easy; the person you're with should make your life easier. If he or she doesn't then it wasn't right in the first place.

When I pull in to the vineyard, Jack is helping unload a shipment from our restaurant supplier. Something he doesn't have to do, but he does it anyway. From the day he arrived, he fit right in, picking up where he left off fourteen years ago, just knowing exactly what to do.

Stopping on the gravel path that leads back to my house, I park my car and wave to him. A strange calm washes over me as I take him in.

He's disheveled from the work around the vineyard; his face smudged with dirt and his clothes stained with purple splotches, his blonde hair rumpled. He's exactly who I pictured I'd someday end up with, someone who wants to be here, someone who loves this place and all its work as much as I do.

Jack says something to the guys he's helping and then jogs over to my car.

"Okay if I get in?" he asks, giving his shoulders a shrug as he holds up his dirty hands.

"Of course. This car has seen its fair share of dirty." As I say it, I laugh, knowing what's about to come next.

"Oh, I'm pretty sure we can show it something far dirtier," Jack jokes, leaning in through the open window to kiss me.

"We'll save that for later," I reply winking at him, but shoving his hand away as he tries to grope my boob, too.

We pull up to my house and he goes around to the back of my car, trying to open the trunk.

"Open the boot," he yells as I'm climbing out of the driver's seat.

"What?" Open what?"

"The boot, silly girl. I need to get your groceries out."

"You mean the trunk?" I ask, as I stand beside him with one eyebrow cocked. "If you're going to stick around here, you gotta brush up on your American dialect."

And in typical Jack fashion he proceeds to feed me a full-on Aussie-filled sentence that makes as much sense as putting my non-existent groceries in a boot.

"No groceries, either," I say, feeling suddenly uncomfortable. I have to explain to him why I went to the grocery store and returned empty-handed.

"I thought you said you were going grocery shopping?" he asks, confused.

"I was but..." I pause trying to figure out how to word this without making Jack jealous or making him think I'm still hung up on Nate. That fucker really knows how to show up at the worst possible times.

Jack's eyebrows scrunch together as he waits for me to finish my sentence, knowing there's more to this conversation.

"I ran into Nate at the store," I finally admit and Jack's face relaxes.

"So where are the groceries?"

"I left them at the store," I confess, looking down at my feet.

"You mean to tell me that fuckwit made you so uncomfortable that you left your groceries at the store?"

"Yeah, and I knocked over a display of potato chips," I say, my face growing warm at my admission of stupidity.

"Aw, Lu, come here," Jack says, pulling me into his arms and pressing a kiss to the top of my head. "I know you said he'll disappear, but I'm pissed he's come round again."

"He will go away. He's harmless and I need to grow up."

"Give me a list and I'll go to the store for you," Jack says firmly.

"Huh?" I say, appalled at his offer. It's probably the nicest thing anyone has ever done for me.

"Write me a list of what you need and I'll go," he repeats, his hands on his hips as if he's waiting for me to drop everything and make the list.

So I head into the house and begin making the list. Jack waits patiently as I think of the things I need and also tells me to add a few things he wants to it.

His list is far funnier than mine, adding all the American things he loved as a kid, which basically amounts to nothing but crappy junk food.

"Jack, that's nothing but crap," I admonish, patting his ridiculously muscular and flat stomach through his shirt.

"This coming from the girl who ate her weight in Tim Tams and managed to make a sex deal based off of them?"

"Touché."

I hand Jack the list, the keys to my car and attempt to give him my credit card, but he shoves it back into my hand, saying it's on him.

I try to argue but it's fruitless because he turns his back on me and walks out to the car as if I'm not even talking.

"You're a stubborn ass!" I yell from the porch.

"But you love it!" he yells back.

And fuck me if I don't, as I hear my mother's words echoed back to me.

The person you're with should make your life easier.

My life has never been easier than it is with Jack in it.

Chapter Twenty-Five

Jack

By the time I head back to the vineyard, it's quiet, the place now closed and all the guests long gone. I'd spent an hour or so strolling around the supermarket, half hoping to run into that fuckwit Nate just so I could tell him to piss off out of Lu's life, for good this time. Unfortunately, he wasn't there, so after I'd finished up, I'd headed back to *Somerville's*.

Just as I'm coming up to the turn-off though, I notice a "For Sale" sign in front of the property that runs along the far border of Lu's. It must be new, because I don't remember seeing it before.

Slowing down a little, I glance at the sign, mentally noting the estate agent who is handling the sale as my gaze moves to the fields of trees that fill the property, the almost new sheds and a tiny farmhouse far off in the distance.

It isn't a winery, but a fruit orchard and as I slowly drive past it, an idea starts to form in my head. A spark that given enough fuel and encouragement could turn into something explosive.

But now, as I park the car in front of Lu's place, I know I'm going to keep these thoughts quiet for a bit. At this stage, it's only an idea, nothing certain and definitely far too soon to start thinking long-term.

"Honey, I'm home," I call out, as I walk in the front door, my arms loaded with shopping bags.

"Out here," comes Lu's voice. I dump the bags on the bench before heading out to the back deck where Lu is stretched out on the sun lounge, a glass of wine in one hand and a book in the other.

"Hey, what's happening?" I ask, standing beside her.

"Uh huh," she replies, not looking up at me, and clearly not listening to me either.

I reach down, take the glass from her hand and lift it to my mouth for a sip. Lu barely even notices. "Good book?" I ask, taking another.

"Yeah."

Shaking my head, I lean down and grab it from her hands, straightening as she scrambles from the chair, reaching for the book. Holding it high, I turn my attention to the page she was just reading, a slow smile spreading on my face when I see exactly what's captured her attention.

"Oh my god," I ask, half laughing. "You're reading porn?"

"No!" she says, even as a small blush starts to creep over her cheeks.

"You totally are," I say, smiling as I flick over the page, taking in the words.

"It's chick-lit," she says firmly. "Not porn."

I chuckle, shaking my head as I read from the page. "*His fingers slide down to my clit, rubbing in slow circles before…*"

"Give me that," she says, snatching the book from my hands.

I turn, reach and pull her against me. "Sure sounds like porn to me, Lulu," I tease. "You miss me that much you had to read this, huh?"

Lu rolls her eyes. "Actually," she says. "It's has an adorable Aussie character," she continues. "He's a perfect boyfriend and amazing in bed."

"Does it now?" I say, leaning in to kiss the end of her nose. "Bet he's not half as adorable as me," I tell her. "Or as good in the sack."

She swats at me with the book in mock annoyance. "He calls his girlfriend, *Pet*," she says. "Why don't you ever call me Pet?"

I burst out laughing. "Fuck me, are you serious?" I ask as Lu nods her head. "Jesus," I say. "Pet is what my eighty-year-old grandma calls the nurse who comes to help her each week," I continue. "It is not a term of endearment, nor something any self-respecting Aussie guy will say."

"Really?" Lu asks, confused.

"Really," I repeat, grinning. "But," I continue, lowering my voice a little. "If you'd prefer I call you Pet..."

"Nope, no," she immediately says, cutting me off. "I do not need you channeling your grandmother when you're talking to me," she says.

My grin widens. "Good answer, Lulu," I whisper, kissing her mouth. "Now, let's go see if we can take advantage of all that porn you've been reading while I was gone."

"It's not..."

"Shhh," I say, cutting her off. "I'm busy thinking about how my fingers are about to slide down to your..."

Now it's Lu who cuts me off as her mouth presses against mine in a hard kiss. Groaning, I take the book from her hand, throwing it on the sun lounge as I wrap both arms around her waist and pull her against me.

Mirroring the words I've just read, I slip a hand into the top of her shorts, under her panties and between her legs where I discover just what reading this book has done to her.

"Jesus," I breathe out, as my fingers slide against her. "You're so..."

Lu groans at my touch, her eyes closing as her head falls back a little, exposing her neck. I press kisses along her jaw and down her neck, along her collarbone to her bare shoulder, biting it gently.

"Let's go inside," I murmur against her skin, even as I'm backing her up to the door, one arm around her waist, one hand inside her pants.

We make it as far as the dining room before I can't control myself any longer, letting go of her waist and undoing the button of her shorts. With fumbling hands, we both push them and her panties down, before Lu rips off her tank top and bra.

When she stands naked in front of me, I step back, running my eyes appreciatively over her body, taking in her flushed skin, her hooded eyes. Smiling, I slowly pull off my own clothes before guiding her back to the table with my hands on her hips.

"Lie back," I whisper, mouth at her ear.

She does and I step closer, a hand on each of her knees as I slowly push her legs apart. Leaning down, I brush my lips against hers before slowly kissing my way down her neck again and between her breasts, stopping briefly to lick and suck each nipple.

Lu arches off the table and I smooth a hand down her stomach, over her hip, urging her back down. Stepping between her legs, I continue my path of kisses, down to her stomach and over to her hip, gently biting the rise of her hipbone before kissing down her thigh to her knee.

Crouching, I kiss a path up her inner thigh until I reach the top, pausing before I press a kiss to the exact place she was just reading about.

"Fuck, Jack," she says, body arching again.

"Mmmm," I murmur as I slowly start to tease her with my tongue, alternating between licking and sucking until she's writhing against the table, fingers in my hair, gripping me tightly as though she's holding me in place.

"Ohh god," she says, her voice husky with desire. "God, Jack..."

She trails off with a moan as I slide a finger inside her and up the tempo with my tongue. I can feel her getting closer, her thighs clenching on either side of me, and goose bumps rising up on her now sweat-slicked skin.

"Tell me," I murmur, slipping a second finger inside her.

"Yes," she says, her voice echoing in the quietness of her house. "Oh god, yes, yes..."

And then I feel her, her whole body clenching around me as she lets go and lust washes over her. I slide my fingers out, moving them to take over from my tongue as I stand up and slide my dick inside her now, feeling the last of her orgasm as it crashes through her.

Leaning down, I cover her mouth with mine, slipping my tongue inside as I slowly start to move my hips against hers. With my free hand, I grab her ankle, lifting it and resting her foot on the table.

She mirrors the action with her other foot, widening her legs as I push even deeper inside her.

"God, fuck you feel so good," I tell her, hand on her hip as I start to move a little faster. She looks amazing spread out beneath me and I can't take my eyes off her, lifting my head so I can watch my fingers as they work against her and see everything this is doing to her.

We fuck for what feels like forever, the table creaking under the weight of our movements. With my fingers, I make her come again, Lu screaming my name as I up the tempo of my hips, my body slamming into hers.

Eventually, I can't hold back any longer, my hands gripping her ankles now, holding her against me as I throw my head back, my body arching into hers as I come and her name falls from my lips in a low growl.

I collapse on top of her, our bodies covered in sweat, both of us breathing hard.

Moving my mouth to her ear, I can't resist saying, "Now tell me your real-life Aussie boyfriend isn't a million times better than that fake one you were reading about...*Pet*."

Lu bursts out laughing, her mouth on my neck as she slides her hands up my back. "You cheeky shit," she says as I lift my head and meet her stare, a huge grin on my face.

"Come on, admit it. You know it's true."

She grins back at me as she locks her legs around my waist and contemplates her answer. "Well," she starts, biting her bottom lip. "Better, yes."

"Better?" I repeat. "Just...*better?*"

Lu laughs. "Well, I might need some further study on the matter," she says, cocking her head in invitation.

I slip my arms beneath her, pulling her up so she's in my arms, legs still wrapped around me and our bodies still joined. "Now who's the cheeky shit," I murmur before walking us back to her bedroom.

A couple of hours later, we're in Lu's kitchen putting something together for dinner, both of us well and truly sated.

"It's kinda quiet without the two O's around isn't it," I say as I throw some steaks onto the hot pan.

"Who?" Lu asks, handing me a glass of red wine.

"The two O's," I repeat. "Oscar and Ollie."

Lu laughs. "Yeah, it is. Same when they go back to school."

I watch as the meat sizzles on the pan, monitoring the time so I can flip them to create the perfect medium rare. "I actually kinda miss them," I admit. "Even if they're nosy little buggers with incredibly bad timing."

Lu doesn't say anything and when I turn to look at her, I see she's leaning against the bench, silently watching me.

"What?"

She shrugs, biting her bottom lip for a second or two before eventually saying, "You're really good with them, you know."

I shrug, because it's no big deal, before flipping the steaks.

"You ever think about having kids?" she asks, surprising me a little.

I keep my eyes on the steaks for a few seconds longer, pressing them with the tongs to check if they're done before switching off the gas. "Yeah, I've thought about it," I say, shooting her a glance. "You?"

"Mmmm hmm," she says.

I slide the pan to the side and leave the steaks to rest for a few minutes before turning back to Lu. Leaning against the bench, I take a sip of my wine before asking, "What does *Mmmm hmm* mean?"

Lu swallows, stalling a little by moving the salad she was just mixing to the island where our plates and cutlery are, not looking at me. When she moves back toward the stove, I reach for her, a hand on her hip as I pull her to me.

"I've thought about it," I say, tilting her chin so her eyes meet mine. "And it's something I want, one day," I add.

Lu nods, her whispered, "Me too," barely audible.

I smile, lean down and brush my lips against hers. "Well, it's good we're on the same page then, isn't it?" I say, before moving back to the stove and dishing up the steaks.

We eat in silence for a few minutes, neither of us elaborating on the somewhat major and potentially life-changing discussion we've almost just had. While it's true, it isn't something I want right now, it doesn't stop my mind from wandering to the future, to a time when there's a mini Lulu running around this house with us.

It feels surreal just to think about it and not just because I have no idea how to make that future a reality.

"Tell me why you took this job?" she suddenly asks, interrupting my fantasy of domestic bliss.

I look up at her, flashing her a smile. "So I could look you up," I say, as though the answer is obvious.

Lu smiles, but I can tell she's not really buying it. "Sure, but why did you leave Australia?" she asks. "I mean, why'd your job end and why were you able to come here?"

I exhale a long, slow breath, putting my knife and fork down as I contemplate how best to answer her. "Generally speaking," I start, "I don't stay at one winery too long. Usually I'm brought in to get things started or fix up a production. I'll do my thing, take someone under my wing and train them up and then move on."

Lu nods. "But this time?" she asks, and I can tell she knows there's more to it than just finishing up a job.

"This time," I say. "I wanted to leave for other reasons. Wanted to get as far away as possible to be honest."

"Why?" she asks, her voice quiet.

I smile at her, reaching for her hand. "I got involved with someone," I say, knowing I owe her some sort of explanation even if it's the last thing I feel like talking about. "It didn't end well and it was awkward as fuck being around her there. I needed a break and this...this came up. It felt like...I don't know, perfect timing, a sign, the right thing to do."

"She worked at the winery?" Lu asks and I know exactly what she's thinking now. Mixing business with pleasure; how if it couldn't work out with this other girl, how the hell is it going to work out with Lu.

I shake my head. "No, she didn't," I tell her. "She was the sister of the one of the workers. She worked in town but we all ran in the same crowds, it was impossible to avoid to her."

Lu exhales, relaxing the tiniest bit when she understands that it's a different situation to us. "How long ago did you break up?" she asks.

I scrub a hand across my jaw, not taking my eyes off her as I answer, "About four months before I came over here," I tell her, even though it feels like both a lifetime ago and only yesterday that it all happened.

Lu nods, biting her bottom lip as she stares back at me. Pulling my stool closer to her, I reach for her other hand, lifting them to my lips and pressing a kiss to the back of each hand.

"It was over long before that," I tell her, knowing it's the truth even if I didn't know it at the time. "And it was over long before I was with you."

She nods again but still doesn't say anything.

"It's nothing like this, Lu," I say, needing her to understand how different this is, how different we are. "You and me, we…we have history and friendship and…" I pause, wondering how best to explain this without freaking her out or admitting more than I think either of us is ready for.

"We have a connection," I say settling on that. "We've always had that."

Lu smiles now, a tiny smile that tugs at the corner of her mouth. "Yeah," she whispers, squeezing my hands.

"I love that about us," I say, skirting dangerously close to unknown territory here. "And I don't…"

My phone ringing cuts through the moment, interrupting my almost confession and startling us both.

"Fuck," I say, glancing at it as it sits on the counter.

Unknown number flashes on my screen, the shrill ring tone cutting through the silence of the kitchen. I make no move to answer it and it eventually goes to voicemail.

Turning back, I find Lu watching me, a strange look on her face that has me wondering if she hasn't read my mind and heard all the things I can't admit to her out loud.

Chapter Twenty-Six

Lauren

The phone rings for a third time, but Jack has now shoved it in the back pocket of his jeans, making no move to look at it.

And when the person calls for a fourth time, I ask, "Do you think you should answer that?"

Jack's usually tanned face has turned a pale shade of white, his eyes telling me that the person on the other line is not someone he's willing to give his time to. There's something he's not telling me.

He lets out a hard sigh before pulling the phone from his pocket and answering with a clipped, "Hello."

He's silent after that, but I watch his already pale face take on an even paler shade of white as I hear the muffled sound of the person's voice on the other end.

Seconds after answering the call, he hangs up and looks back at me, making me question what just happened.

"Who was it?" I ask, my curiosity eating away at me, building something up in my head that's probably far worse than the reality.

"Just one of those recordings. Something about a car warranty," Jack replies, but he struggles to get the words out, and the color has yet to return to his face.

"You sure you're okay?" I ask, not trying to pry, but this is the first time I've seen Jack react anything but casually.

"Yeah, yeah, all good."

I don't push the conversation any further. As much as my thoughts are swirling, and I know the phone call was more than just a telemarketer by the look on Jack's face, I can't bring myself to ask anything more.

I take our empty plates from the table and walk over to the sink as Jack comes up behind me and slips his arms around my waist. He presses his lips to my neck and I turn in his arms, my back now against the sink.

"So, why'd you and Nate break up?" Jack asks and the question catches me off guard.

"You jealous?" I ask, deflecting the question away.

"Me jealous of that fuckwit? Never," Jack says pursing his lips and giving me a side eye as he tips his head and begins biting at my neck. "I just want to make sure you know you're mine," he growls in my ear and something about it is so fucking hot.

"Jack," I warn, because he knows exactly what he's doing to me.

"It took me this long to get back to you and I'm not going lose you again."

"You never lost me," I reply, pushing against him as I feel my heart hammering in my chest as the rest of the words settle heavy in my throat. They rest on the tip of my tongue, waiting to be said, but I swallow them down.

"Confession," I whisper, my heart slamming harder, wondering if Jack can feel everything he's doing to me. "You're the only guy to ever…" My lips are parted and it's difficult to get the words out, my breaths coming hard and fast. "To ever turn me on so fucking hard. Even when we were kids."

I had no idea what I was feeling at fifteen, but I knew I wanted Jack, that something about the way he teased me, about how angry he made me, made a fire burn inside my body. I wondered what it would feel like to have his hands on my body, to have him touch me, to explore me.

"Fuck, Lu," Jack hisses, his mouth now sucking and biting at my neck as his hands slide under my shirt. "You were so fucking hot at fifteen and time has been really good to you. I dreamt about you, about your body, about one day being inside you."

Jack's words, his accent, his hard muscled body pressed against me, everything about him sends my body into a tailspin.

"I had no idea it would be this fucking hot. You were worth the wait," Jack adds, his words low and deep and sexy as hell.

Neither one of us says another word.

We wake early the next morning, Jack going out for a run and me heading to the office before the property is busy with tours and visitors. With Ellen gone, I need to pick up the slack and payroll needs to be sent off to the bank along with making sure everything for the restaurant has been ordered.

I also have the couple who's wedding I booked a few weeks back coming in for a tour of the property and go over a few things with them like choosing a caterer and finalizing numbers.

My life is weirdly calm and the normalcy of having Jack here is something I've grown quite accustomed to. A part of me begins to wonder if he really will go back to Australia. We've created a life together in just a few short months.

The couple arrives just before nine o'clock. They're young and cute and excited, and I feel like they're exactly the reason I finally started booking weddings again.

They sit down across from me in the two chairs I have set up in my office and we begin to go through the day, the number of guests and the catering options. I share with them the promotional pictures we have on file of the multiple weddings we have hosted to give them an idea of chair set-ups and locations.

Everything is going smoothly and suddenly the door to my office opens, but I don't think much of it. People come and go throughout the day, especially Penny and our summer tour operators; dropping off invoices, picking up paychecks, and now with Jack here, he pops in from time to time.

But when I look up, I find Nate standing in the doorway, that smug smile on his face as he leans against the doorway.

I'm speechless, as I look back at the prospective wedding clients who are staring at Nate. I'm sure they're wondering exactly the same thing I am. *Why is he here?*

This is getting out of hand, and as much as I'm a consummate professional, I want to yell out *what the fuck* right now.

"Planning your wedding?" he asks nonchalantly, like he has a place in this conversation. "It's a beautiful place to have your wedding. We're having our wedding here too," he adds, motioning between him and me.

I'm absolutely fucking appalled at his audacity and his stupidity. He can't possibly be this self-absorbed and unaware of the body language and tension that is now filling the room.

"Oh my gosh, I didn't know you were getting married too," the young bride-to-be squeals. Like we're part of some ya-ya sisterhood traveling pants engaged girls tribe. Something I now realize I'm not sure I ever want to be a part of.

I guess I'm the only one giving off the *what the fuck* vibe.

"I'm sorry," I interrupt, glaring at Nate as he winks at me from his now posted position in the doorway. "You'll have to excuse me for a second." I shove away from my desk and walk to where Nate is standing and mutter, "Can I speak to you outside?" Keeping my voice low, but allowing my animosity to be felt through the bite in my words. I'm not exactly giving off an aura of excitement.

"I like to surprise her here at work," Nate says, chuckling a little as I shove past him. "She is my fiancé after all." He's smiling at the couple, but their faces are a cross somewhere between bewilderment and disgust. It's what I imagine my face looked like the first time Ellen explained to me that our parents had to have sex in order for us to be born. A conversation that goes down in my record books as one of the worst. But it's possible the one I'm about to have now just might top it.

When we're finally outside, away from my office and out of an earshot of the couple, I spit out, "What in the actual fuck are you doing here?" My foot stomping the ground with each word. "First of all, I'm with clients and this is so not appropriate. Second, we are not in engaged, we are not getting married, and I've asked you repeatedly to go away."

"How long are we going to do this, Lauren?" Nate asks, but it's his tone that pisses me off even more. It's casual, like I'm playing hard to get and he's just waiting around for me to come to my senses.

It's taking everything in me not to lose my shit and kick him in the dick.

"*We're* not doing anything," I hiss back. "We're nothing. This is all you, and I want no part of it."

"Fine, fine," he says, holding his hands up in defense as if he's going to concede that easily. "What's it going to take for you to forgive me? Just tell me and I'll do it."

I let out a long slow breath trying to control the anger that's burning inside me as I cross my arms over my chest.

"I forgive you," I say, my words laced with venom, sliding from my tongue. "And what I need from you," I watch as Nate nods his head, blissfully unaware of my hatred, "is for you to forget me, because as of this moment you're dead to me."

I stomp off, leaving him standing there, hopefully he's been knocked down a few pegs and finally gets it through his thick skull that I give no fucks about him.

Luckily the couple seems unfazed by Nate's unannounced and misguided appearance, and we continue uneventfully.

After gathering all the information we need to continue with the booking, we head out to the wedding ceremony site.

The last wedding it was set up for was mine. Everything has been stored in the shed off to the side for the last year; collecting dust and waiting for the moment when I had finally recovered.

I owe that moment to Jack. I know I made some mistakes, some big ones, but those mistakes led me to Jack. He was never a mistake.

I'm carrying a book of photographs that have been taken of the numerous weddings we've hosted. It gives the clients a better idea of what the empty space will look like or what it can look like on the day of their wedding.

Right now the space is just grass and grapevines and flowers, trees and tiny twinkling lights that don't shine as brightly in the daylight.

"The date you are looking at is totally open," I tell the couple, knowing that honestly every day for the next twenty years is open. Something I hope to change soon though. I think once I get through this first one, the rest will come more easily.

"We can do a day ceremony or a twilight one. I know it's hard to picture at twilight, but I have…"

"It's stunning at twilight," I hear Jack's voice call out and I watch him walk out from between a row of grapevines.

I'm smiling so wide my cheeks begin to hurt and when he walks up, I slip my hand into his giving it a quick squeeze before I let go.

"I've seen it done a bunch of times and it's far better than a day wedding. Show them the pictures, Lu," Jack says, tipping his head in the direction of the book I have tucked under my arm.

As I flip to the pages in the book, Jack walks over to the shed and unlocks it, pulling out a few chairs and setting them up.

We take a seat and the couple begins to thumb through the pictures, commenting and discussing as Jack fills them in on all the benefits to having a twilight wedding.

"The vineyard closes early on wedding days, so your guests will have full access to the property," I chime in, not that I think I need to sell them on it. They're both enamored.

"We also have two locations for the reception that will fit your party size. We have a fully restored barn or there's our restaurant. Like I said, the property will be closed to the public," I continue, as Jack also joins back in the conversation.

"Personally, if you go for the twilight wedding, the barn pairs well with it. Why don't we take a look at it? That cool, Lu?" Jack asks and I'm still smiling like an idiot as I watch him so naturally fit into this environment.

Jack and I take them through the barn, but don't move on to the restaurant as they decide they want the twilight wedding along with the reception in the barn.

It's a perfect choice for an August wedding and despite the short notice we should be able to pull it off beautifully.

"It was wonderful to meet you both," Jack says, shaking their hands. "But I have to get back to work; my boss is a bit of a stickler," he adds, tossing a thumb in my direction and giving me a wink. "I can't wait to see your wedding. I'm sure it will be stunning."

The couple thanks Jack for his help and I'm just as grateful as they are. I didn't realize I needed it, but having someone by my side, helping with these kinds of things, takes the stress off.

Jack just makes everything in my life easier.

"That's the one you're going to marry," the girl says, her face lighting up as she nods her head with certainty. "Not that other guy. You're perfect together."

"Thanks," I reply not sure exactly what to say. "The other guy is my ex and I'm really sorry that he showed up like that. But I'm glad we were able to take you around the property and get things settled for you. Like Jack said, your wedding is going to be stunning."

"I have no idea why you chose us to be the first wedding at the property, but we are beyond thankful. This is the only place I wanted my wedding and we've been holding out and hoping."

"You can thank Jack for that."

Chapter Twenty-Seven

Jack

I'm lying on my back, staring up at the darkened ceiling, unable to sleep. Lu lies beside me, a hand resting on my stomach, her long even breaths telling me she's in a deep, peaceful sleep right now.

I hadn't been entirely truthful last night when I'd finally answered my phone and for the past twenty-four hours, it's been bugging the hell out of me. The problem is, I don't know how to explain it to Lu, not when I can barely even understand it myself.

Jack, it's me, Mel, she'd started, stunning me into silence even though deep down, I knew it was going to be her when I answered. *I don't know why you're ignoring me, but you've left me no other option. I'm coming to see you. There are things you need to know, things...*

It was at that point that I'd hung up, too shocked to say anything, too freaked out to possibly believe it was true.

Could she really be coming here?

Although I'd acted like it was nothing, just an automated call from some warranty company or whatever, I could tell Lu didn't buy it. But I hadn't said anything more and instead, fired off a quick email to my parents as soon as I'd woken up this morning, asking them exactly what they'd said to Mel when she contacted them. I still hadn't received a reply and so I had no idea what or how much they'd told her. They knew we'd broken up, they knew the reasons why, but fuck knows what Mel had said to them. Had she made up some bullshit that somehow convinced them she needed to see me and so they'd told her exactly where I was.

"Fuck," I mutter, scrubbing a hand down my face in frustration.

Mel showing up here is the absolute last thing I need, and I knew, no matter what she had to say to me, nothing was going to change my mind about her or what had happened between us.

A repetitive ringing noise is what drags me from sleep and when I force my eyes open, I can see it's now daylight. It feels like I've been asleep for about five minutes and it takes me a second or two to realize what it is that's woken me.

By the time I put two and two together, the ringing has stopped. Reaching for my phone, I see the same *unknown number* message on my screen, signifying the missed call that I know has to have been from Mel.

I'm grateful Lu is in the shower, the sound of running water drifting through the closed door of her bathroom.

The phone rings again and I almost drop it in shock, fumbling a little as I quickly move to answer it.

"Hello?"

"Jack," comes my name, a long exhale telling me she's relieved I've answered this time.

"What do you want, Mel?" I ask, not bothering with a hello. "Why the fuck do you keep calling me?"

"Because you won't respond to my messages," she says, as though it's obvious. "You didn't even tell me…"

"I thought I'd made it abundantly clear I didn't ever want to speak to you again," I say, cutting her off. "I don't care what you have to tell me, Mel and I sure as shit don't want to see you."

"But, Jack," she says, her voice pleading. "I need..."

"No," I say, cutting her off again. "I don't give a fuck about what you think you need. You and I are over, so please, stop calling me."

"I..."

I hang up, just as the shower cuts off. My heart is pounding in my chest as I flick my phone to silent in case Mel still doesn't get the message and decides to call again. Guilt flashes through me at the secret I know I'm keeping from Lu, at how much it will hurt her if she ever finds out. Fuck, I can't even imagine what would happen if Mel does show up here and Lu discovers that I knew it was a possibility.

"Hey, sleepy," she says, smiling as she opens the door and walks into her bedroom, a towel wrapped around her body.

"Hey," I say, dropping my phone on the bed as I reach a hand to her.

Lu takes my hand in hers, sitting beside me as she leans in and kisses me. "You okay?" she asks. "You don't look so good."

I shrug. "I'm okay," I tell her, offering a small smile. "Just didn't sleep that well last night."

It's not a lie. Not exactly.

Lu returns the smile, leaning in to press a kiss to my lips again. "Why don't you stay in bed," she whispers against my mouth. "Try and get some more sleep?"

I slip my other hand into her hair, holding her against me. "I'll stay if you stay," I whisper, brushing my lips against hers.

She sighs, squeezing my hand. "I don't think you'd get much sleep if I stayed," she says.

"But it would be fun," I offer, kissing the corner of her mouth.

Lu pulls back, offering me an apologetic smile. "It would," she agrees. "But I can't. With Ellen away, I've got to…" she trails off as I sit up to face her, cupping her jaw in my hands.

"It's okay, Lu. I get it, seriously."

"You should stay though," she says, eyes flicking over my face as she smooths a hand over my cheek. "Take the morning off, boss' orders."

I smile even as I lean into her touch. "No, things to do, it's all good," I say, kissing her once more before I throw off the covers and head into the shower.

I spend the day on edge, my nerves frayed as I imagine every car that pulls into the carpark as being driven by Mel. I can't believe I'm even contemplating the possibility of her showing up here, but I know I have to. I know it's something she's capable of and the only thing I know is that I need to tell Lu about it before it actually happens.

The last thing I need is those two coming face to face with each other.

"Jack?" comes Tommy's voice, forcing me back to the present.

"Yeah," I say, walking out of the shed.

He nods, his expression neutral as he walks up to me. Although no more has been said about the whole Lu and me thing, I know he still has issues with it. Our conversations are strictly work related these days, but they're tense and it's obvious there's an unspoken hostility there, on both sides.

And while I know now it doesn't come from a place of jealousy, but as more of a big brother protective type of thing, it still pisses me off that he thinks I'm not good enough for Lu. That I could ever hurt her like he assumes I will.

"Looks like those parts have finally arrived," he says, handing me an invoice. "Earlier than we thought," he continues, even as my heart starts to pound in my chest at what this really means. "Means we can get that crusher back up and running and you can…"

"I can what," I say, my words harsh as I cut him off.

Tommy stares at me, his mouth set in a firm line. Eventually he shrugs, offering a, "get back to whatever it is you were doing before this," as though that's what he's really thinking.

I shake my head, shoving the invoice into my back pocket. "Where are they?" I ask.

Tommy tilts his head. "Up at the office."

I nod, swallowing hard as I wonder if this now means Lu knows they're here too. "Thanks," I say, before turning and walking off.

When I get up to the office, I see the two huge boxes sitting outside Lu's office. She isn't inside though, and I can't help but say a silent thank you that maybe she doesn't yet know.

Even though it's going to take me a week or so to install them, another week to put the crusher back together and maybe a week of tests, I know we've both been silently dreading their arrival. As though their delivery puts an end date on this thing that's been going on between us.

It's not what I want, not by a long shot. But at the same time, I'm still no closer to finding a way to change that.

Exhaling, I know staring at these boxes is not going to give me the answer, so I rope one of the guys into helping me and together we carry them back down to the shed. The invoice is still in my pocket, burning a hole there because I haven't left it on Lu's desk like I normally would.

After we unpack the boxes and I check everything is there, I call it a day, finishing up earlier than I normally would, because my mood has gone from on edge to well and truly pissed off.

As I walk back to Lu's house, my brain turning over the events of the last twenty-four hours, I can't help but think back to the other day and the tiny idea I had as I drove home from the supermarket. Pulling my phone from my pocket, I call up google and type the details into the search bar. When I get the information I'm looking for, I type in the number and hit call on my phone.

It's answered immediately, the woman announcing the name of her company and asking how she can help. I quickly explain what I'm after and we set up a time to meet later this afternoon.

After I'm done, I head inside to check over some figures on my laptop before sending an email to my dad, asking for both his advice and his interest in what I'm thinking about doing.

It's a ballsy move, but one I'm suddenly realizing, I'm actually prepared to take. And while it might actually be an answer to one of my seemingly ever-growing list of problems, I'm still not quite ready to tell Lu about it yet.

So after I grab the keys, I quickly type out a text letting her know I'm running some errands, before I jump in her car and head out to meet this woman, all the while the guilt of keeping yet another secret from Lu burns a hole in my gut.

On my way back from town, I stop off and grab us some dinner. I'm later than I thought I'd be and I'd texted Lu a few minutes back telling her I was on my way. She didn't ask what I'd been doing all afternoon and as much as I wanted to tell her, it was still too soon, for so many reasons.

So instead, I stop in and grab us a couple of pizzas and garlic bread, as well as a tub of her favorite ice cream before heading back to *Somerville's*.

"Hey," she says, as I walk into the kitchen where she's already pouring me a glass of wine.

"Hi," I say, leaning in to kiss her. "Should we eat outside?" I ask, nodding toward the back deck.

"Okay," she says, giving me a strange look, as though she's trying to decide whether she should ask. She doesn't and instead picks up our wines and some plates and follows me outside.

We silently grab some pizza and bread, an awkward silence settling around us. Eventually though, we both speak at the same time. Lu's, "Is everything okay?" almost lost in my confession.

"So, the parts arrived today."

"What?" she asks, pausing with a slice of pizza halfway to her mouth.

I swallow. "The last of the parts arrived today," I repeat, pulling the invoice from my back pocket.

Lu lowers her pizza to her plate. "Oh," is all she says, her eyes falling to the sheet of paper in my hands. She doesn't take it though and eventually I set it to the side. "So how long do you think it's going to take you to finish fixing it?"

I shrug, pulling off a piece of bread and putting it my mouth. "Couple of weeks," I say, chewing what now feels like a hard lump in my throat. "Couple more to make sure it's all okay."

Lu nods. "So, a month then."

She's still not looking at me, her hands in her lap now as her eyes stare at the invoice on the table.

"Lu," I say quietly. "Look at me. Please."

She finally lifts her head, her eyes meeting mine. Even in the low light of the setting sun, I can still see they are filled with tears.

"Babe," I say, reaching for her. She doesn't move though, doesn't lift her hand to meet mine like she'd automatically do every other time. "Lulu," I say. "Come here, please."

She stares at me for a few seconds before eventually standing, walking around to my side of the table and letting me pull her onto my lap. I press a kiss to her temple as I wrap my arms around her, pulling her close.

"This doesn't mean the end," I whisper, my mouth against her skin.

Her fingers knot together in her lap, her knuckles white. "But it does mean you're leaving," she says, and I can hear the sadness in her voice.

I press another kiss to her before gently turning her so she's facing me. "But not leaving you," I tell her. "I'm not leaving you."

A tear falls down her cheek now and it breaks my heart seeing her like this. I reach up, brushing it away with my thumb as she says, "But how are we going to make this work, Jack. We've spent every night together since this started and now what? You go back to Oz and I stay here and we spend every night apart until one of us can find a way to visit the other?" She stops, swallows hard before continuing. "That's not a relationship, that's not..." she pauses, swiping angrily at her eyes before meeting mine. "It's never going to work and I'm not sure either of us can make it work, regardless of how much we might want to."

I lean in and kiss her lips, silencing any more of her words. She whimpers at the touch, her body leaning into mine despite everything she's just said. I feel her fingers tighten in my shirt, my own arms as they tighten around her, both of us clinging to each other as though we can't bear the thought of ever letting go.

Eventually I pull back, knowing I owe her some sort of explanation, even if it's nowhere near to a solution.

"What if I said I was trying to come up with a plan?" I say, brushing the hair back from her face.

"What?" she asks, eyes searching mine.

"It's early days," I admit. "And nothing is sorted or set in stone, but I'm trying, okay?" I tell her. "Can you trust me that I'm trying, believe that I want this with you?"

Lu nods, even as a thousand questions flash across her face.

As much as I want to tell her what I'm doing, I know it's far too early and everything is still way too uncertain that I don't want to risk getting her hopes up, only to crush them when everything falls through.

"Do you trust me?" I ask, my words low.

"I trust you," she eventually says, biting her bottom lip.

I smile, lean in and brush my lips against hers. "And do you believe me?" I ask. "Believe that I want this, want you?"

Lu nods, her lips still pressed against mine as she murmurs, "Yes," before deepening the kiss.

And I kiss her back now, desperately, both of us seemingly overcome with some sort of urgency, as though we're hoping for the best, but preparing for the worst. Dinner is all but forgotten as Lu's hands slip under my shirt, mine doing the same, relishing the smooth warmth of her skin.

But despite the desire that now takes over, nagging at the back of my mind is the other secret I'm keeping from Lu. The one that has the power to destroy everything I'm trying so desperately to protect, to save.

Mel.

Chapter Twenty-Eight

Lauren

My morning is consumed with replanting an entire row of grapevines that were overtaken by last year's drought. Things like this went on the back burner after the wedding debacle, and even though I could have delegated these types of jobs, there was something in me that couldn't give up what I had done for so many years.

It was something Tommy and I did together, we always had and without question he joined me again today.

"Things feel normal again," I said as we worked side by side in a quiet steady rhythm.

"Things are normal again," he replied back and the conversation about what was once is finally laid to rest.

It felt really good to be out in the fields getting dirty and knowing that the normalcy of my life is back. My routine, something I thrive on, something I love, is creating exactly what I need and there's a familiar buzz within my body, an aliveness in my chest.

I'm back in my office when Jack shows up covered in grease and dirt and grape stains, at exactly 11:30, the time that has become designated as our lunch hour together.

"How's it going with the crusher?" I ask, trying to sound vague and casual. While knowing it's a long process, I also wonder how much longer he'll be around. I'm fishing for an answer to appease myself.

"Okay. It's still a mess, but I think I should be able to have it up and running in a week or so," Jack tells me, but continues as he takes in the look on my face. "But I'm going to need to stick around for at least two weeks afterward to make sure it's working properly."

I smile at him, and in the back of my mind I can't help but think he's dragging out his time here. There's no way it's going to take two weeks to see if the machine is working. He'll know the first few cycles if it's acting up, but I don't question his logic.

While my sigh of relief isn't an exhale of everything I'm holding on to, it is for the moment a relief of sorts.

A thought tugs at the back of mind as we eat, something Jack mentioned last night; an idea, a plan in the works, something that I gather is his attempt at salvaging what we've started here. We both know a long-distance relationship isn't feasibly possible; the distance too vast.

"Stop looking at me like that," Jack says plaintively, but a smile tugs at the corners of his mouth.

"Like what?" I ask, feigning innocence because I know he can see the wheels turning in my head, he knows I'm obsessing over him leaving and his lame ass story about needing to stay several weeks after the crusher is repaired.

"Like you know I'm lying," he admits and we both get a good laugh out of his honesty.

"You are lying, but I don't care. If I get to keep you around a little longer then lie all you want."

"Lu, I'll stay as long as you want me too."

His words make my heart skip a beat, fluttering in my chest and making my cheeks grow warm.

"We both know that's not true. I think you've got twenty-four months max since you're here on a J1 Work Visa."

My words hit me like a ton of bricks, smacking me in the face and the first thing I picture is Ellen. Ellen had to sponsor his visa. She's a damn liar too!

Jack's riotous laugh rings out in my tiny office and he leans over my desk, his hand slipping so he's cupping the back of my neck.

With his lips nearly touching mine he murmurs, "Guess you just realized Ellen set us up, huh?"

He presses his lips gently to mine, his tongue slipping out to trace my bottom lip and for a second I lose myself in him, forgetting that I want to murder Ellen in her sleep.

"You knew about this too?" I ask, my forehead resting against his, my thoughts clouded by Jack and his amazing mouth.

"Nah, but I hoped like hell you'd be here." His words are placating and calming, and he brushes his thumb against my cheek as he pulls back. "Ellen's last name isn't Somerville anymore so I assumed your family sold the business."

"You said you were going to look me up?"

"If you weren't still here, I totally was going to look you up."

"How?" I question, thinking after all these years I could've been married, changed my name like Ellen, left the state.

"Stalk you," Jack jokes and once again that playfulness is back between us.

As soon as Jack leaves my office, I pick up my phone and call Ellen. There's no way I'm letting this wait until she's back from Disneyland. She set me up and she damn well knows it, and while things definitely turned out for the better, I didn't need her inserting herself into my life. I was doing just fine on my own.

"Everything okay?" Ellen asks as a way of greeting me, not even realizing this has nothing to do with the vineyard and everything to do with her nosiness. Wonder where her kids get it?

"Here at the vineyard, yes, but with you and me, no," I snap, but as annoyed as I am with her for lying to me, I'm finding it difficult to keep up this feisty persona. Every time I want to lay into her, Jack's beautiful face pops into my head and I'm stunned into silence.

"What are you even talking about?" Ellen asks, letting out an annoyed huff and sounding very much like our mother.

"I'm talking about you lying to me."

"Lying to you about what?" she asks, but I know she's scanning her brain for all the times she's bullshitted me in the past.

Being the younger sister means you get shit on. It's the way the world works or at least the way it worked in our house.

Ellen outgrew clothes, and they became mine. Ellen stayed out past curfew, so mine was moved up an hour. Because she was the oldest she was privy to all the quiet little details that were whispered between her and our mother.

"You set me up and then you lied to me about it. You knew you hired Jack because you had to sponsor his visa. You knew it was him all along and you played dumb."

I hear Ellen exhale hard into the phone, the sound of her breath loud in my ear, as she says, "Listen Lauren, yeah, I knew it was him, well at least I thought it was, but there's way more to this..."

"More to your lies? Holy fuck, is this like one of those shitty teen comedy romances where you and Jack are in cahoots, like you paid him to date me but then he really falls in love with me." I'm pacing my tiny office, coming to the end of the room in about six steps and having to turn back around instantly.

"For fuck's sake, Ellen, you better not have made me the next nerdy outcast!"

"Jack *is* in love with you," Ellen cuts in trying to distract me from the real reason for my call.

"So you did set this up with him?" I ask, my voice coming across in a high-pitched whine, hating the fact that this wasn't possibly as organic as I thought it was.

"No. Shit, Lauren, settle down. Can you let me explain?" I nod my head in response to Ellen's question even though I know she can't see me. I'm trying to process this whole thing.

"When you asked me to find someone to fix the crusher I called Dad. I know we don't like to involve them in the business any longer, but we clearly had no idea who to contact to help us get that damn thing fixed. That's when Dad suggested I reach out to Tony, Jack's dad."

"Why didn't you tell me any of this?" I ask, wondering why she would keep this all from her business partner.

"Seriously, Lauren? I kept it from you because I knew you would be irrational, since you were still carrying around your unrequited crush on Jack Wilson." She laughs a little and I don't find her teasing funny in the least.

"Whatever," I respond, dismissing her and the idea that I would be irrational about anything.

"Can I finish now?" Ellen scolds, like she's talking to one of her kids.

"Yes," I reply annoyed.

"So, I was able to track down Tony through some old business associates that he and Dad have in common. Which led him to tell me he's also retired, but to contact his son. Now he didn't tell me his son's name and in my defense when I filled out the paperwork to sponsor Jack's visa, his name isn't actually Jack, it's John. I assumed it was possibly his brother or something."

"He's an only child," I tell her growing more annoyed with her stupid lengthy explanation. "Can you get on with it? You're getting old, Ellen. You tell stories like Mom does."

"Well, whatever. I felt like you could use a distraction from all the bullshit with Nate, something to remind you that you loved the vineyard and that you once loved someone other than Nate. So, I went through with it and hoped like hell it was Jack."

"That's the same thing he said to me," I mutter, my voice catching in my throat at her words as I realize maybe this was exactly how everything was supposed to play out.

"Said what?"

"That he hoped like hell it was me."

"Maybe some things are just meant to be," Ellen says, a kindness in her voice, a soothing tone that makes me feel like I might cry. "I didn't set you up, Lauren. I promise I didn't. I just wanted you to be happy again and if going out on a limb with a hunch I had was the way to it, I was willing to give it a try."

I don't know if I should thank her or cry or run and find Jack and confess that I do love him. I'm huge fucking mess right now thanks to Ellen and her meddling.

"Do you really think he loves me?" I ask her and she busts out laughing.

"Oh my god, not this shit again. You sure you don't want to send me a million emails detailing everything he's said to you so I can analyze it?"

"Fuck off," I say, laughing through the tears that have pooled in my eyes.

"I gotta go. Will drank this sangria in a glass the size of a fish bowl and is about to get on this spinning tractor ride with the kids. I'm pretty certain there will be puke, but I'll keep you posted."

"Send pictures if there is! And thanks Ellen."

"No problem. Glad I could talk you off the ledge."

"Fuck, why do you always have to have the last word?" I hiss, still living the life of the little sister at thirty.

"Because I'm older," she retorts and hangs up before I can say anything more.

Moments after I hang up with Ellen, Jack pops his head into my office.

"Hey sweets, I gotta run out and pick up a few tools that you're missing. Tommy's gonna go with me since we might have to hit up a few home improvement stores to find them."

"Glad to see you're getting along with Tommy," I say back, giving him a wink.

"Yeah, he's not so bad. You okay though? You look like you were crying."

"Nah, I'm all good. Just allergies, I guess. When do you think you'll be back? Don't forget we're closing up early today. We've got that private party."

"Oh yeah, thanks for reminding me. I'd guess we'll be back by five."

"Dinner?" I ask, standing up from my desk and making my way to the doorway where Jack is still standing.

"Of course," he replies leaning in for a kiss before he heads out the door.

I spend the rest of the day organizing the last minute details for the private party, like going over the menu with the chef and making sure the servers are prepared. The party will run itself and I leave my staff to do what they do best.

But just as I'm about to leave for the day a knock comes on the door to my office. It's a quarter to five and the party is set to arrive in fifteen minutes, so assuming it's a staff member with a last second question, I call out, "Come in."

The door opens slowly and in steps a tall leggy blonde with a bronze glow and piercing blue eyes.

"Can I help you?" I ask, wondering if she's with the private party and maybe she's taken a wrong turn.

"I'm looking for Jack Wilson," she says, her accent unmistakable. "The woman up front said I could find him here."

I fall silent and take her in. She's stunning and even though I can see the faint look of dark circles under her eyes, she's still far prettier than the average woman.

"Do you know where I can find him?" she asks again, seemingly growing impatient with my lack of response.

I shake my head waiting for my mouth to catch up with my brain and willing it not to boldly ask who she is and what business she has with Jack.

"He's not here right now."

"Do you know when he'll be back?"

She's very audacious for someone who has just shown up here unannounced, making it obvious that she and Jack have some history.

"We're closing in fifteen minutes, so you'll have to come back another time."

"I didn't ask when you were closing. I asked if you knew where I can find Jack," she chides, a hand now going to her hip as she straightens up, looking even taller than she already is. Her eyes growing narrow as she now rakes her gaze over me.

"I'm sorry, but whatever business you have with Jack will have to be done another time seeing as he's not here and we're closing."

It's now me standing with hands on my hips but looking far less menacing and far less beautiful. She's like *Land Down Under Barbie.*

She lets out an annoyed huff and runs a hand through her long blonde hair. "Can I leave a message for him then?"

"Sure," I reply, knowing this is the perfect way to find out exactly who she is without turning into a version of Ellen's nosy sidekick. I hand her a pen and a pad of paper and wait.

It only takes her a few seconds to jot down her information and she hands it back to me.

"I'll pass the message along to him," I tell her, possibly lying though my teeth.

"Thanks," she answers back, but her words are cold and she definitely isn't thankful she ran into me. Without saying anything more, she leaves.

I wait about a half a second before my eyes immediately dart down to what she's written on the paper, and it's then that I realize I'm holding my breath.

Chapter Twenty-Nine

Jack

It's almost five by the time Tommy and I pull back into *Somerville's*.

"You want to keep working tonight?" he asks as we head down the long drive toward the offices and sheds.

"Nah," I say, shaking my head. "Let's pick it back up first thing tomorrow," I say. "I've got dinner plans tonight."

"With Lauren?" he asks as he turns into the carpark.

"Of course," I say, glancing over as he switches off the engine. "Who else would my plans be with?"

Tommy turns in his seat, arm resting on the steering wheel as he stares back at me, an unreadable look on his face that I'm sure means he's about to lay into me again about my relationship with Lu.

"Look," I start, a hand up as if to preemptively stop anything he's about to say.

"Jack," Tommy says, cutting me off. "What is it that's going on here?"

"What the fuck does that mean?"

Tommy exhales, swallowing hard as though to calm himself down a little. "I mean, what exactly is going on with you and Lauren?"

Now it's me exhaling. "And how exactly is that any of your business?" I ask, wondering how the fuck we can go from being totally amicable in town to practically wanting to punch each other in face right now.

"There's stuff you don't know," he says, a weird look on his face, almost as though he's happy about the fact that he knows more about Lu than me. "Stuff with…"

"With Nate?" I cut in, an eyebrow raised.

"You know about him?" Tommy asks, obvious surprise on his face.

I nod, not bothering to elaborate.

"So, you know how he…"

Tommy's words are cut off by someone knocking on the window behind me. I see Tommy's eyes move to whoever it is, a look of confusion flashing across his face.

I turn, everything somehow in slow motion now as I take in the person standing outside my door, the pissed off look on her face as she stares down at me, hands on her hips.

"Fuck," I mutter.

"Who is that?" I hear Tommy ask, but I don't bother answering as I open the door and get out of the car.

"What the fuck are you doing here?" I ask, standing up.

Mel moves closer, as though to kiss my cheek and I instinctively pull back. "Jack," she says, a sadness in her voice that I just don't believe.

"What are you doing here?" I repeat, moving to the side so I'm not trapped between her and the car.

"You wouldn't answer my calls," she says, fingers playing with her hair. "Or my emails."

I let out a humorless laugh. "What and you didn't get the hint?" I ask.

I hear Tommy get out of the car behind me and I know that as much as I don't want to talk to Mel right now, I absolutely do not want Tommy talking to her or witnessing any of this either.

Turning, I stare at him across the roof of the car. "You mind giving us a sec?" I ask, gesturing behind me. "I'll catch you tomorrow?"

Tommy's eyes move from me, to Mel, then back to me again, an unreadable look on his face. Eventually he nods, his simple, "Sure," doing nothing to relax my nerves or reassure me that he isn't going to go straight to Lu and tell her about this.

I nod and he turns and walks away, glancing back once as though he still isn't sure what he's doing is a good idea. When he's far enough away, I turn back to Mel.

"Listen, Mel," I start. "You have no right to come here like this, no right to confront me about not answering your calls or..."

"I'm pregnant," she blurts out.

My stomach immediately turns, bile rising in my throat as a thousand images flash through my mind, none of them good.

"You're what?" I say, the words catching in my throat.

"I'm pregnant," she repeats, hands moving to her stomach.

My eyes travel down, resting on her hands clasped over her still flat stomach. "Well, it's clearly not mine," I say, swallowing the knot of tension. "You and I haven't..."

"It's Aiden's," she says, as though that somehow explains everything.

"Who?"

Mel takes a deep breath, looking down at her feet before finding my eyes again. She offers a small smile, which I don't return. "Aiden's," she repeats. "He was one of the fruit pickers."

I shake my head. "No idea who he is," I say. "Or why the fuck this has anything to do with me."

"Jack," Mel says, stepping toward me, a hand out as though to reach for me. My hands go up automatically, as though to stop her from coming any closer. She lets out a long breath, nodding once before continuing. "He and I were together only a few times," she says. "And then he left, moved on when the season ended."

My head falls back as I suck in a deep breath, pinching the bridge of my nose. When I lower my head, I see Mel is watching me, a mix of sadness and apprehension on her face.

"Why are you here?" I ask again. "Why do you think any of this has anything to do with me?"

She moves closer again, slowly this time and I freeze, mentally willing her to stop, to back the fuck up and not come anywhere near me. Not to touch me. "I miss you," she says now, her words barely audible. "What we had was good," she continues. "And I miss that."

A hard laugh escapes me. "You miss me?" I ask, incredulous. Mel nods. "Right," I say, my voice dripping with sarcasm. "And what we had was so fucking good that you had to go and cheat on me?" I continue. "With my best fucking friend."

"Jack," she says, reaching for me again, her hand surprisingly quick and strong as it latches onto my arm. "I love you," she whispers.

I shake my head, pulling my arm from her grip. "No, you don't," I tell her. "You miss the idea of us, of someone being there for you," I say. "But you know what, I'm done with that. I was done the day I walked in on you and Matt."

Mel stares at me, a look of hurt and confusion on her face. "But that was a..."

"Go home, Mel," I say, cutting her off. "Just go home."

I turn now, not wanting to hear another word. My eyes move to the door to Lu's office, where Tommy is standing, arms crossed over his chest as he watches us. I have no idea what he's still doing here or worse still, how much of this he's heard, but I don't bother to stop and find out.

Instead, I slide my hands in my pockets and head down the long drive, past the sheds and toward Lu's house, unsure if I should head back to my place or head inside and see her.

I'm not sure if she knows Mel is here looking for me or not.

And I'm not sure how the hell I'm going to explain it anyway.

By the time I reach the cottages, I've decided to head inside and take a shower, stalling a little longer while I try to get my thoughts and head together.

"Hey," Lu calls out and turning, I see her stand from the chair she's sitting in on her front porch.

"Hey," I say, forcing a smile as I subtly turn and head toward her place.

"You okay?" she asks, hands on the railing as she watches me take the stairs.

I nod, not trusting myself to voice the lie. She watches as I walk up to her and pull her into my arms. I feel Lu's hands slide around my waist and for a second, I can almost forget that my cheating ex-girlfriend has shown up here, pregnant with another man's child and somehow still expecting me to take her back.

For a second, I can almost believe it's just Lu and me still.

"Jack, what's wrong?" she asks, pulling back a little. "You're shaking."

I swallow hard, unable to look at her. "Yeah," I start, swallowing hard. "It's um, I…"

I feel Lu's hands slide up my sides, curling around my ribs. "Is it something to do with the woman who came looking for you today?"

My head shoots up. "How…what…" I stammer, not sure which question I want to ask her first.

Lu's hands drop to her sides now, no longer touching me as she takes a step backward, the small gap she creates between us suddenly feeling huge.

"She came into the office," she says, eyes on her feet. "She was looking for you, was asking about you."

"Lu," I murmur, reaching for her.

She steps back again. "Who is she?" she asks.

"Lu," I repeat, reaching for her hand and pulling her back to me. "She's no one," I add, as I tilt her face to mine.

Lu shakes her head. "She isn't no one, Jack," she says sadly. "She's come all this way, all this way for you."

I take a deep breath, never turning away from Lu as I nod once. "I don't know why she's come here," I say. "Truly, I don't."

"Who is she?" she repeats.

"She's my ex," I admit. "The one I broke up with months before I came here."

Lu stares up at me, her eyes sad as they search my face. "If you broke up with her, why is she here?" she asks, as though she can't possibly understand. As though she actually thinks I'm lying to her about the status of my relationship with Mel.

"Babe," I whisper, stepping even closer, desperate for her to believe me. "I'm not with her. I haven't been with her for a very long time," I say, my words pleading. "And I have absolutely no desire to be with her now or ever again. It's you I want, Lu," I whisper, leaning down so my forehead rests against her. "Only you."

Lu's head falls forward now, so it's resting against my chest. I lean down and press a kiss to her hair, inhaling the now familiar scent of her shampoo.

"She's very beautiful," she says, her words quiet.

I step back, cup her face in my hands as I lift her eyes to mine again. "What did you say?" I ask, needing her say it again so I can make sure she hears my answer.

"She's very beautiful," she repeats.

"Lu," I start, pausing as I lean in and press a soft kiss to her lips. "You are the only woman I see, the only woman I want to be with, okay?" I say. "And to me, you are the most beautiful woman in the world."

Lu stares up at me, her eyes filled with a sadness that breaks my heart. "Really?" she whispers.

I smile now, leaning in to kiss her again. "Really," I say against her lips. "More than anything," I add, before deepening the kiss as I try to prove it to her.

Later that night, we're lying in bed, the darkness of her room occasionally interrupted as the light breeze blows the blinds, lifting them and letting in the moonlight.

Lu lies against me, her body pressed into mine, her arm lying across my stomach. I trail a hand up and down her spine, neither of us saying anything, but neither of us able to sleep either.

I feel her sigh against me, her hand sliding over my ribs.

"What do you want to ask me?" I murmur, my lips pressed to her hair.

"What?" she asks, lifting her head a little.

I smile at her, brush the hair back from her face before she lowers it to my shoulder again. "What do you want to ask me about her?" I ask again.

Lu says nothing for a minute or two, but I know that's only because she's trying to work out what to ask. Beside me, I can feel her heart, pounding in her chest as it lies pressed against mine.

"Why did she come here?" she asks, repeating her question from before.

I exhale, long and low as I push a hand through my hair, my eyes on the ceiling as I try to work out how to answer that question.

"Honestly," I eventually say. "I'm not really sure," I start. "She says she wants us to get back together, but I don't actually think that's true."

"Why?" she asks, shifting a little so her chin rests on her arm, which now lies across my chest.

"Why what?" I ask. "Why she wants to get back together or why I don't think that's true?"

Lu shrugs. "Both, I guess."

I smile a little, my fingers brushing against her cheek as I stare at her. Despite the darkness, I can still make out her features, her wide blue eyes as they stare up at me, waiting.

"I don't think Mel knows what she wants," I start. "And I think she often thinks it's the things she no longer has, the things she threw away when she got bored or whatever."

"Is that what she did with you?" Lu asks. "Threw you away?"

I chuckle, but it's without humor. "Sort of," I say. "Although I don't think she actively tried to do that, she just fucked up and that's what ended up happening."

"What exactly did she do?"

My thumb smoothes across her cheekbone, my calloused skin rough against the softness of hers. "She cheated on me," I finally admit. "A lot."

"Jack," she says, lifting a little as she shuffles closer. "I'm sorry," she says, a hand on my cheek now.

I offer her a smile. "It's okay, seriously," I say. "We were never going to work out anyway."

"Why?" she whispers.

I slide my hand down her spine and around her waist, pulling her up my body so her mouth is against mine. "Because she isn't you," I say. "And you are all I've ever wanted. Ever since I was fifteen years old."

Lu whimpers now and I silence any more of her questions with a kiss, my lips hungry against hers, desperate for her to believe me.

She moves, rolling her body so it's on top of mine, her skin warm, her heart still pounding in her chest, mirroring what's happening in mine.

"I want you, Lulu, only you."

Chapter Thirty

Lauren

It's still early but the light from the rising sun is beginning to cast its shadows around the room as it filters though the slats in the blinds. But it isn't this that woke me. It's my obsessive tendency to focus on Jack's ex-girlfriend and the reason she's flown across the damn Pacific Ocean to find him.

She's the upgraded version of me, the better model with all the bells and whistles. She's Lauren 2.0; the hot Australian version because hell, there must be something in the water there to crank out people who look like Jack and his femme bot ex.

I have far more questions than I'm willing to let myself ask and I try to flush them from my mind as Jack stirs next to me.

"You up already?" Jack asks, his voice hoarse with sleep as he reaches his arms above his head and stretches.

"Yeah, I should probably get an early start with the party last night and everything."

I'm trying to be casual, but what I really want to tell him is that of course I'm up already. I've been up for the last hour wondering who the hell Melissa is and why she's come and uprooted what has become my new normal.

I never gave Jack the note she left him, not that it said anything, just her name and a phone number. It's still folded up in the back pocket of my jean shorts waiting for me to be honest with him and hand it over.

"You okay?" Jack questions, his hand sliding over my bare stomach as he rolls toward me. "I know you're not so don't tell me you are."

I shift away from him and climb out of bed. Grabbing for my shorts that are lying on the floor next to the bed, I pull the note from my pocket and hand it to Jack.

I can't look at him while he reads it over, but I hear him crumple it up and toss it over to the small wastepaper basket. It lands with a soft thud and my eyes are drawn to it.

"That note is no use to me," Jack announces, his tone now harsh. "I have no interest in what she has to say."

"But she wants to talk to you."

"I don't care."

Jack is now sitting next to me on the bed, his arm slipped around my waist and my head falling softly against his chest.

"I've told you everything," he whispers into my hair. "I wouldn't lie to you. You're all I've ever wanted, and it doesn't matter if she comes back a million times, the answer will always be the same."

I nod slightly and Jack shifts, his fingers under my chin as he lifts my face so I'm looking at him.

"You have my heart, Lu. It's been yours for fourteen years. She can't take what was never hers to begin with."

Again I nod, remembering what it's like to lose something even when it was never yours. But this time, I'm certain this loss would destroy me.

The morning passes slowly and at our regularly scheduled time, Jack appears in the doorway to my office wearing his cheeky smile and holding two takeaway containers.

"You free for lunch?" he asks, teasingly holding up the containers.

"For you, I guess," I reply back shrugging my shoulders and giving him a hard time, but making his smile grow. Any visitors?" I ask as Jack sits down.

"Nope and hopefully there won't be."

"I agree," I say, this time adding a firmness to my voice that is my attempt at convincing myself to move on. Dwelling on this is getting me nowhere and Jack has never once shown me that he isn't fully committed to what we have together.

I'm done being stupid.

Jack and I chat while we eat with Jack filling me in on how things are going with the crusher and his attempts at dragging out his time here. He's still eluding at some big plan, but won't give me all the details.

"Well, I gotta get back to work," Jack says, collecting up our garbage as he leans over and kisses me.

"We should go out to dinner tonight," I say, smiling at him and getting in another kiss before he walks away.

"Yes, let's."

Just as Jack is walking out Tommy is walking in. He greets Jack with a curt nod of his head but neither of them says anything.

If Jack's going to stick around, this shit has got to end.

"Lauren, you got a minute?" Tommy asks, glancing over his shoulder to see if Jack has walked away.

"Yeah, what's up?"

"You know we're like family, right?"

"Yeah."

"So last night when Jack and I got back from picking up the tools a girl was waiting for him out front."

"Yeah, I know," I reply, trying ease Tommy's mind that something isn't going on behind my back.

"Oh good. I wasn't trying to rat on Jack, but with what happened in the past, I didn't want you to be left in the dark."

"She came to the office looking for Jack, but you guys were gone. And then later on Jack and I talked about it. She's his ex."

"I think she's pregnant," Tommy says, catching me off guard and suddenly my legs feel like I'm standing in a stream of rushing water. They're weak and struggling to keep my body upright.

"What?"

"I overheard a conversation between them, so I don't have the full details."

I'm now staring at Tommy. He's never once done something to hurt me and right now I'm wondering what his motives are for sharing what he overheard.

"I don't want you to make the same mistake you made before; putting everything you have into a person and have them turn out to be not what you expected."

"That's all this is?" I ask, my mind spinning with everything that is happening. "You're not trying to get rid of Jack, because that's what it feels like."

"Lauren, I didn't come here to argue with you or upset you. We both know that having Jack here has brought out all the good things in you again."

"So why'd you tell me then?"

"Because I think there's more to this ex-girlfriend story than Jack's letting on."

"Well, I'm going to go find out then," I shoot back, my sudden rush of shock now replaced with anger as I push away from my desk and storm out of my office.

"Jack," I call out, my voice echoing across the vineyard as I watch Jack walk back toward the sheds.

He doesn't hear me so I shout again, my hands cupped around my mouth, but this time I hear someone call my name in return.

When I turn around I'm face to face with Nate in a well-tailored suit and an idiotic smile on his face.

He has got to be fucking kidding me!

Between Jack's ex and now mine, this nightmare is never going to end.

"What do you want, Nate?" I hiss, my eyes darting away from him as I watch Jack make his way back over to us. He didn't hear me the first time I called him, but obviously he did the second time, the time that I didn't want him to.

"I want you, Lauren and I'm determined to win you back."

I roll my eyes but watch as Nate drops to one knee and pulls a small box from his pocket.

"What the fuck are you doing? Seriously, Nate. Get up!"

It's all happening in slow motion; Jack walking toward us, Nate down on his knee as he pulls the engagement ring from the box. I watch his lips move, but hear nothing he says. And as if the universe is trying to fuck with me, Jack's ex Melissa appears out of nowhere too.

This is not happening to me.

"Lauren, Lauren," Nate calls as if I'm standing miles away from him. "Will you marry me...again?" He thinks this whole thing is one big fucking joke, and he clearly can't read the expression on my face.

At this point he's now standing in front of me, reaching for my hand, but I pull it away.

I look to where Jack was and he has now stopped, taking in the scene as it unfolds in front of him. He's far enough away that he can't hear what's being said and his eyes flick from me to Nate and then to Melissa who is walking over to him.

In my confusion, Nate takes my hand and that's when Jack storms over with fury written all over his now redden face.

But he doesn't stop, just walking right past the shit show of stupid Nate in his suit with my old engagement ring in his hand.

"Jack," I call after him, jogging to catch up, but Melissa steps in between, setting herself up in my way like the seemingly immovable Amazon woman force that she is.

"Let him go. I think you've done enough, don't you?" she says, her accent as apparent as the condescending tone in her voice.

"Me?" I hiss, my face only inches from hers as I push up on my toes. "You're the one who showed up here unannounced and unwelcomed..."

I feel a hand grab the back of my arm and tug me away from her, but I pull away from it.

I whip around and this time shout, "And Nate, get the fuck out of here! I can't say it again."

This is my place of business, this is my relationship and I'm watching it all go down in flames with this embarrassing display of chaos.

I walk away from both of them, following in the direction that Jack went in hopes of finding him and salvaging this mess.

But after several hours of driving around looking for him, multiple text messages and non-stop calling, I come up short. A part of me even toyed with the idea of reporting the car Jack left in stolen just to get the police to track him down.

When I finally return to the vineyard Melissa is gone but Nate is sitting on the steps to my house.

I'm absolutely floored at his audacity and his ability to not read a situation for what it is.

"Nate, you need to go. This is over," I say, making an attempt to step around him to get to my front door.

"At one point you were going to marry me, Lauren. It wasn't that long ago," he says, desperation dripping from his words.

"It was a long time ago. A year ago practically and there's a reason it didn't happen. It was never meant to happen, Nate."

"I made a mistake," he pleads.

"So did I. It was that I ever agreed to marry you in the first place."

It's with those words that I move past him and into my house, slamming the door behind me.

I can only hope that this is the last I see of Nate, because there's no way Jack is going to stick around while I deal with my idiot of an ex-fiancé.

Hindsight is twenty-twenty; you hear it said all the time, but it's so damn accurate. Even if Jack weren't in the picture, I wouldn't consider the idea of getting back together with Nate.

I see things for what they are now, and at the time, I think I knew Nate was cheating on me, that he would never be faithful. That he couldn't understand my dedication to the vineyard or my relationship with Ellen or that above all, I just wanted to feel a completeness with someone else.

In the end it was all of those reasons why he didn't show up to our wedding. And maybe he knew all along that I gave my heart away a long time ago. I was an easy target.

I walk into my bedroom, pulling the long white box from under my bed and staring at it as I wonder why I even kept it.

It's the one thing I didn't purge from my life.

But that's about to change.

The bottom of the dress is still speckled with a pale shade of green from where the grass brushed along it. There was no point in getting it cleaned; I was never going to wear it again.

I step into it, sliding my arms in and taking a quick look in the mirror before the tears start.

It was stupid of me to even keep it, a strange attachment to the dress, but not to the event or the person, but the dress and only the dress.

And I'm sitting on the floor of my bedroom in my green stained wedding dress ugly crying when Jack walks in the door.

Chapter Thirty-One

Jack

Of all the ways I thought today could've gone down, this is not it. I'm not sure exactly what I expected when I woke up this morning, especially given my ex-girlfriend had decided to jump on a plane and inform me that she wanted another shot, despite the fact she was pregnant with another man's child.

It was bad enough when Lu's fuckhead ex had decided to make an appearance, dropping to one knee in what I'm assuming he thought would be some romantic display of his intentions. But to have Mel show up and once again fuck things up, well I thought that was going to be the icing on the fucking cake.

But as pissed off as I was with everything that had gone down today, when I'd disappeared this afternoon, it was so I could get my plans in order and finally prove to Lu that she was all I wanted and that here with her is exactly where I want to be.

Never in my wildest dreams did I imagine that things could get any worse.

But no, they could. They could actually get a lot fucking worse.

"So not just an ex-boyfriend then?" I say, standing in the doorway as I stare down at Lu, sitting in a wedding dress on her bedroom floor, her cheeks wet with tears.

"Jack?" she says, her head shooting up.

I watch as she stands, furiously wiping under her eyes as she makes her way toward me, the look of hurt and confusion that crosses her face when I hold up a hand stopping her from coming any closer.

"Tell me, Lu," I say, my words harsh as I feel a vice wrap itself around my chest. "Are you still married to him or have you actually gotten divorced? Because I'm not one for sleeping with married women."

"Jack," she says again, stepping closer me. "It isn't like that," she adds, tears still streaming down her cheeks.

"Oh," I say, eyebrow raised. "What's it like? You're separated then?"

Lu nods, a small hiccup stopping whatever she was about to say.

"I see," I reply, taking a deep breath as I scrub a hand down my face. "And when exactly did it all end?" I ask. "Because married or not, I'm not really into sleeping with women who are still involved with other men either. I thought after what I'd told you last night, you'd have understood that?"

Lu stares at me, anger flashing across her face as her hands go to her hips. "Seriously?" she asks, practically spitting the word out. "You seriously think that's the kind of woman I am?"

I shake my head but say nothing.

Lu laughs, but the sound is harsh as she looks away. "Right," she says. "Well, I guess I didn't take you for the kind of guy who abandons his pregnant girlfriend either."

"What?" I half yell, stepping toward her. My hand finds her chin and I turn her face so she's forced to look at me. "What did you say?"

Lu stares defiantly back at me. "Your pregnant girlfriend," she says, the words cold, devoid of emotion.

"How the fuck did you know that?" I ask.

Lu cocks an eyebrow at me, as though how she knew is the last thing I should be worried about. "Tommy told me," she says, stepping back so my hand drops to my side.

"Fuck's sake," I mutter, both hands in my hair, gripping it tight. "That guy needs to mind his own fucking business when it comes to you and me, Lu."

"Oh, really?" she says, hands on her hips. "Because Tommy is one of the few people who's been here for me," she says. "When everything went to shit, he was here for me, keeping things running when I could barely drag myself out of bed."

I laugh, even as I shake my head in amazement. "Oh right, amazing wonderful Tommy," I say sarcastically. "If he's so damn amazing, why don't you get him to fix your fucking crusher. Then maybe you could start a relationship with him too and all your dreams will come true."

The smack is hard, the loud crack of skin against skin echoing in her room as she slaps me hard across the face.

"Fuck you, Jack," she says, her words quiet and filled with hurt, before she turns and walks out of her room.

I storm after her, reaching for her arm as she walks into the kitchen. "You do not get to walk away from me," I say, spinning her around to face me. "Not now, not after all this," I add, waving a hand in front of me as though that explains everything.

"And what exactly is this?" Lu asks, hands on her hips again as we stare at each other. "The whole me in a wedding dress thing or the pregnant Aussie Barbie femme-bot that's shown up here demanding you take her back?"

"The what?" I ask, unable to stop the smile, even as my cheek still stings with the reminder of what she just did.

Lu's jaw tightens as she stares back at me, refusing to budge.

I exhale, exhaustion suddenly washing over me. "Look," I say, hands out, palms up as though in surrender. "I have no idea what's happening here," I add. "But I do know that the child is not mine. I haven't been with Mel in over six months, Lu and even though it's been a long time since I studied biology, I'm pretty sure women are starting to show by the time the six-month mark rolls around."

Lu continues to stare at me, still not saying anything.

"And besides," I continue, walking over to her and closing the distance between us. "She told me who's it is. Actually admitted it wasn't mine."

Lu swallows hard now as she takes in my words. I can see all of the questions and emotions battling it out in her eyes as she dares herself to believe what I'm telling her.

"She cheated on me, remember?" I say, needing her to understand, to know what happened between us and why I will never ever want her back. "She did it a lot, with my best friend for fuck's sake. It's why we broke up."

Eventually Lu nods, her eyes softening a little as my explanation sinks in.

"I'm not that kind of guy, Lu," I continue. "I don't treat someone I care about like that and I sure as shit don't walk out on my responsibilities."

Lu's shoulders drop now, her hands sliding from her hips and falling to her sides. "I know you're not," she eventually says. "I'm sorry I thought that about you."

I nod, stepping a little closer and closing the gap between us. We aren't touching, neither of us quite ready to do that yet, but at least the hostility has dropped.

"So, you gonna tell me what this is all about?" I ask, waving a hand over the dress she's still wearing.

Lu looks down, her eyes moving over the white material. When she looks up at me, she bites her bottom lip, a move I now know means she's either nervous as hell or trying hard not to laugh. In this instance, I know it's the former.

"It's my wedding dress," she eventually says. "From when I was going to marry Nate."

I nod, even as I force myself to take a deep breath. "Right, so you were married to him then?"

"No," she says quickly, shaking her head as she steps near me.

"No?"

"No," she repeats. "We never actually got married."

"But you were going to?" I ask.

Lu nods now and I once again feel the blood pounding through my veins, an anger building not just at the idea she was ready to commit to someone else but that she couldn't even tell me about it.

After everything we've been through, all the years we've spent apart, both of us wanting the other but neither of us knowing how to make that happen. When I'd finally come over here and told her exactly how I felt about her, I'd thought we were both on the same page with what we wanted and how we felt about each other.

Confessing all the things that Mel had done to me last night felt like we'd reached a new level of commitment, that by admitting our past mistakes and fuck ups to each other, we were truly saying we trusted each other.

"Why didn't you tell me?" I ask.

Lu shrugs. "I don't know," she admits. "I guess a part of me was embarrassed about how it all went down," she says. "And that it didn't matter anymore because Nate was gone and you were here."

I shake my head as a harsh laugh escapes. "What, so because you and Nate were over and you and I were now together, the fact that you were going to get married is of no consequence? Fuck, Lu, you don't think I might have deserved to know that you were once engaged to someone else, were committed to spending the rest of your life with someone else!?"

I can feel my heart pounding in my chest again, my blood racing through my veins as my lungs fight to draw a breath. I can't even work out what it is that pisses me off the most right now. All I know is that I need to leave before I say something I regret.

"I don't think I can stay here right now," I say, shoving a hand through my hair as I turn and walk to the back door.

"Jack, wait," Lu cries, her hand on my arm.

I look back, shaking my head. "I need some space, Lu," I say, peeling her fingers from my arm, even as the tears start to fall down her cheeks again. Then I turn and walk out the back door, my heart no longer pounding, but instead feeling like it's cracking wide open inside my chest.

I don't go back to my place, but instead head over to the sheds, looking for something, anything to do that can distract me from the shit fight my day has turned into.

I'm relieved to see that Mel is not around and I can only hope she's finally gotten the message and pissed off back to Australia. What I really hope is that I never have to see her again.

It takes a second for my eyes to adjust to the darkness, but when they do, I see Tommy, standing beside the crusher as he attempts to install one of the parts.

"Fuck's sake," I say, walking over to him. "Can you not?" I ask, yanking the wrench from his hand.

"What the hell's your problem?" he asks, turning to face me.

I shake my head. "Jesus, really?" I ask in mock surprise. "Because you think sticking your nose into other people's business and telling Lu half-truths about shit you know nothing about, isn't bad enough?" I ask.

"What the fuck are you talking about?" he asks, hands on his hips.

I throw the wrench on the ground as I step toward him, mirroring his stance. "Telling her about Mel being pregnant," I bite out through gritted teeth.

"She deserves to know," Tommy spits back at me.

"It's not my fucking kid!" I shout back at him. "Did you ever stop to consider that before you decided to open your big fucking mouth?"

A look of genuine shock crosses Tommy's face. "What?"

I stare back at him, breathing heavily. "Yeah," I eventually say.

"But I heard, I..."

"You heard half a story, Tommy," I tell him. "From a woman who is well versed in spinning epic amounts of bullshit."

"Fuck," Tommy says, half turning away as he scrubs a hand down his face. "Shit, Jack, I'm sorry, really, I am."

I shake my head, unsure if I can really believe him. "Why'd you do it?" I ask. "Does me being with Lu really piss you off that much?"

Now it's Tommy shaking his head. "No," he says, turning back to face me. "The opposite," he admits.

"Then why?" I ask, confused.

Tommy exhales, hands sliding into his pockets as he meets my stare. "That guy, Nate," he starts, head nodding outside. "He and Lu were engaged once," he says, even as I nod in acknowledgement. "He left her at the altar, Jack. Couldn't even show up and admit what a spineless fucking shithead he was," he adds. "Just texted his mom and then fucked off, breaking Lauren's heart in the process."

"Shit," I mutter, my body sagging a little as his words sink in.

"Yeah," Tommy says. "She was a wreck for months after it happened," he says. "Even more so when she found out he'd been cheating on her too."

All of the anger I've been directing at Lu disappears in an instant, replaced by a burning rage that is directed squarely at that fucking arsehole of a man she used to call a fiancé. "I'm gonna fucking killing him," I say.

Tommy chuckles a little. "Yeah, join the line buddy."

I find myself pacing the shed a little as Tommy's words and the events of today all start to sink in. I can feel him watching me, saying no more as he gives me the space to try and make sense of it all.

Eventually I stop. "So why has he shown up here again?" I ask, confused about this last part, about what I saw today. "Why the fuck was he proposing to her?"

Tommy shakes his head. "Because he's a shithead," he says. "And he can't stand the thought of Lauren being happy, especially if it's not with him."

"Jesus Christ," I mutter, as I start my pacing again.

"She is, you know," he says.

"What?"

"Happy," he says. "With you," he adds, gesturing toward me. "She's different with you, Jack, we can all see it."

"What do you mean?" I ask, confused.

Tommy exhales. "With Nate, it was always just going through the motions, you know. As though she was settling for something that never quite fit. But with you, it's like, I don't know, you're just so in sync, it's impossible to imagine her with anyone else."

"Oh, fuck," I mumble, as I realize just how epically I might have fucked this all up. "I gotta go," I say, practically running to the shed doors. “Thank you,” I add. “And stay away from my crusher!”

When I get back to Lu’s house, the place is quiet, empty, with no sign of Lu or where she might have gone. Grabbing a sheet of paper, I scrawl out a note for her, telling her where to find me and begging her to give me a chance to explain everything to her. To apologize for being a dick about this whole thing with Nate.

Then, I walk out the door, hoping like hell she sees it and comes and finds me.

Chapter Thirty-Two

Lauren

Like being caught crying in my wedding dress wasn't embarrassing enough; I've misconstrued why Jack's ex is here, lied to him and now I've pushed him away. I did the one thing I didn't want to do, but a part of me wonders if this was my way of making him leave on my terms.

He didn't leave me.

I made him leave.

After I flung off my wedding dress, leaving it in a heap at my front door, I desperately chased after Jack. But in my haste to remove the toxic relationship-ruining dress, I gave Jack enough time to lose me.

I searched the vineyard for what felt like forever, but with a place this massive, it's easy to find a place to hide, and I wasn't about to go asking around to see if anyone had seen him.

With my red-rimmed eyes and swollen lips, it's obvious that I'd been crying and I didn't need any of my employees delving too deeply into my personal life. That's already happened once before; no need to make a habit of it.

I left in my car shortly after, driving to all the places I thought Jack might be, trying to remember what he loved when he was here all those years ago. But in the end, I come up short and eventually find myself pulling back into the vineyard on the verge of another breakdown.

When I reach my front door and open it, a gust of wind blows through, ruffling the white silk and tulle that lies crumpled on the floor. I kick at it with a rage that burns inside me.

I hate this fucking dress and everything it once symbolized.

I yank it from the floor, taking everything I feel inside me out on the dress, but damn this well-made piece of shit, because when I try to tear through the fabric with my bare hands, it doesn't budge.

"What the fuck!" I scream out loud, shaking the dress in front of me like a ragdoll.

Turns out it's far easier to destroy a wedding than it is the dress, but that doesn't stop me.

Dragging the dress behind me in a blind rage over how majorly I fucked up with Jack, and with how angry I am at myself for lying to him, for keeping this stupid dress in the first place; I heave it out the back door.

I return to the house paying attention to nothing but the fury I have and my need to rid my life of this fucking dress.

I grab a shitty bottle of red wine from the rack, knowing I'll never drink it, not even remembering where it came from, and I twist off the top as I widely stride to the open door that leads to my backyard.

Dragging the old metal garbage can from behind the shed, I shove the wedding dress into it as I hold the bottle of wine in my other hand, careful not to spill a drop.

Once the dress stuffed in, I take one long pull from the bottle of wine and pour the rest over the dress, watching the deep red color saturate the bright white.

Taking it in, symbolic of the death of everything I've grown to hate, I light the match and toss it in.

The wine is an unnecessary accelerant, because the tulle goes up like a field of hay after a ten-year drought, and the flames practically reach the height of the small cottage's roof.

I chuckle to myself as I watch it burn, finally feeling lighter and freer than I have in years.

But all of this is at the expense of my relationship with Jack, and while I feel like I have finally rid Nate from my life, a weight still presses down on me; the guilt and enormity of losing Jack.

I feel the tears fall through the laughter that still comes from my lips and when I turn around, I find Ellen watching me from the doorway.

Shaking her head, she says nothing, just walks over to me, her eyes closing in a slow blink as she embraces me.

"Jesus fucking christ, Lauren. What the hell is going on?" she asks as we separate and both take in the raging makeshift bonfire.

"What does it look like? I'm burning my wedding dress," I state matter of factly. My hands now on my hips as the tears spill from my eyes, noiselessly and cathartic.

"Who would've thought it would burn like that?" she says, giving me a little smile as she pokes my side.

"It wasn't even made in China," I say in all seriousness, but my voice still has a playful tone to it. It's not like Ellen or me to take anything seriously, and maybe that's how I got myself into this whole mess in the first place.

"Do I even want to know what this is about?" Ellen asks after a few seconds of silence, both of us mesmerized by the flames that dance in front of us.

"I fucked up so badly, Ellen. Like the worst I've ever done," I start and the tears return, falling hard and fast as I unload everything on her.

After listening to me ramble on about everything that has happened in the past week since she's been gone, she smiles at me, but nothing about it is remotely comforting.

I know what I've done. I was given a once in a lifetime chance with Jack after all these years and I went and fucked it up.

"He's not gone," Ellen says, pulling a slip of paper from her pocket and handing it to me. "This was on the floor by your front door when I came in."

It's wrinkled from being shoved in her pocket and as much as I'm pissed at her for keeping it from me, she somehow knew I had to let it all out before I'd be ready to handle what now needs to be said to Jack.

I look down at the note, my eyes welling with tears, tears that I feel should have long since run out, but I let out a deep sigh when I see what Jack has written.

He's in the one place I should have known to look, the one place I skipped over so quickly because it was far too easy.

And in my frame of mind just a short time ago, thinking he had long since left me, I would never have believed he had made this about me. I looked for him in all the places he loved, all the places I thought he would go. I never once stopped to think he'd be waiting for me in the place I loved.

"I have to go," I tell Ellen, thanking her for finding the note and being here while I fell apart.

"I know you do and it would be great if you could stop being such a hot mess for just a second." She shrugs her shoulders and laughs a little at her own joke, making it hard not to laugh along with her.

I practically sprint across the vineyard with everything in me willing Jack to still be where his note said he would be. I have no idea how much time has passed since he left the note, but I'm holding out more hope than I ever have.

I make it there in record time, winded but with my heart racing, and when I round the last row of grapevines and the open field with the rose-covered trellis comes into view, Jack isn't there.

I practically collapse; barely making it to the swing that hangs from the willow tree. My ass hits the seat and for a split second I laugh out loud. I feel like my life is one of those never-ending TV series where the writers are just making ridiculous shit happen to me just to keep the show going long after it should have ended.

I bury my face in my hands knowing that at some point all my stupid decisions were bound to come back and bite me in the ass.

I guess this is that moment.

I push my feet off the ground sending the swing swaying slightly under my weight, my eyes now closed. And as I rock back and forth shakily on the swing, I swear I hear Jack whistling.

I drag my feet on the ground, stopping the swing along with my breathing, I call out, "Jack!"

And what comes next makes my heart come to a screeching halt in my chest.

"Come find me, Lu!" he yells back and I'm smiling through the tears that fill my eyes.

Fourteen years ago, I chased him through these vines, fourteen years ago he hid from me in a game of tag that left both of us breathless as he raced to the swing.

I leap from the swing, racing down the first row of vines, a smile plastered on my face making my cheeks hurt and as I reach the end of the row, Jack steps out.

I nearly crash into him, our bodies colliding hard as I throw my arms around his neck, jumping to wrap my legs around his waist.

His arms instinctively move to hold me against him, and when our lips connect it's hard and needy and desperate.

Our kiss saying all the things we should've said to each other all those weeks ago, hell all those years ago.

"Jack, I'm so sorry," I murmur, my forehead resting against his as he slowly releases me from his arms. "I should have told you about Nate, about the wedding, but I was..."

"You don't need to say anything more," Jack whispers against my mouth, his lips lightly brushing mine. "I'm so sorry too, Lu. I never meant to keep anything from you either."

I stand clinging to him, never wanting to let go because it's taken me fourteen long years to realize this is where I was always supposed to be.

"I gave my heart to you a long time ago and I never got it back. I've spent the last fourteen years of my life pretending I didn't, but nothing compares to what I have with you, Jack."

"I never wanted to leave you, and I never did. We may have been in different places, but everything in me belonged to you, Lu. Not a day went by that I didn't think about you," Jack says, his lips once again covering mine in a needy kiss, a kiss that means more than either of us can ever express. "And it doesn't matter who came before or after, you have always been mine, and you always will be."

Despite the fact that it has only been a couple of months, it's hard to imagine my life without Jack in it. I can't imagine waking up without him next to me or seeing him as I work through my day at the vineyard, but more than any of this, I can't even fathom what it will be like without his unwavering support in all that I do.

I never had this with Nate. He didn't understand my attachment to this place or all the happiness it brings me despite its struggles. He wanted me to leave the only thing that I ever felt understood me. But now I have Jack, and even if we live on different continents and this whole thing might be totally crazy, it somehow works.

"Lu?" Jack says, a shakiness to his voice, a questioning tone that draws my eyes to his. I feel his heartbeat quicken and a moment of silence hangs between us as I slide my hand to his chest, feeling his beating heart.

His tongue slips between his lips, running it along his bottom lip as he bites down on it and draws in a long slow breath.

"I love you, Lauren," he murmurs, his voice catching as he says my name and his eyes shining with tears.

"Oh Jack, I love you too," I reply back as the tears fall quickly through the smile that stretches across my face.

I've waiting for this moment for as long as I can remember and it far exceeds my wildest dreams.

As we make our way back to my house, Jack's hand interwoven with mine, he says, "By the way, what was with the wedding dress?"

"Don't worry about that," I say, flicking my other hand into the air. "I doused it with a bottle of cheap red wine and lit it on fire."

Jack stops, an eyebrow raised as he looks at me, "You've always been crazy, but fuck if I don't love it."

Chapter Thirty-Three

Jack

By the time we get back to Lu's place, my heart is pounding, my hands itching to rip her clothes off and have my way with her.

Like I said, when I woke up this morning, this is not how I expected my day to go, but fuck me if it hasn't taken a huge turn for the better.

I love her.

I fucking love her and it's something I should have told her weeks ago, hell, years ago if I'm being honest.

"What are you smiling at?" Lu asks as we take the steps to her front door.

Grinning, I spin her around, backing her up against the door as my hands slide to her waist. "You," I tell her, my fingers slipping under her top. "You, me, this, US!" I practically shout.

Lu laughs and it's the greatest sound in the world.

"I really do love you, Lulu," I say, leaning down to kiss her. "I wish I'd told you that sooner."

She grins, her mouth against mine. "We should've done a lot of things sooner," she whispers. "But we're here now, exactly where we're supposed to be."

I pull back a little, eyebrow cocked as I look down at her. "Almost," I say, biting my bottom lip.

"Almost?"

My smile widens. "Well, you do have far too many clothes on for my liking," I add, letting go of her waist as I open the door behind her and we both tumble inside.

Lu's hands grab my arms as I walk us inside and down the hall to her room, the smell of burnt synthetic fabric wafting in the window.

"Jesus, you weren't kidding about setting the dress on fire."

She shakes her head, even as her hands are pulling my t-shirt off. "That dress, that man, that whole relationship are all dead to me," she says, throwing my shirt on the floor and moving to my belt buckle.

I grin, pulling off her top as I back us up to the bed. "Same for me with Mel," I say. "I don't want her back," I continue, unbuttoning her shorts as she shoves my jeans down. "I will never, ever want her back," I add, unhooking her bra. "Because you," I say, pausing as I slip my fingers into the edge of her panties, "are the only woman I want."

Lu gasps as I fall to my knees, sliding her panties down her legs to her feet. I press my lips to the warm skin of her thigh, inhaling her scent. Two seconds ago, I was itching to tear her clothes off and have my way with her, but now, suddenly, I want everything to slow down. To savor this moment with her that feels like another new step in our relationship together.

I feel her fingers in my hair and I look up, find her staring down at me with a look on her face that I've never seen before.

"I love you," she whispers, smiling.

"I love you," I reply, kissing my way over her hip, her stomach, between her breasts and up her neck to her mouth where I whisper, "So fucking much."

Lu's arms slide around my neck as I ease her back onto the bed, following her down so my body now covers her, skin to skin, nothing between us anymore.

My hand, resting on her hip, slides slowly up her side to her rib cage, thumb brushing against her breast and making her moan.

"God, I love that sound," I whisper, my mouth against hers.

Lu's hands slide into my hair, holding me against her as she kisses me, her tongue slipping into my mouth in a way that has me groaning now. She smiles against my lips, her hips pressing up off the bed and against me with a sense of urgency.

"I want you," she whispers.

I smile, moving my hand higher, my fingers brushing against her cheek as I continue to kiss her, my body falling between her legs as they widen to accommodate me.

"Jack," she moans, hand moving down my back to my arse, urging me closer. "Please."

I lift up my hips, brushing my dick against her before sliding slowly inside. "Fuck," I murmur. "God, fuck you feel so good."

Lu's body arches beneath mine, her chest pressing against me, a long exhale falling from her lips as I slowly pull out before pushing back inside her again. It feels torturous moving this slowly, but at the same time, like the greatest sensation in the world.

I don't ever want to stop.

We move together in a slow, perfect rhythm as though we were made for this, made for each other and this exact moment. I keep my thrusts slow, long and gentle as I pull almost all the way out before sliding slowly back in again, inch by inch.

Every time I do, Lu groans beneath me, her kisses never stopping as she holds me against her, her legs wider now as though urging me deeper and deeper.

I feel my body grind against hers, pushing her closer and closer to the edge. I can tell by her breathing, her long exhales now turning to hard, deep gulps of air, as though breathing is almost an afterthought to what we're doing and where I'm pushing her to.

Her legs wrap around my hips as hers push against me, her nails digging into my back, which is slick with sweat.

"I'm so close," she murmurs, her kisses growing harder, hungrier as she catches my bottom lip between her teeth and gently bites.

"Yes," I whisper, my arms planted on the bed beside her, my body pushing into hers and urging her closer and closer.

She groans, long and low, her mouth finally leaving mine as her head pushes back into the pillow, her neck arching as she cries out my name.

My mouth slides down her throat, sucking at her skin as I pull out, pushing inside her one last time as she moans again and explodes around me, pulling me right over the edge with her.

My heart pounds in my chest as I finally collapse against her, my arms sliding beneath her shoulders as I pull her close. We lie together, our bodies entwined, connected in all the best ways and we both slowly start to come down from this high.

"God, make-up sex is awesome," I say when I finally catch my breath.

Lu giggles beneath me, her hand squeezing my arse as she says, "That wasn't just make-up sex."

I lift my head, my eyes meeting hers. Her face is flushed, her eyes bright and alive as she looks up at me. "No?"

Lu shakes her head, a cheeky grin on her face. "No," she repeats. "That was make-up and I-love-you sex, all rolled into one."

I grin, leaning in to kiss her again. "Then let's have make-up and I-love-you sex every day."

"Every week," she replies.

"Every month."

She squeezes my arse again. "Every year?" she adds almost in question.

I pull back a little, brush a thumb across her cheekbone. "How about, For. Ever?" I suggest, any more words cut off as she slams her mouth hard against mine.

We wake late the next morning, tangled in the bedsheets, which we spent all night rolling around in. I lost count of how many times I made Lu scream out my name, but I know it was a lot.

"Morning," I grin, as she rolls her body on top of mine.

"Morning," she whispers, her voice husky from sleep, even though we've barely had any.

I slide my hands down her back to her arse, pushing her hips against mine and my morning wood. "Please tell me we're not working today?" I whisper, licking her neck.

"We're not working today," she moans, her mouth finding mine.

I grin against her mouth. "God, I love fucking the boss," I tease. "So many perks."

Lu stops, pulling herself up so she straddles my hips as she swats at my chest. "Perks?" she says, the smile on her face giving away the mock annoyance she puts on.

I grin up at her, my hands lifting her hips a little. "Yeah, perks," I add as my dick now slides inside her.

"Hmmm," Lu replies, the sound more of a groan as she narrows her eyes at me, even as her hands flatten against my chest and she slowly starts to move. "Well, just as long as you remember I'm in charge."

"Oh, Lulu," I say. "I'm…"

My words are cut off by the sound of the front door flying open, the simultaneous cry of "Aunt Lulu, Uncle Jack!" echoing down the hall to her bedroom.

"Fuck," Lu whispers, scrambling against me, even as I hold in her place. "Jack, shit," she adds, grabbing for the sheet when she realizes it's too late.

"Busted," I say, winking at her as the Two O's suddenly appear at her open bedroom door.

"Get out!" Lu says, turning to face them as she pulls the sheet around us, hiding the extremely compromising position the two of them have just found us in.

And as embarrassing as it is, I laugh, relieved that her niece and nephew's uncanny knack for bad timing is now the biggest issue we have to contend with.

"Hey!" I say, when neither of them says anything or moves, the shock on their faces seemingly rendering them speechless for once. "Why don't you guys head out to the kitchen and give us a sec, we'll be out soon?"

Oscar's mouth hangs open, even as Ollie rolls her eyes, grabbing him by the arm and dragging him away.

"Oh my fucking god," Lu says, falling against me. "I swear we *have* to start locking that damn door."

I chuckle, holding her against me. "Oh, I'm pretty sure that moment right there means they will never bust in on us again."

"You think?" she mumbles against my chest.

"Yep," I say, pressing a kiss to the top of her head.

She exhales, pushing herself back up. "We should probably get up," she says, staring down at me.

"Well," I say, fingers squeezing her hips," first things first, baby," I add, laughing at the look of horror she gives me.

"You can't be serious?" she hisses.

I grin. "When it comes to sex and you, Lulu," I say, "I'm very fucking serious. But I'll compromise," I add, sitting up as I swing my legs over the edge of the bed. "How about I fuck you in the shower instead," I whisper, pushing up off the bed, Lu still wrapped around my hips. "God knows we can't go out there reeking of make-up and I-love-you sex now, can we?" I add, kicking the bedroom door shut as I walk us into her bathroom.

By the time we reach the kitchen, the kids have unbelievably got a pot of coffee on and are attempting to make breakfast, but are in actual fact creating a huge mess.

Laughing, I shuffle them both over to the kitchen island, ordering them to take a seat and fill us in on their trip to Disneyland while I take over. Lu gives me a grateful smile, squeezing my arm as she moves to grab some mugs.

We both know the longer we keep them distracted by their holiday talk, the less likely the questions about what we were doing this morning will get asked.

"Hey, it's just me," Ellen calls out, just as we're sitting down to bacon, eggs, toast and waffles. I'm almost positive our morning activities are now long forgotten.

"Hi," I say as she walks into the kitchen.

Ellen stops, smiling as she looks from me to Lu and back to me again. "So," she starts, eyebrow cocked as she turns to Lu. "You found him then?"

Lu blushes and it's fucking adorable. "I found him."

I watch as Ellen takes us both in, her eyes moving between us, a small smile on her face. "Good," she says, nodding once before moving to pour herself a cup of coffee.

"We found them in bed," Oscar says before shoveling a fork full of eggs into his mouth.

"Fuck," Lu whispers, a mouthful of coffee spilling out of her mouth and onto her breakfast.

I shake my head, laughing as I reach over to wrap an arm around Lu's shoulders and pull her close. Ellen pisses herself laughing so hard she has to put her mug down on the bench before she drops it.

"It's true," Ollie says, nodding. "They were in bed and naked."

"Oh, my fucking god," Lu mumbles, burying her head against my chest. "We are definitely locking the front door."

Later, after everyone has left and it's just Lu and me, I pull her into my arms. "I'm just gonna run back to my place for something," I whisper, mouth against her ear.

"Tim Tams?" she asks, pulling back a little.

I chuckle. "Yeah, okay, those too."

Lu gives me a questioning look, but I lean down and press a kiss to the end of her nose. "I'll be back in a sec."

Over at my place, I grab one of the two things that I was attempting to sort out yesterday when I left *Somerville's* after Mel and Nate showed up. I'd hoped to have both things finalized, but I knew that was too much to hope for in such a short time frame, so for now, this would have to do.

Holding the box in one arm, I walk back over to Lu's where I find her in the kitchen.

"Last two packets," I say, sliding the Tim Tams across the bench to her, laughing as she pouts in genuine sadness. "Don't worry, baby," I add. "I'll always get you Tim Tams."

Her eyes light up as a smile breaks out on her face. "Yeah?" she asks, making me laugh. "What's that?" she asks, suddenly noticing the box I'm carrying.

"This," I say, pushing the box over to her, "is a present for you. Proof that from something bad, something really good can always come."

Lu looks up at me, a confused look on her face as she tries to work out what I'm talking about.

"Open it," I say, nodding my head at the box.

I watch as she does, her eyes widening as she takes in the twelve bottles of red wine. She reaches in, pulls one out, her jaw dropping when she sees what it is, the name I've given it.

"What...what is this?" she whispers.

I move toward her, pulling her into my arms. "This is your wine, Lu," I say, kissing the top of her head. "From the grapes you thought we'd have to throw out when I first got here. From something bad, came something good."

Her fingers brush over the front label, the four gold letters that spell out her name, the name I've given the wine, across the front. Turning it, I watch as she takes in the back label, the words I put together that describe so much more than just the wine.

Lulu – Cabernet Sauvignon

A lush and complex fruit-driven wine with absolutely no hint of residual tannins or bitterness. Aromas of cherry and dark-chocolate dominate and are perfectly undercut by subtle, yet lush earthy undertones.

On the palate, the wine is rich and full-bodied, evoking a powerful and all-consuming flavor that both surprises and deeply satisfies.

Strictly limited edition, this one-of-a-kind wine is superb to drink right now, but promises endless rewards if cellared and cared for properly.

A wine to enjoy today and for many years to come.

"Oh my god, Jack," she whispers, her eyes shining with tears as she looks up at me. "You did this?"

I nod, my thumb brushing away a tear as it slides down her cheek. "I did, I love you, Lu," I say.

A sob falls from her as she crushes her lips against mine. "Jack," she murmurs between kisses. "You made wine for me, you did this, *for me*."

I smile, pulling back a little so I can meet her eyes. "I did," I tell her. "I'll always make wine for you," I say, lowering my mouth to hers.

One down, one to go.

Chapter Thirty-Four

Two Years Later...

Lauren

The alarm rings out and we both let out a long groan as I reach over and press the center button on my phone silencing its shrill cry.

"You'd think after two years I'd be used to the tone of your alarm," Jack says, his voice gruff and sleepy. "You know you can change it to something less annoying?"

"You know you've told me that practically every morning for the last two years, right?" I mutter back, my face buried in my pillow.

His arm slips around my waist, his fingers slide along the bare skin of my stomach as his lips trail a series of small kisses across my shoulder blades.

It's been two of the fastest years of my life, and I owe everything to Ellen who continued to sign Jack's paychecks until yesterday. She kept him on the payroll and kept his visa up to date despite his diminished presence at the vineyard.

Today is hard for me, harder than I expected it to be, as I lie in bed with Jack's warm body pressed against mine, reminding me what it feels like to always have him here with me.

"Tomorrow you won't have to worry about the sound of my alarm," I say, swallowing back the lump that has formed in my throat.

"I may just change mine as a reminder of you," he replies, but any sleepiness that was lingering in his body has faded as he slips a knee between my legs, pressing himself against my ass.

He begins sucking at my neck making me move against his knee as it presses exactly where I need it.

"Jack," I moan, needing him more in this moment than I ever thought I could need someone. "Please…"

"How can I refuse you?" he asks, sliding his hand down the inside of my thigh, reaching my knee, pushing it so I open myself to him. "Especially today," he adds as he slides inside me.

He's slow and methodical, taking his time and when he slips out of me I cry out in protest as he moves me onto my back and hovers over me.

My arms reach out to pull him closer, to feel his skin against mine again, but he shakes his head and pins my arms above me.

"Don't move," he commands and I watch him for a second, his eyes raking over my naked body. "I just want to look at you, commit every curve of your body to memory, every fucking inch of you."

I can never have enough of him or him of me. His hands explore my body, touching every inch of bare flesh as if he's never felt me before. His fingers trail up my sides, brushing my breasts and making me moan out his name. But he doesn't stop, grazing my stomach as he makes his way with the lightest of touches to the inside of my thighs.

My breathing is erratic and my heart is pounding wildly against my chest. Everywhere he touches feels like my skin is on fire. It's screaming for relief as the sensation finds its way to just one part of my body. He runs his fingers between my legs, only lightly brushing against me, making the need worse.

"This is it, Lu. The last time I'll have you like this, because after today, everything changes."

I nod my head, unable to speak as Jack slides back inside me, my eyes closing in response.

"Open your eyes, Lu," he says, his words laced with demand and my eyes flutter open. "I want you to watch, watch as I fuck you, watch as I make you come."

Every dirty word that falls from his lips is like fuel to my fire and I push up and watch as he slides in and out of me, my eyes focused on where our bodies are connected.

His movement is slow and deliberate, taking his time and it makes me grow more needy with every passing second. I push against him, willing him to pick up his pace, and I know he can't hold out like this much longer, wanting me as much as I want him.

I watch as his need takes over, and his arms pull me against him, moving faster until I'm calling out his name, moaning for him.

We finish together, both of us breathing heavily as we collapse back on the bed. With my head resting on his chest, Jack presses a kiss to my hair, moving to look up at him, he kisses me softly, three small kisses in succession and with each touch of his lips, my heart grows larger. To feel what it truly means to be loved is an amazing feeling, so deeply satisfying and all consuming, and I never want it to end.

"I need you, Jack."

"I'm right here, baby. I'll always be here."

He swipes his thumb over the tears that slip from my eyes and kisses where they just touched.

"No worries, right?" he asks and I shake my head and confirm his words back to him. "No worries, Jack."

The day has gotten away from us and by the time we leave the bedroom it's nearly ten o'clock.

"Breakfast, Miss Somerville?" Jack asks, a cheeky smile on his face as he enjoys his own words a little too much.

"Don't call me that," I reply, cocking my head to one side and winking at him as I grab a few tomatoes from the basket on the counter.

"I call you Lulu and you tell me you hate it. I call you Lu and you tell me to stop. So I call you Miss Somerville and you hate that too. If I wasn't certain you loved me I'd be getting a complex."

Jack leans over the island, resting his elbow down and slipping his other hand behind my neck, he pulls me closer until our lips are nearly touching and whispers, "I've got something else I can call you."

I smile against his mouth knowing exactly what he's thinking and despite all my reservations, I know it's what we need to do. He needs his job and I need the vineyard, and we will make this work.

I slice the tomatoes as Jack works on frying eggs and bacon, grumbling about American bacon not being as good as Australian, and we get into our regular morning debate about American coffee versus Australian.

"Our last morning like this," Jack announces looking around the house before his eyes fall on me.

"Why do you keep reminding me?" I ask, again that lump forming in my throat at his words and my thoughts begin to swirl with all the possible scenarios.

"Because everything is going to be just fine," he says, tucking a piece of loose hair behind my ear. "And because I know you're stressing. It's written all over your beautiful face. It's that love/hate thing we do, Lu." He winks at me and my heart flutters in my chest.

We finish up breakfast and ready ourselves for the rest of the day with Jack heading off to finish up some work and me off to meet with Ellen.

We're standing on the front porch together and Jack slips his hand in mine giving it a little squeeze.

"See you tonight for dinner?" I ask, reassuring myself that we're still on, as that ever-present clock ticks away the minutes. Each one that passes bringing us closer to the time we sort of agreed upon.

It was more Jack's idea than mine and since he's way more confident about it all, I let him have his way.

"You can just stay," I say, seemingly out of nowhere.

"But what fun would that be?" he retorts, knowing exactly what I'm talking about.

"This isn't much fun for me," I whine, hoping to get my way. "Or I could come with you," I try and Jack shakes his head slowly, a firmness to his decision and I push my lip out still trying for a win.

"You keep pouting like that and I just might give in," Jack replies, leaning down and taking my bottom lip in his teeth. "You're a terrible distraction, Lulu."

"You mean I might win this?" I ask, my voice teaming with excitement as I fling my arms around Jack's neck.

"Not a chance, beautiful girl."

He kisses me quickly and steps off the porch giving me a flick of his hand as a way of good-bye.

"Love you!" I call out and when Jack looks over his shoulder his stunning blue eyes focusing on me, I convince myself that everything will be just fine.

By the time I get back to the house everyone is already there. I'm running late since I spent most of the afternoon sorting out a bunch of housekeeping shit that I left in limbo for the last few months. I had spent so much time with Jack over the last two years; finally letting a few things go here at the vineyard. It was probably much needed.

Jack has taught me how to let things go, how to delegate better and how to take care of myself without losing what I love about the business.

Olivia runs to me the moment the door opens, throwing her arms around my waist and squeezing me.

"This is the best day ever!" she yells throwing her head back and laughing as she wraps her hand around my wrist and tugs me toward the backyard.

"Why's that?" I question as we make our way to where I can already hear Jack and Will talking loudly about some football draft or something.

"Because Mom let us get two cakes. We never get to get two cakes," she says bouncing up and down and now clapping her hands.

I smile at her, but I'm struggling, wondering if this is really happening and I tease her with, "Mom said you couldn't eat the cake until tomorrow though."

"What?" she says stopping in her tracks and then bolting out the back door screaming for Ellen.

"Would you stop riling her up!" Ellen yells from the back deck and when I appear in the doorway she glares at me. "Just because you're anxious doesn't mean you get to get to bring the kids with you."

"I'm not anxious," I insist, knowing I'm lying through my teeth.

"Whatever," she replies and starts to round everyone up pushing them to the table that is already set for everyone to start eating.

If it wasn't for Ellen I don't know how this would have all come together this quickly. Our parents arrived yesterday and Jack's came in a few days ago. They always said they wanted to visit, and they made it just in time.

We chat and eat, and it's simple and quiet and calming. It's just what I hoped it would be and when the night starts to wind down, I'm once again overcome with emotion.

I choke back the tears, not wanting to cry in front of everyone, especially the twins. The questions will fly out of them like water from a tap and if they see me upset they'll think something is wrong. That's not at all the message I want to convey to them.

Ellen gives Will a slight tip of her head and he gathers up the kids and we all head back through the house.

"Say good-bye to Jack," Ellen tells Oscar and Olivia and in their usual flourish, they cling to him, laughing and demanding he pick them up.

It's never a short good-bye and this one is no different with Ellen and Will eventually having to peel the twins off of Jack.

After my parents share their goodbyes, hugging us both I can see the smile on my mom's face, but I can see the worry in her eyes. She worries about me even though I've told her I'm going to be okay.

This is happening.

Last to leave are Jack's parents and they're all smiles, not a trace of nervousness shown on their faces. They haven't seen Jack in ages and right now that's their focus, him and his happiness.

When they're finally gone, Jack heads into the bedroom and grabs his bag, and I take a long slow breath, reminding myself that it's all going to be okay.

We find ourselves precisely where we were this morning with Jack pulling me into his arms and kissing me.

"Bye, baby. I love you," Jack says, his lips next to my ear.

"I love you too," I respond, as he slips from my arms knowing that if it isn't quick we won't be able to follow through with this.

I watch him walk down the steps to the waiting car, tossing his bag in the back; he climbs in and waves good-bye.

"Bye, Jack," I say, even though I know he can't hear me and I watch until his taillights disappear.

I can do this.

Chapter Thirty-Five

Two Years and a Bit Later...

Jack

The wait feels endless, testing my rapidly fading patience at what feels like the longest moment of my life. My feet shuffle, itching to pace but unable to. I just want this to be done already, just want it to be finished so everything is finally sorted.

"You okay?" I hear someone ask and when I turn, I catch my dad smiling at me.

I grin, nodding. "Yep, I'm good."

Dad chuckles. "You sure, cause you kinda look like you're shitting bricks there."

Now it's me laughing. "No, Dad," I say. "I'm all good."

"You're allowed to be nervous, you know," he says, elbowing me in the side.

I roll my eyes. "I'm not nervous!" I tell him. "Can't you go find something else to do?"

Dad laughs. "Whatever, I'm going," he says, hands up in surrender as he wanders off.

I turn to the guy standing behind me who raises an eyebrow at me, the look on his facing suggesting he can see right through my bullshit.

"Don't you start," I murmur.

But despite my charade, there's a small part of me that is nervous about all of this. Not about doing it, just about…I don't know, wanting it to be done already. Finalized, sorted, set in stone so nothing can undo it.

The past few years have been filled with so many changes, some of them very unexpected and some of them desperately wanted. But none of them compare to the change I'm about to make today.

"Showtime," I hear my dad mutter as somewhere, some music starts to play.

I take a deep breath, before turning to quite literally, face the music. Next to me, Will catches my eye, grinning because apparently, he too, can see that I'm full of shit.

I subtly flip him off and he chuckles before nodding to the end of the drive and the car that has just stopped.

I see Oscar and Ollie climb out first, practically bouncing up and down with excitement as they jump and wave at me, huge grins on their faces as though it's been forever since they last saw me.

Ellen soon follows, trying to get them under control, even as she glances up in my direction, as though to confirm I really am here.

I nod at her, grinning as she almost visibly exhales before turning back to the car.

Lu comes next and despite her claims yesterday that she wasn't anxious, that she believed me when I said everything would all be okay, I watch as she lets out a long, slow breath, her whole body relaxing when her eyes meet mine.

I wink at her and she smiles, and that's all it takes for my nerves to disappear.

I watch as Oscar practically runs toward me, Ollie desperately trying to slow him down by grabbing his arm. He ignores her though and when he reaches me, we go through the same handshake routine we've been doing for the past two years, before he heads over to stand beside his dad.

Ollie soon follows, her cheeks blushing a little as she walks up to me and I crouch down and wait for her. I give her a hug before she moves to the other side and waits for her mum.

When Ellen reaches us, she gives Will a quick smile before turning back to me and murmuring, "Guess I don't have to cut your balls off after all."

I chuckle. "Please, my balls are strictly reserved for your sister," I say, leaning in to kiss her cheek as she shakes her head at me.

And then it's Lu.

Walking toward me on her Dad's arm. She's dressed in a simple white dress, nothing like the monstrosity she set fire to two years ago. This one's strapless, her bare shoulders covered with nothing but her long blonde hair and she looks fucking beautiful.

"Hey Lulu," I say, when she finally reaches me, taking her hand in mine as I press a kiss to her cheek. "You okay."

She exhales, the shaky, "Yes," barely audible as her fingers squeeze mine.

I don't remember much about the ceremony. Not until the end when, with her hands in mine, and a ring firmly placed on her finger, the celebrant finally tells me I can kiss my wife.

I pull her into my arms, dipping her backward and kissing her hard on the mouth as all around us, I hear the sounds of our family and friends, cheering and clapping.

Many of them have come from Australia, my parents and other relatives included. Everyone making the journey all this way to help celebrate something that's been over sixteen years in the making. It's great to see them all and as much as I miss the country I grew up in, I know that this, right here, is exactly where I want to be.

"You believe me now," I whisper, our foreheads touching.

Lu chuckles. "I do," she says, smiling up at me. "But thank you for last night," she adds. "You didn't need to do that, but I loved it, so thank you."

Last night...

After I'd left, taking an Uber into Napa and checking into a hotel, I'd called her, knowing she'd be back at our place freaking out. As much as I know she believed me when I told her I wasn't going anywhere, that I'd absolutely be showing up today, I knew that past hurt still lingered. That it would be impossible for her to picture this day without remembering what happened last time.

We'd chatted for an hour or so, but when we eventually said goodbye, I realized I didn't care about us not seeing each other the night before we got married. What did it matter? So, I'd called another Uber and gone back home, sliding into bed beside her as she lay awake, staring up at the ceiling.

She'd been surprised, but I knew it had been the right call when she turned into me, her head resting on my chest and finally drifted off to sleep. I'd woken early this morning, confident this whole not seeing each other before we got married thing was total bullshit as I rolled her beneath me. But then she kicked me out, refusing to let me have my way with her.

"Come on, baby," I'd said, sliding my hand up her body. "One last shag before we're married."

"No," she'd replied firmly, hands against my chest. "Out, quick, before anyone sees you," she'd added, pushing me out of bed.

I grin at her. "You've always been a terrible liar Lulu Somerville."

She pinches my side. "Lulu Wilson now," she says, before kissing me again.

We go for photos in the grounds of *Apple Jacks,* the orchard and cider house I now own. I'd bought this place not long after I saw it driving back from Napa one afternoon, the day that fuckhead ex-fiancé of Lu's had walked in and tried to get her back.

Seeing this place for sale that day had started an idea in my head. It wasn't wine making and I'll admit, I'm new to the whole brewing thing, but I had a great team behind me and I still got plenty of opportunities to make wine at *Somerville's.*

So I'd gone for it and this became the other half of my plan to convince Lu that staying here with her was something I was very serious about.

It had taken the better part of the last eighteen months to get it up and running and even though we didn't open for another month, having our wedding here felt like the perfect way to get things started.

Afterward, we all move into the newly created tasting rooms for the reception. A band is playing music from the eighties and people are already dancing, others laughing over drinks as we walk into the room.

It's informal and relaxed, exactly the way we wanted it to be and we both move around the room talking to all the people who've come to share this moment with us.

Sometime toward the end of the night though, I lean over and whisper in Lu's ear, "Come with me," pulling her over to the doors leading out to the back.

We walk down the steps from the balcony overlooking the fields of fruit trees and over to the boundary line, the fence that separates *Apple Jacks* and *Somerville's.*

"We should take this down," Lu says, running a hand along the fence.

I chuckle. "Yeah, I was kinda thinking the same thing," I tell her. "Cause you're really stuck with me now, Lu, you know that right?"

Lu turns to face me, her arms slipping around my waist as she steps closer. "Good," she replies.

I lean down to kiss her, the two of us alone in the dark, surrounded by nothing but rows of apple trees and grape vines. "So, you gonna tell me where we're going?" I ask, referring to the honeymoon we leave for tomorrow afternoon. I'd let her decide where it was, not caring about anything except the fact that it would be just the two of us, alone somewhere.

She grins, excited about whatever it is she's planned. "Nope," she says, and I haven't the heart to tell her I know she's taking me back to Australia, the email alert I got reminding me of my upcoming flight to Sydney ruining the surprise.

It'll only be the second time I've gone back since I got here two years ago. The last trip a quick four-day thing so I could pack up my house and get things squared away. Lu hadn't come with me and I know she struggled while I was gone, wondering if I'd change my mind and never come back.

This time though, we're both going and it's going to be Lu's first trip Down Under. But I know that's not the reason she's done this. A small part of her still worries that I'll miss living there now I've committed to being here with her.

And I will, but I know we'll go back there from time to time and in any case, I've made a life here now, a life with her that I wouldn't give up for anything.

"Okay," I say, feigning ignorance as I lean in to kiss her again. "How about we sneak off and go have sex somewhere then, really christen this place?"

Lu bursts out laughing. "Of course you're thinking about sex," she says, swatting my chest.

"What?" I ask. "It's been so long since we have, baby," I whine.

Lu shakes her head at me. "It's been twenty-four hours, Jack," she says, the smile not leaving her face.

"Twenty-four hours too long," I tell her.

A cheer rings out from the reception and Lu glances over. "Come on, we should go back," she says, grabbing my hand.

I pout, pulling her back to me. "This whole getting married thing better not mean the sex stops," I say.

"Oh Jack," she says, pushing up on her toes and kissing me. "You know I only married you for the sex, don't you?"

I grin, smacking her on the arse as I say, "Yeah and I only married you for the green card."

She laughs now, her mouth once again finding mine. I pull her closer, deepening the kiss as she melts into me. "Come on," I whisper. "Let's go do it."

She smiles, lips against mine. "Fine," she says. "But you better order me some more Tim Tams," she adds.

Now it's me laughing. "Oh and now the real reason you married me comes out!"

Lu winks, her fingers weaving with mine as she pulls me further into the darkness, an enticing look in her eye and a cheeky grin on her face.

"They were always my biggest weakness," she says. "And the love of my life."

"I know what you mean, baby…"

I know what you mean.

Acknowledgments

First and foremost, thank you to our readers. We appreciate you more than we can express, but we're eternally grateful to anyone who reads our books, leaves reviews, or contacts us.

To our husbands, thank you for being hilarious and always giving us material. But beyond that, thank you for supporting our crazy dreams. We love you.

This book was a stray from our usual romantic suspense that we started out with.
We hope you enjoyed it as much as we enjoyed writing it, because we had a lot of laughs over the things Lauren and Jack did and said.

Stay tuned because we're just getting started. Big things are coming.

Join Us:
www.claireraye.com
clairerayeauthor@gmail.com

Made in the
USA
Middletown, DE

74948113R00187